E. M. Kkoulla

Prey of the Huntress

Ships of Britannia, Book 2

Copyright © 2021 E.M. Kkoulla

All rights reserved, including the right to reproduce this book, or portions thereof in any form. No part of this text may be reproduced, transmitted, downloaded, decompiled, reverse engineered, or stored, in any form or introduced into any information storage and retrieval system, in any form or by any means, whether electronic or mechanical without the express written permission of the author.

This is a work of fiction. Names and characters are the product of the author's imagination and any resemblance to actual persons, living or dead, is entirely coincidental.

The views expressed in this work are solely those of the author and do not necessarily reflect the views of the publisher, and the publisher hereby disclaims any responsibility for them.

ISBN: 9798510652673

PublishNation
www.publishnation.co.uk

DRAMATIS PERSONAE
Mortals
Maia Abella – Naval candidate, Ship training programme.
Helena Quintilla – Matrona, in charge of candidates at the Naval Academy.
Branwen – servant.
Master Sulianus – An old tutor at the Academy.

Marcia Blandina – Maia's former mistress and murderess (deceased).
The Cyclops – her henchman (executed).
Chloe – Blandina's cook and abused slave.
Xander – slave.

Captain Lucius Valerius Vero– Captain of the Livia, husband to Aura, father of Maia (deceased).

HMS *Blossom* – A three hundred year old training Ship.
Her crew:
Gaius Plinius Tertius – Captain.
Marcus Laevinius Durus – First Lieutenant.
Heron – Mage.
Robin – apprentice Mage.
Campion – Adept.
Danuco – Priest.
Big Ajax – large, quiet crewman.
Scribo – crewman.
Hyacinthus – crewman.
Cap'n Felix – Scribo's foul-mouthed parrot.

Admirals
Lord High Admiral, HRH Cei (pronounced Kay) Julius Pendragon Mordrawd, uncle of the King.
Lucius Albanus Dio – Senior Admiral and father of Tullia Albana, now HMS *Regina*.
Florus Helvius - Senior Admiral.
Blasius Cadogus – Senior Admiral.
Aeron Silius Fortus –Admiral and Head of Supernormal Liaison Section (SLS).

Agents
Milo – former apprentice Mage, now one of the Government's
chief troubleshooters. Nicknamed Ferret.
Caniculus (Little Dog) – friend of Milo.
Foxy, Hart – fellow Agents.
Favonius – civil servant and spymaster.

Ships
HMS *Patience* – formerly Briseis Apollonia, Maia's best friend from the Academy.
HMS *Regina* – formerly Tullia Albana – daughter of Admiral Albanus.
HMS *Persistence* – an old Ship, friend of the *Blossom*.
HMS *Cameo* – also close to *Blossom*.
HMS *Augusta* – the oldest Ship and the Flagship of the Royal Navy
HMS *Diadem*, HMS *Victoria*, HMS *Imperatrix*, HMS *Justicia*, all Royal Ships.
HMS *Livia* – executed for murdering her Captain in a fit of jealous rage. She returned as a Revenant to claim Maia as her own, but was destroyed.

Priestesses of the Mother Goddess
Ceridwen – High Priestess.
Modren.
Arianrhod.
Rhiannon – a little girl, daughter of Arianrhod and sister to baby Mabon.

Mages
Raven – an ancient, blind Master Mage.
Bullfinch – Prime Mage, head of the Londin Collegium.
Lapwing, Kite, Yellowhammer – Bullfinch's supporters.
Sparrow, Dunnock, Chough – friends of Raven's. Not supporters of Bullfinch.

Royals
King Artorius the Tenth – recently ascended to the throne after the death of his grandfather, Artorius the Ninth.
Admiral Pendragon, his uncle (see above).
Prince Marcus – his cousin, Pendragon's son.
Princess Julia – his older sister.
Prince Julius – his father, killed in a hunting accident some years previously.

Miscellaneous
Gnaeus Proculus Aquila – Chief Priest of Jupiter, Londin Temple.
Vibia Laelia – High Priestess of Juno, Londin Temple.
Speedwell – An Adept.
Emrys Brigantius Silvius – Captain, HMS *Regina*.
Magonius – proprietor of Magonius' Naval Outfitters.
Morgan – a worker at Magonius'.
Seren – proprietor of Coventina's Cavern.
Inspector Cyndrigus – Londin Polis.
Crispus – Royal Interrogator.
Thistle – Adept, Londin City Pathologist.
Senator Madoc Britannicus Rufus - Advisor to the King and Raven's friend.
King Parisius – the elderly King of Gaul.
Quintilian – wealthy landowner.
Efa – a housekeeper.
Poppy – an Adept.

Immortals
The Twelve Olympians
Greek names in brackets
Jupiter/Jove (Zeus) – The Thunderer, Ruler of the Olympian Gods and God of the Sky.
Juno (Hera) – Queen of the Gods and Jupiter's sister wife. Patron of marriage and childbirth.
Neptune (Poseidon) – God of the Sea.
Pluto (Hades) – God of the Underworld.
Minerva (Athena) – Goddess of Wisdom.

Mercury (Hermes) – Messenger of the Gods, patron of merchants
and travellers.
Mars (Ares) – God of War.
Ceres (Demeter) – Goddess of the Earth.
Vulcan (Hephaestus) – God of Fire and Artificers.
Apollo – God of Music and the Arts, Light and Prophecy. Bringer of plagues. Associated with the sun.
Diana (Artemis) – Goddess of the Hunt, protector of maidens. Twin sister to Apollo. Associated with the moon.
Bacchus (Dionysus) – the God of Wine.

Other immortals
Aura – Goddess of the Breeze and Maia's mother. Wife to Lucius Valerius Vero.
Pearl – a Tempestas, spirit of the air.
Cymopoleia – Goddess of Storms. Aura's sister.

TIMELINE
AUC (AB URBE CONDITA) – from the founding of Roma, as Maia's dates are reckoned.
Dates from our world in brackets – Before Common Era/Common Era

Year 1 AUC
(753 BCE)
Founding of Roma.
698 AUC
(55 BCE)
Julius Caesar visits Britannia.
743 AUC
(10 BCE)
Emperor Augustus makes a pact with the Sea God, Neptune. Sacred oak branches begin to be grafted on to vessels.
796 AUC
(43 CE)
Emperor Claudius invades Britannia.
814 AUC
(61 CE)
Boudicca (Boadicea) leads a rebellion against the rule of Roma.
875 -881 AUC
(122 - 128 CE)
Building of Hadrian's Wall.
1146 AUC
(393 CE)
Birth of Artorius Magnus.
1163 AUC
(410 CE)
Roman Empire in crisis. Civil war in Britannia as rivals vie for the throne.
1165 AUC
(412 CE)
Civil War ends. Artorius acclaimed High King of the Britons and forms Britannic Legions. Merlin gathers Mages and forms Collegium. Artorius and Merlin lead the Legions

on a march to Roma and rescue the Empire. Goths and Vandals bought off and retreat to the East.

1167 AUC
(414 CE)

Empire stabilises. Major Fae return to Britannia. Artorius returns with his Legions.

1170 AUC
(417 CE)

Great Fae Wars. Artorius receives Excalibur.

1174 AUC
(421 CE)

Major Fae defeated at great cost and driven overseas to Hibernia. Merlin disappears.

1210 AUC
(457 CE)

Artorius dies. His son, Mordrawd becomes king.

1436 AUC
(683 CE)

Northern Alliance formed between Scandinavian, Baltic and Germanic peoples. Hostilities increase.
First Ship, the *Britannia*, created.

1548 AUC
(795 CE)

HMS *Augusta* installed.

1567 AUC
(814 CE)

The Great Blight.

1579 AUC
(826 CE)

Battle of the Oceanus Germanicus

1730 AUC
(912 CE)

Jupiter's decree bans the creation of demi-gods.

2028 AUC
(1275 CE)

HMS *Livia* executed. Maia born.

2044 AUC
(1291 CE)

Marcia Blandina is killed. Maia enters the Naval Academy.

The story so far, as told in Wrath of Olympus: Ships of Britannia, Book 1

The Province of Britannia has been part of the Roman Empire for over two thousand years and is ruled by descendants of King Artorius Pendragon.

Maia Abella is a sixteen year old foundling living in the large city of Portus, the major port on the south coast of Britannia. She is forced to go on the run when something unseen murders her cruel mistress and she is blamed. Wary of arrest, she makes a precarious living doing odd jobs in a local tavern, aided by her nondescript appearance and manner.

The Naval authorities, alerted by the supernormal killing, find Maia and take her to the Polis offices in Portus. There, she is questioned by an ancient blind Mage, Raven, but she can tell him nothing about the killing. Suspecting that she was responsible for her mistress' fate and has hidden power, the Royal Navy becomes involved. It is constantly on the lookout for girls or women showing signs of divine heritage, which manifests as precognition, psychokinesis or telepathy. Candidates are recruited to train as living Ships; their spirits, or *anima*, being split from their bodies and merged with wooden vessels that they can control through the grafting of ancient oak from the sacred forest.

These Ships are faster, more magically powerful and able to communicate across the miles with ease. This gives the Britannic Royal Navy an advantage over the rest of the Empire and their enemies, such as the Northern Alliance, consisting of Scandinavian and Germanic peoples, with whom they currently have an uneasy truce.

Raven can find no evidence of power, or Potentia as it is called, but a mysterious Priest of Mercury, Nuntius, convinces the naval authorities to admit Maia into Ship training, saying that it is the will of the Gods. Meanwhile, Raven orders Milo, a government Agent, to try and find her family but the trail has gone cold.

Maia begins her training, along with two other candidates, Briseis and Tullia, who progress to being installed in their own vessels. Briseis, her best friend, becomes the HMS *Patience,* whilst Tullia, daughter of a senior Admiral, becomes the more impressive HMS *Regina.*

After a couple of years, Maia is assigned to the HMS *Blossom* to be trained and slowly begins to understand just what it takes to be a Ship, caught between immortals and humans. Just as she is completing her training, her name is connected to the sudden and brutal death of the Overseer of her foundling home. It soon becomes clear that an extremely powerful elemental force is on the loose and is trying to get to Maia. It turns out to be a Revenant, a spirit of vengeance – all that remains of a Ship called the *Livia,* which was condemned to be destroyed for the murder of her Captain, Valerius.

The *Livia* kills a young Mage on land before reaching the *Blossom,* who is out at sea just off Portus. She forces her way aboard and claims that Maia is her child by her Captain, which is patently false. The Revenant is clearly mentally and physically damaged but has great power to destroy. Meanwhile, the source of the *Livia*'s power has been tracked to the corpse of her Captain, in which she secreted a splinter of her Shipbody, formed from the living wood and anchoring her to the world. Milo is called upon to disinter and destroy the Captain's remains, but Maia is badly burned protecting her friends from the entity before he can complete his task.

When Maia is well enough, she is sent to the Temple of Jupiter in Londinium for testing by the scientist-healers, known as Adepts. It is discovered that she has one immortal parent, which puts her life in danger as Jupiter, the King of the Olympian Gods, has forbidden the creation of demi-gods. Fortunately, the God shows pity in the light of her parents' punishments; her father, Captain Valerius, was murdered and her mother Aura, Goddess of the Breeze, is forbidden any contact with her daughter.

Jupiter offers Maia a choice – die or continue to train as a Ship, where she will be bound and controlled. He orders her to hide her origins, which she agrees to do, while informing her that she has a sister and that Cymopoleia, the unpredictable Goddess of Storms, is her aunt.

However, as Maia has come to realise, another God is summoning forces to destroy her before she can reach her goal.

BRITANNIA
N
W
E
S
PICTS
CALEDONIA
MARE GERMANICVS
HADRIAN'S WALL
GAELS
HIBERNIA
OCEANVS HIBERNICVS
EBORACVM
VERBEIA
MONA
DEVA
LINDVM
LETOCETVM
RATAE
VERVLAMIVM
GLEVVM
CORINIVM
ABONA
ISLE OF THE DEAD
LONDINIVM
AQVAE SVLIS
THAMESIS
DVBRIS
DVRNOVARIA
PORTVS
ISCA
KERNOW
NOVIOMAGVS
VECTIS
OCEANVS BRITANNICVS
GAVL
AJN

I

Jupiter had spoken.

There had been no mercy in the golden eyes or sympathy for her plight, just a cold balancing of odds and probabilities as he calculated how her fate could benefit him. No wonder the other Gods were terrified of provoking his anger.

Even as those around her were congratulating Maia on her good fortune, all she wanted to do was run far away and hide her disfigurement from the world, where nobody had heard of Ships or Olympians. Perhaps there was somewhere on the planet that had kinder Gods, ones who didn't treat humanity like toys to be broken on a whim? Maia snorted inwardly at the idea. That wasn't likely.

She remembered the dream she'd had while recovering from the Revenant's attack. She knew the couple on the beach had been her parents, but why had the vision been sent to her? They had been so happy, oblivious to the horrors that lay in their future. How could they have known that her mother would be disgraced and her father murdered by his own Ship?

They'd also been unutterably stupid to think that they could get away with breaking Jupiter's decree on half-Divine offspring and, as a result, they'd condemned Maia too. At the very least it was negligent; at worst it was criminal, especially if her father hadn't known about her mother's Divinity. Aura, Goddess of the Breeze, had abandoned her to fend for herself in a world where every hand was against her and with a powerful enemy intent on her destruction.

Diana, Goddess of the Hunt and once her mother's best friend had been so jealous of Aura that she'd brought about the latter's ruin. Now the Goddess' enmity was directed at her daughter.

Daughters. She had a sister.

Her sibling had saved her life by dragging her murderous mistress away and crushing her with a statue of the God Mercury, who had taken Maia's side for some reason. But why had her sister kept her Potentia when hers was blocked? There had been a brief glimpse of ethereal arms around Blandina's waist, then nothing. Did she not have flesh of her own?

Maia's life had always been difficult, but at least it had been hers. Given time and opportunity, she could have made something of herself, maybe even had a husband and children. She wouldn't have spent all her life swilling latrines and doing rough work for a handful of coppers.

Now she would never know where that path might have taken her.

*

"I'm concerned for Maia."

Raven, the ancient, wizened Master Mage was back at the Temple of Jupiter. Maia had returned to the Admiralty, with Matrona hovering around her anxiously. She had hardly spoken since receiving Jupiter's judgement the previous day.

"Understandably," Aquila replied. The High Priest still looked drawn and exhausted from being possessed by his God. "You were brave to speak up for her."

Raven snorted.

"Brave? No, not at all. What could he do to me? Strike me down? That would be a relief. No, I simply have little left to lose. Besides which, the Gods should be used to me by now."

"Hmm. What did you tell everyone?"

"I had to think quickly," Raven admitted. "In the end, I lied through my teeth and said that Maia had been rewarded with some Potentia for her actions."

"That's not too far from the truth," Aquila pointed out. "The God has hopefully released enough for her to undergo initiation."

"Yes. What worries me more is the comment he made about the *Livia*."

"I know." Aquila poured them both a glass of wine and Raven accepted it with gratitude. "Is it true that the Ship had Potentia of mind?"

"She did. She could Send to people from an early age and pick up their thoughts as well. It was a dangerous combination, more so because of her obsessive nature. I'm surprised that she didn't realise that Valerius was in love and intending to leave her. Perhaps Aura blocked her?"

"But she found out, nonetheless."

"I think someone made sure she did."

"The Huntress is an implacable enemy," Aquila mused, "single-minded and indefatigable in her pursuit. I'm afraid that Maia's trials aren't over yet."

"I agree, but surely even the Goddess wouldn't interfere with the Mother on her home ground?"

The Priest shrugged. "The Huntress is wily enough and she'll push the boundaries. We just have to hope that the girl survives."

"Maia has a trick of memory too," Raven told him. "She remembers everything. She'd have made a great storyteller."

Aquila raised an eyebrow. "Interesting. I wonder if that was passed on from the *Livia*? She would be mind-to-mind with her Captain and I hear that occasionally traits can leak from one to the other."

"That's true. I knew of a Captain who never touched certain foods before he linked with a Ship and then he couldn't get enough of them. After he left her, the craving ceased. I don't think it's something the Navy's really looked into."

"Maybe they should. In the meantime, what's going to happen to Maia?"

Raven thought for a moment. "She'll be returned to the *Blossom* to finish her training. At least that will enable her to be out of body most of the time. My main concern is her relatives. The Lady of Storms is part Titan and you know how volatile they can be."

"And this sister. Do we know anything of her?"

"Only that she was possibly the cause of Marcia Blandina's death, back in Portus. The woman was a homicidal maniac, so it was a blessing."

"Strange how Maia ended up in her household," Aquila said, pointedly.

"Or maybe not. Watching your own daughter be strangled while you're helpless to do anything about it is a terrible punishment. Can you find out anything about the sister?"

Aquila shook his head. "The God said he would allow 'limited contact', so things may soon become clearer. I just hope that Cymopoleia is mollified now and calms down or we'll all have to batten down the hatches."

Raven grimaced. "Indeed."

The High Priest glanced over at an ornate timepiece above the mantel.

"I have to go to the palace shortly. I've a meeting with the King."

"How are you finding him?"

Aquila sighed. "Young and, as you know, the young are easily swayed. It was a cruel blow when his father was taken too soon. Julius Mordrawd would have been ripe for the throne."

"No-one can escape their fate," Raven said, sadly, "and Atropos has been no friend to me. Klotho spins and spins and still her sister stays her hand. Lachesis must be sick of measuring my thread by now."

"Even the Gods are subject to the Moirae. I will do what I can to mitigate Artorius' excesses. It wouldn't do to lose him too, but the boy will insist on hunting as much as possible."

"While his cousin waits in the wings. He needs to produce an heir."

"I hear negotiations have already started," Aquila confirmed. "And for his sister, also. We need to strengthen our ties with the Empire. There's too much talk of separation these days."

"There's always talk," Raven said, "and always will be. It would damage trade."

"Still, we should be wary," Aquila said. He closed his eyes for a moment, preparing for the ordeal ahead. "Well, no rest for the wicked."

He finished his wine, heaved his great bulk out of the chair and rang the bell for a servant.

"I hope you can talk some sense into His Majesty," Raven said.

Aquila grunted. "So do I, old friend. So do I."

*

Maia stared at the food on her plate. Normally she would have tucked in with a will, but since her visit to the Temple her appetite had deserted her.

The initial relief at not being blasted into the underworld by Jupiter's Divine wrath had faded into a dull acceptance of the path her life would take. She would follow her peers, Briseis and Tullia into a life of service and obedience as a living Ship, controlling a vessel of His Majesty's Royal Navy and doing whatever her Captain required of her. There would be no more eating as her flesh body would be stored away, leaving her *anima* to inhabit whichever vessel was deemed appropriate at the time. She would be given a new name and, over the centuries, the one she had now would be consigned to some dusty list that nobody cared about.

Who remembered what the *Augusta* had been called after five hundred years, or any of the others for that matter? She would remember Briseis and Tullia, but they were now the *Patience* and the *Regina* and would remain so, probably forever.

Her burned hands lay in her lap, under the table where she couldn't see them. The skin had healed but the scars would never fade, just as the ones on her face and body were a constant reminder of the vicious hatred of her enemy and her parents' recklessness. Part of her wished that she'd died that night, drowned in the sea along with the *Livia*'s Revenant, then she wouldn't have to feel this pain any longer.

A little breeze crept into the room, brushing her face as if trying to console her, but she jerked her head away, glaring around the room with angry eyes.

"I hope that's not you, Mother!" she spat to the empty air. "Curse you for the pain you've caused!"

She felt it falter, withdrawing through the open door and felt justified in her condemnation.

Someone entered the room and she flinched, but it was only Branwen, her maid, coming to take away the dishes.

"Oh, miss. You haven't eaten anything!" The woman's face creased in concern. "You must try something, or you'll be ill."

Maia kept her head down.

"I don't know what they did to you at the Temple," Branwen continued, "but you can't punish yourself like this. To Hades with the lot of them, eh?"

Lost in self-pity, Maia didn't have the energy to reply. The maid fetched a blanket and tucked it around her thin shoulders.

"There's a nasty draught in here. Someone must have left a window open." She bent over, to see Maia's face. "What about some cake?" she said encouragingly. "I've never known you turn that down."

Maia shook her head dumbly. All she wanted was to be left alone in her grief. She heard Branwen sigh, then the tray was taken away and the maid left.

Matrona was waiting outside.

"She hasn't eaten anything," Branwen told her. "What can we do? She doesn't even want cake."

"I don't know," the older woman said wearily. "I was hoping that she'd snap out of it, especially now that her course is set, but it seems to have had the opposite effect. Maybe I should consult with the Adepts?"

"It can't do any harm," Branwen said thoughtfully. "There was that one that came before. Speedwell?"

"Oh, yes." Matrona brightened. "He was so helpful. I'll send them a message and hope that he's free to visit. It will have to be soon, before we all return to Portus."

Branwen agreed, returning to her duties and Matrona bustled off to her room to find pen and paper. She was rummaging through a drawer when there was a knock at the door.

"Come in."

It was the young Adept. She blinked in surprise.

"Oh, Master Speedwell! I was just about to call for you and here you are!"

His smile was as charming as she remembered.

"I heard a whisper that my services were required. I've brought more tonic and I thought I might examine the young lady as well, this time."

"I'm glad you're here," Matrona confided. "She hasn't been the same since coming back from the Temple of Jupiter. Not a word since and she won't eat anything."

She gazed imploringly at the Adept, who nodded reassuringly.

"Yes. It's quite common for there to be side-effects when mortals come into contact with Gods. This medicine should help and we can have a little chat at the same time."

"She's in her room." Speedwell followed her as they made their way along the corridor. "I don't think it helps her to be in an unfamiliar place as well. She'd never left Portus before coming to Londin."

The Adept nodded. "It must be overwhelming for her."

Matrona rapped on the door and went in. Maia was still sitting at the table, staring at nothing. She didn't look around when they entered.

Speedwell smiled at Matrona and gestured for her to leave. The older woman raised her eyebrows but then she found herself agreeing with him. It was best if he spoke to Maia alone. Any objection she might have had about propriety disappeared and she found herself returning to her own quarters.

Once there, she looked at the open drawer in bewilderment. What had she been doing? It seemed to have slipped her mind. She shook herself mentally, then remembered that she was going to invite Captain Plinius over for dinner. Yes, that was it. She'd do it now.

*

Maia heard the door open and the sound of footsteps, but found that she didn't care to see who it was. Branwen must have got Matrona to come and try to cheer her up, but she knew that it wouldn't work.

"No, I'm not Matrona," a male voice said. "She's gone back to her room. It's just you and me now."

Her head shot up and she half turned, hands raised instinctively to ward off an attack. She saw the blue robes first – an Adept then. It made sense that they'd call for medical help because of the state she was in. Then she saw his face.

"Priest Nuntius?"

Her face showed her shock. How could he be both Priest and Adept?

"Of course. You never forget a face. Or anything, really."

The young man crossed to where she was sitting and pulled up another chair. As he sat, the illusion cloaking him fell away, the blue robes disappearing to be replaced by a shimmering silver tunic. He leaned back in his chair and crossed his sandalled feet, while removing the winged helmet from his curly hair.

"Hello, Maia," Mercury said. "You can close your mouth now."

Maia spluttered for a few moments, while she tried to get her jaw under control.

"It was you all along!" she got out at last.

The God nodded.

"I was asked to keep an eye on you. I acted when I saw the interference in your life. You didn't think that you'd been sent to Blandina's by chance, did you?"

"I thought it was my bad luck," Maia said bitterly.

"Not entirely. I have no proof, but my half-sister can be excessively devious when she puts her mind to it and when she gets hold of something, she's like a terrier with a rat."

His tone was casual, but Maia shivered.

"And I'm the rat."

"She would like you to be. However, even Gods don't get things all their own way sometimes."

"I just want to know why," Maia said.

"Why?"

"Why were my parents so...so...stupid?"

The God's eyes filled with sadness. "That would be Venus. Maybe. She's been very quiet about the whole thing, but I personally believe that it was because Aura took proper human form for the first time and for an extended period. She's usually quite incorporeal and her emotions must have got the better of her. Of them both. As for stupid, well, I would call it only human."

"Most humans aren't that idiotic."

Mercury laughed. "You'd be surprised! Also love is a kind of madness in itself."

"But to have a child, or children I should say. What were they thinking?"

"I doubt they were. 'It just happened' is the usual excuse."

Maia thrust her arms at him. "And this is the result!" She touched her scarred face, a wild hope forming in her mind. He dashed it at once.

"I'm sorry. I can't interfere to that extent. It would provoke my half-sister to outright war and I can't afford for that to happen. There's enough trouble brewing without having to deal with her as well."

"If you know what's going to happen, can't you do something about it?" she asked him. She knew that was strange, but talking to him felt almost normal, as if he were a friend she hadn't seen for a while.

He shook his head. "It isn't like that. It's more in the nature of presentiments and shadows of things to come. Fate rules all and the Moirae can't be bribed. Believe me, I've tried."

Unexpectedly, she laughed.

"Yes, I got into trouble over that one," he replied, joining in. "There, that's better. I've been ordered to calm your auntie down as well. She was ready to march into Olympus and take Diana on herself for the insult to her sister and hang the consequences. She's got a vile temper."

"I heard she appeared off Portus when I was ill," Maia said. "Briseis, I mean the *Patience* was spared by her."

"Because she's a friend of yours," Mercury said. "And the quick thinking of her Priest helped because Cymopoleia needed the Potentia the sacrifice would generate. I swear she was ready to wade in and throw some punches!"

"What's she doing now?" Maia asked. It was strange to be talking about a Goddess as if she were some fierce old lady ready to brawl in the street with an annoying neighbour.

"Skulking to the west of Hibernia," Mercury said. "I had to do some fast talking there, I can tell you."

"And my sister?"

"Ah, yes. Your sister. As you have been bound into purely mortal flesh, so she was totally denied it. One child was bad enough, but twins? Diana was for destroying you both, but something stayed our father's hand and I don't think that it was entirely due to your mother's pleading. Valerius' fate was a grisly one and it broke her."

"It hasn't stopped the Thunderer before," Maia said. She knew the old tales of death and destruction.

Mercury sighed. "I know. I'm not really into all that vengeance stuff myself, though I'm sent to carry it out often enough. Don't blame the messenger, eh? Perhaps it's because I've always got on well with humans and I deal with them on a regular basis. Trade and commerce are vital for civilisation and I'm not one of those Gods who'd like humanity to be reduced to simple goat-herders trembling at every sign in the heavens. I love all the new machines and devices! I've just bought one of those new steam carts and I can't wait to try it out."

"Not up and down the streets of Olympus, I hope," she said, daringly. His eyes widened.

"Now, there's a thought! Bacchus would be up for that."

They grinned at each other, before his face became serious again.

"You'll have to make your own way from now. There's not much more I can do to help you for various reasons, though I think you'll be seeing your sister soon. Be patient with her. She's very shy and hasn't had much to do with mortals, but she'll be able to communicate with you."

He reached into the folds of his tunic and pulled out a gold pocket watch.

"Time's up, I'm afraid. Places to go, people to see."

He offered it for her inspection, his face alight with enthusiasm. "A new acquisition, offered to me by a merchant friend. Nice, isn't it?"

She leaned over to peer at the intricate device. "Very."

"I love these things. People are so clever and stupid, often at the same time. Don't be too hard on your mother. She did what she could to save you, remember that."

Maia nodded. Even if she couldn't quite forgive Aura, she had a better understanding of what she'd been through. Maybe one day she could come to terms with it.

"Thank you," she said simply. Mercury smiled and she saw little lights glinting in his dark eyes.

"My mother was called Maia too, you know. Stay strong and never give up hope! Oh, and I brought you these."

He placed a cardboard box on the table, tied with a pink ribbon. Maia picked it up and undid the bow. Inside, nestled in delicate little cases, were half-a-dozen cakes, dusted with sugar and candied rose petals. She opened her mouth to thank Mercury again, but when she looked up he had vanished.

The cakes were delicious.

*

Dinner that evening was a happier affair. Captain Plinius appeared with Campion in tow, and Maia was delighted to see them both. She didn't know what had been in the cakes that the God had given her, but her low spirits had lifted and she felt better prepared to face her future.

She caught Campion giving her some appraising looks over the food and smiled back at him. "I'm much better now."

"I'm glad to see it," the Adept replied. "You had us worried, young lady."

She hadn't mentioned her visitor to anyone and Matrona seemed to have forgotten all about it.

"*Blossom* sends her love and is overjoyed that you'll be returning to us," the Captain said. "You'll make a fine Ship, all being well."

"I can't wait, either," she answered.

"Yes, you need to keep busy," Campion told her firmly, waving a half-eaten chicken leg. "Too much time moping about doesn't do anybody any good. The busier you are, the better you'll feel."

"When can I leave?"

"The day after tomorrow," Plinius replied. "Why don't you take the time to look around the capital while you're here?"

Maia shook her head, reluctantly.

"No, seriously. There are zoological gardens and art galleries – or there's the theatre."

"I've had quite enough drama lately."

"There are comedies."

"No thank you. I'll be happier when we're out at sea." Maia secretly hoped that it wouldn't be too traumatic to return to the *Blossom*. Her time there had been marred by memories of pain and fear, but there wasn't another training Ship and both *Blossom* and her Captain would be hurt if she showed any reluctance to sail in her again.

"You won't be too far from us, either," Matrona said, smiling. "You'll be getting visitors."

"I'll look forward to it."

The older woman leaned forward.

"I must tell you. You and I have had an invitation to lunch aboard the *Regina*; from Admiral Albanus, no less."

Maia's face fell. How could she see Tullia, no, the *Regina*, in her condition? It would have been different if it had been the *Patience*.

"Your physical shape doesn't matter," Plinius interjected, on seeing her expression. "Ships can look like anything they please. Take the *Scorpion* – she has pincers, eight legs and a sting. And the *Hippocamp* is just that, complete with fish tail."

Maia squirmed. "But I'm not a Ship yet."

"You're a Ship-in-training and, moreover, the only one we've currently got, so I wouldn't worry about the *Regina*. You'll also be able to eat in front of her and she'll be jealous, believe me. It's a Ship thing."

So, *Blossom* wasn't alone in her dislike of watching her crew eat. Interesting.

"Albanus has just been appointed second-in-command of the entire Navy," he continued. "It's useful to keep up the connection, as he has the ear of the King. There's also the official version of events to consider, in which you were injured saving the Ship. You deserve to be the heroine of the hour."

Maia pulled a face.

"It happens to be true," the Captain told her. Naturally, the full story would only be known to a few. It was yet another secret she would have to keep. The only mortals who knew of her Divine blood were the Adept who tested her, Raven, Aquila, Vibia and herself and if Maia wanted her friends to be safe it would have to stay that way. She would never be able to forgive herself if anything happened to them because she couldn't keep her mouth shut.

Maia knew that the Captain didn't like politics, but it was good advice. Part of her wondered if there'd been whispers about her encounter in the Temple but she couldn't mention it here. She'd have to ask the Master Mage when she saw him next. She had a certainty that she'd be seeing him again before too long.

Suddenly the zoological gardens seemed a much more attractive prospect.

"I don't suppose I can send my apologies?"

"Best not to," Matrona said sympathetically. "Remember, it's not just because of you, but what you represent."

It was as if her old self was dying. Some strange alchemy was about to transform her into something else, leaving her suspended between Divine and mortal; an object to be revered. All these people wanted to use the power she represented, desperate to be near her like so many street beggars. And just as unwanted.

"If it benefits the Navy," she sighed.

The others nodded. "It will," Plinius said. "Every candidate is a blessing on the country."

She knew he meant well.

*

Maia had expected that they would be travelling to the *Regina*'s berth by carriage, but instead she was escorted to the river, where a Naval barge awaited them.

"It's much quicker than trying to get across the city by road," Matrona explained.

Maia was bundled up against the cold, as her damaged skin had to be protected from the chill winds that blew on the water. The oarsmen saluted as she stepped aboard and she saw the same awe in their eyes that she'd seen on the *Blossom*. She'd already been elevated to the status of national icon.

She seated herself under the canopy and Matrona tucked a warm fur wrap around her. The trip down the river was interesting and she admired the fine buildings on either side, though it seemed more open to the south. She tried not to look at the Temple of Jupiter, focusing instead on the river traffic that plied its trade up and down the waterway. Small boats darted in between larger wherries, taking goods upstream from the docks, where the bigger vessels anchored. Shouts rang across the water and crowds of people hurried along the banks on business of their own. Children were playing on the foreshore, whilst others picked through the detritus that was washed up there in the hope of finding something to sell. Away from the centre, more factories and warehouses appeared. Maia couldn't believe how big it all was; stretching for miles with the great river at its heart. A pall of acrid smoke hung over all in the grey winter sky.

Matrona pointed out various sights, including several new bridges. One was decorated with shields, on which was displayed a rampant bear.

"That's Senator Rufus' family crest," Matrona told her. "He paid for the whole thing, though there is a small toll charge. Most people are happy to pay it because of the convenience. He's a very important man in the Senate."

Maia stored the information away for later, knowing that she would be able to recall every detail of her journey.

Vessels crowded almost every inch of the waterfront, just like in Portus but in greater numbers. Galleys from the Mediterranean were berthed next to merchantmen from every country in the Empire. There were even some distinctive Northern Ships with their carved prows seeming to snarl at their neighbours. She wondered if they talked among themselves as Britannic Ships did, or if they could only howl and grunt like wild beasts.

It wasn't long before she spotted the masts and spars of Ships, clustered together in their own section of the river. Flags and banners proclaimed that they were entering the area of the Royal Dockyards reserved for His Majesty's Navy. Maia wished she had her earring, then she could have listened in on the conversations that would be passing from one to another.

She studied their names as she passed. *Fortuna, Vigilance, Cornucopia, Leopard, Dauntless, Unicorn*, the list was almost endless. Some would be re-provisioning after long sea voyages, or exchanging crew. Others would be in for repairs, or re-fitting, like the *Diadem* and *Swiftsure* had been, down in Portus. That would mean that the Ships would be assigned to the main Admiralty Offices in Londin while they were out of action. The Navy had several dockyards around the coast, not just the ones in Londin and Portus.

Maia looked for anyone she might have met through *Blossom*, but there was no sign of the *Cameo* or the *Persistence*. She'd been out of the link for so long that she didn't even know where they were now and she realised that she found the thought vaguely unsettling, as if part of the Ship had stayed with her despite her absence.

"There she is!" Matrona announced as they rounded a small bend.

The *Regina* was huge. The *Blossom*, as a mere fourth-rate, would be dwarfed next to the enormous warship that was anchored next to the dock. Her black and yellow paint, still fresh, glistened in the light and her name gleamed golden along her bow. Maia couldn't even count how many guns she had, but knew that there must be about a hundred. The barge angled across the current to dock at some steps. They would be walking to the Ship and Maia was glad that she wouldn't be hoisted aboard like she had been when she first went to the *Blossom*.

"What a magnificent vessel!" her companion announced. Maia had to agree.

"Is she a Royal?"

"She isn't. As you'll recall, Tullia was installed just after the old King died and his grandson hadn't been crowned. Bad luck for her, otherwise her father would have made sure she was."

"Couldn't he make her one now?"

"It isn't done that way." Privately Maia thought that it must be galling for the *Regina* not to be in the top rank of Ships, but what she lacked in status, she more than made up for in weaponry and power. The older Ships must be looking on with envy and planning their next refits.

The oarsmen helped them both out of the barge. They would have a harder journey on the way back, she thought, then sensed that the tide was about to change. Perhaps it wouldn't be that bad after all?

She adjusted her veil, glad of the anonymity it afforded her. The soft kidskin gloves that protected her hands had been a present from the Captain and were a boon on a day like this, though she would have to take them off to eat.

She followed Matrona to the vessel's gangplank, where they waited for the invitation to proceed.

"Welcome, ladies! You have my permission to come aboard."

Tullia's voice was still recognisable, though Maia thought that it had lost some of its shrillness. They ascended the ridged wooden walkway and entered amidships.

Waiting to greet them was the familiar figure of Admiral Albanus, resplendent in his uniform, whilst behind him was the man she presumed was the *Regina*'s Captain. They both saluted and the Admiral introduced the *Regina*'s new commander.

Captain Emrys Brigantius Silvius was a dark haired older man, with narrow lips, piercing black eyes and a stiff bearing. His gaze raked Maia, who was mostly hidden under her layers and he afforded her a polite smile. She guessed that the expression was one he rarely adopted. Maia was glad that he hadn't been assigned to her and speculated about how he was getting along with his Ship. He didn't look the sort to stand for any tantrums.

The *Regina*'s Shipbody was standing on the quarterdeck. Tullia had been quite pretty in the flesh and had accentuated her features when she became a Ship so that now she was dazzling. She was holding a jewelled crown as her *tutela*, with another in her stiff golden locks, while smiling like the cat that had got not only the cream, but an entire dairy.

"Matrona, Maia, how lovely to see you both!" she trilled. "So, what do you think of my new vessel? Isn't it wonderful?"

"It's amazing!" Matrona said and Maia nodded her agreement.

"It has all the latest devices and the new breech-loading guns, too," the Ship proclaimed. "I'm so fortunate to have such an advantage."

She beamed at her father, who smiled back with paternal pride.

"My daughter has done well," he said. "She's also fortunate to have such an experienced commander."

"Oh yes," the Ship agreed, though Maia fancied that a fleeting shadow crossed her face at the mention of her Captain. So, there'd been clashes already. She wondered whether *Blossom* knew anything about it, though she had the sense that they hadn't bonded well during their partnership. *Regina* was hardly likely to unburden herself to her – maybe *Patience* would know? That was something to find out about later, as Ships loved to gossip.

The dining room was as splendid as the rest of the vessel. Slaves hurried about, bringing wine and dishes of food as they reclined on couches to eat. Maia assumed that they had been brought in specially, as, when at sea, chairs were used. Matrona complimented the Captain on the elegant arrangements.

"The *Regina* is state-of-the-art," he told her with pride. "Better than anything the Northern barbarians have and far superior even to the Imperial ships. She can travel farther and faster than any Ship to date."

Matrona looked suitably impressed. The *Regina* took up station to one side, presiding over the occasion as the Admiral offered the customary toasts to the Gods and the King.

Maia took a deep breath and lifted her veil. Albanus' face twitched and she saw his throat jump as he swallowed, but Silvius barely blinked. The *Regina*'s gasp of horror could be heard across the room. The Ship controlled herself immediately and shot a chastened glance at her Captain.

So, she's just had a telling off. Ships were supposed to control themselves at all times. Still, it must have been a shock for her to see Maia this way. She took her time stripping off her gloves.

"It all looks lovely, Admiral," she said, calmly, looking him straight in the eye. "It's such a pleasure to meet you again after your kindness to me."

"We're honoured to welcome the heroine of the *Blossom*," he replied, suavely. "Your actions were exemplary, and your sacrifice honours us all."

"Indeed," Captain Silvius said, his precise vowels echoing his superior's. "It is our highest hope that we may serve our country to the utmost of our ability."

He gave her a look of approval and raised a glass. The others all followed suit and Maia nodded as graciously as she could. She had the distinct feeling that this wasn't going the way the *Regina* had planned. She felt a flash of sympathy for the Ship, remembering her desperate attempts to evade this fate.

"Your vessel is truly a marvel," she told her. The *Regina* smiled apologetically.

"Thank you, Maia. I hope that when your time comes, you get one that's just as good."

For a second it was as if they were both at the Academy, making up after one of Tullia's strops.

"I pray to the Gods that it be so. I'm so happy for you, *Regina*," Matrona said. "You have the opportunity to make a difference and protect Britannia's interests across the world."

"Hear, hear!" Albanus raised his glass in salute. "And I trust that when her time comes, Miss Maia will do the same. Sister Ships working to advance all our prospects, eh?"

He gestured to a servant and the meal began. Maia enjoyed the dishes, noting out of the corner of her eye that the *Regina* was watching every mouthful. She had to admit that it added a certain piquancy to the experience.

*

"Well, that was interesting," Matrona said to Maia, as soon as they were back on the barge and heading upstream. Maia looked ahead to where the centre of Londin was appearing over the heads of the oarsmen.

"It certainly was. I think that Tullia has met her match in her Captain."

Matrona raised her eyebrows, knowingly.

"He's very experienced and stands for no nonsense, by all accounts. Just what a young Ship needs to guide her through her first missions."

"I didn't think she'd be so *big*."

"Nor did I. The Navy is in a war of armaments and technology with just about everybody, even if technically we're at peace. The old King must have given his approval for her vessel. There have been several upgrades over the past few years and progress is speeding up with all the new inventions that keep appearing. I can't keep track of them these days!"

"I should have asked whether she has the new kraken detector Heron and Robin were working on," Maia said. "They must have finished it by now."

"It needs to be tested and approved before it can be fitted," Matrona told her.

"The *Regina* can test it," Maia said innocently. Matrona tried to look stern, but her mouth twitched.

"I don't think they'll use a brand new Ship to tempt krakens. They're more likely to use a smaller, older one, just in case, or possibly an inanimate on a long line, remotely monitored."

It all sounded very interesting and Maia decided to ask Heron all about it when she got back to the *Blossom* – if she had a couple of hours to spare. He'd happily talk all day about his pet project.

She spent the rest of the journey mulling over the unexpected reaction of others to her scarred appearance. There was a kind of Potentia there too and one that she could use to her advantage.

If she was forced to become a Ship, she wanted a vessel like the *Regina*'s.

Only better. And Royal.

II

Back in Portus, *Blossom* welcomed Maia with open arms, her huge smile white against her dark skin.

"I've missed you, girl! You must tell me all about your trip to Londin, where you went and who you saw. I've not been up there for ages!"

Ships were always hungry for news.

"I've a lot to tell you," Maia said, thinking about all the things she couldn't talk about as well.

"Were the tests difficult?" her friend asked in concern. Maia remembered the crushing weight of Jupiter's presence and nodded.

"One was, but it didn't last long. The Adept had some complicated devices and I had to give blood and hair."

The Ship looked impressed. "Fancy that. They're always inventing new things. Plinius told me that you're Valerius' daughter after all. I'm so sorry about what happened to your family."

Matrona must have told him.

"It's all right," Maia said. "I never knew my parents, so it's hard to feel a connection to them. I can only hope that the whole thing is over and done with so I can move on."

"So do I," *Blossom* said fervently. "By the way, I've moved your cabin. I didn't think you'd want to go back into your old one. Durus has been using it instead, so you can have his. Oh and do you know that we've got a new Priest?"

"No! What happened to Cita?"

"It all got a bit much for him. He was due to retire, anyway. He went back to Neptune's temple in Portus. The new one's called Danuco. He seems competent enough."

Maia nodded. She wasn't surprised. Cita had been terrified by the Revenant's appearance and was a bit too fond of the bottle. She was also grateful to *Blossom* that she'd been allocated another cabin. She hadn't been looking forward to going back into her previous berth. The memory of the thing forcing its way in to seize her was still too raw. Her eyes moved involuntarily to the rail where she had dragged the *Livia* into the sea, but there were no scorch marks now, only newer-looking wood.

Blossom moved closer to her, but Maia flinched at the touch of her hand. The Ship backed off immediately.

"I'm so sorry. It's too soon, I know. It will be better when you have your own Shipbody."

"No, I'm sorry," Maia told her, feeling guilty. The *Blossom* wasn't the *Livia*, but the memory of being imprisoned in unyielding wooden arms still made her shudder.

The Captain joined them on deck, smiling. "Here you are. Has *Blossom* told you about your move?"

"Yes. I'm glad, really."

"Excellent. The next thing we have to do, as soon as you're rested, is to give you back your earring and put you to work."

"Can we do it now?" Maia asked him hopefully. He looked surprised for a moment, then nodded.

"Good idea."

"I'll tell Heron," *Blossom* offered. She paused for a moment. "He says to come to his quarters and he'll do it right away. It should be easier this time, Maia."

"Is Robin still here?" she asked.

"Yes, but not for too much longer. He's being put in charge of the kraken detector tests."

"It's a great honour for one so young," the Captain said, "but he has an aptitude for devices. He'll probably end up as a Mage Artificer, like Heron."

"I don't think anyone's like Heron," Maia laughed and the others joined in.

It was good to see familiar faces again, greeting her as she passed. Big Ajax, never a man to say much, beamed all over his weathered face and even Scribo's expression was less grumpy than usual.

"Here comes trouble!"

A screech from his shoulder told her that Cap'n Felix was still going strong. She'd been told that he'd kicked up a fuss just before the Revenant had forced her way aboard and she reminded herself to ask *Blossom* to use him as an early warning system in the future.

"Hello, you naughty bird," she told him.

"Behave yerself," Scribo growled at the grey parrot, who was bobbing excitedly on his shoulder. "Yer not fit fer respectable company, are yer?"

"Go to Hades!"

"That's mild for him," Maia remarked. "He's behaving, for once."

Scribo grinned at her, his four remaining teeth leaning like broken posts. "'E likes yer, ma'am. Glad yer back."

Cap'n Felix fixed Maia with a beady eye.

"Monster ahoy!" he screamed.

Scribo rolled his eyes.

"Yer daft pillock!"

Maia laughed.

"I'd better get on. I'm having my earring refitted."

"That's good to know, ma'am, an' yer'll feel better fer it."

Down below, Heron was waiting. This time there was no ceremony; the earring slid into place without a problem and Maia was ready as her senses expanded. The immediate mental links with *Blossom* and her Captain were familiar and reassuring and she felt the tightness in her chest loosen.

"There you are," the Mage said, approvingly. "Nice and easy, eh?"

"How are you both?" she asked.

"Oh, we're fine, though naturally we were worried about you. Isn't that right, Robin?"

The young man gave her a shy smile. She saw that he had graduated to full Mage's robes, with the sign of the Artificers' Guild attached at his collar.

"It is," he answered.

"I can see that congratulations are in order," she said, and Robin blushed.

"Thank you. I'm glad I stayed here long enough to see you again," he said carefully.

"We've been working on his stammer," Heron said proudly. "It's almost gone. Fascinating process, you know, retraining the mouth."

Robin glanced at his old Master and rolled his eyes.

"When do you leave?" Maia asked him.

"Next week," Robin said. "I'm to present the detector at the Admiralty, then I should get the go ahead to field test it."

"Won't that be dangerous? Matrona said something about a vessel being controlled remotely."

"It will be a challenge," the young Mage admitted, "but we're bound to get lucky at some point."

"And the creature doesn't have to be actually attacking," Heron interjected. "If one simply passes within range it should be enough to set it off. We've already had some success. I hope it gets approved in time for your new vessel, Maia."

"So do I," Maia said. "I could be the first Ship to have one."

The Mages were pleased but she could sense that they were in the middle of something complicated, judging from the contraption taking up a good deal of the floor. It looked like a large metallic sausage with coloured wires trailing from it.

"What's that?"

"Top secret!" Heron said, his eyes alight with enthusiasm. "A combination of magic and mayhem, eh, Robin, with a sting in the tail?"

"It will be, if I can get the propulsion systems working," Robin said seriously.

"Well, I'll want one of those too," she said. "I'm sure you'll work it out."

Before she left them to tinker, she crossed to where the giant Nile crocodile was fixed to the wall. He looked long dead and mummified, but Maia knew that if he hadn't come to her aid, she would have drowned in the depths of the ocean.

"Hello, Sobek," she said. "I'm back. I have a present for you."

The expensive incense had come from a market in Londin, procured by Matrona at her request. She burnt it before him, arms upraised and saying the ancient words of praise that Heron had taught her. Did his eyelid move, just a little? She decided that it had.

"I suggest you rest and eat, then I'll be along to check your link to *Blossom*, if you like," Heron said, smiling his approval. "It's about time you got back to work."

Maia thanked him and set off to her cabin. She stopped before her old door for a moment, before moving further down to what had been the Lieutenant's quarters, reminding herself to thank him for vacating so readily. The new cabin was a mirror image of her old one and all her familiar belongings were there, including her sea chest and her bed. She sat down on the latter, feeling it swing beneath her. She much preferred it to a stationary bed and had missed the gentle rocking when on land, though she hadn't as yet had to cope with much stormy weather.

Her thoughts turned to her Divine relatives. So, Cymopoleia had been angry at her treatment? Come to think of it, her time at Marcia Blandina's had been marked by a number of severe storms. The Goddess should have just blasted the woman – one well-aimed bolt of lightning would have put paid to the evil harpy once and for all.

Whatever. She had survived, thanks to her sister. Wherever she was. Perhaps she'd find out soon?

Now it was time to complete her training.

*

<There's someone here who wants to say hello.>

Maia was practising her tacking skills when *Blossom* broke off her instruction.

<Hello, Maia!>

It was her friend Briseis, now the *Patience*, a third-rate sloop on diplomatic duties in the Mediterranean.

<*Patience*! I'm so glad we can speak again. How are you?>

<I should be asking you that,> her friend Sent. <I'm all right. Still ferrying ambassadors and their retinues and currently anchored off Neapolis.> Maia felt her mime a yawn and giggled.

<I'm fine, thanks,> she replied. She felt *Blossom* take back control of the vessel so that they could chat without being distracted. <I'd rather be here than in Londin, though the weather's been miserable.>

<It's nice here,> her friend replied. <Much sunnier than Portus. I hear that you were invited aboard the *Regina*. How is Queen Tullia?>

Maia snorted. <Having to knuckle down under her new Captain, though her vessel's wonderful!>

<I've seen it,> *Patience* said. <We always knew that she'd be given the best.>

<Don't you wish you'd got a first-rate too?> Maia asked, though she sensed *Patience*'s contentment through the link. She'd never had an envious bone in her body.

<I'm happy enough with my vessel, thanks. We can't all be enormous great warships and I can go places she can't because of my shallower draught. There are few wharfs that can accommodate her, so she'll usually have to stay offshore. And I'm lucky to have Fabillus as my Captain. We're well suited.>

Maia told her about her encounter with the *Regina* and *Patience* listened sympathetically. <Oh yes, Silvius will have his hands full all right,> she said. <I'm glad he's keeping her in check. I must admit that it's hard to remember to be calm at first. You need to practice detachment now so it will be easier for you later. Just let your mind glide over everything and try not to get too involved. There'll often be little dramas on board but it's best to rise above them and never take sides, unless it's to back up your Captain and crew when needed.>

<I can always rely on you for words of wisdom,> Maia said, gratefully. <Though you were always so calm and poised in the flesh.>

<I think some of that is down to my early training,> *Patience* admitted.

<So your name is apt, then?>

<Like Tullia's. She always wanted to be a queen.>

<She's lucky they didn't call her the *Madam*,> Maia said tartly. <Now that would have been a good name for her. HMS *Madam*!>

Even *Patience* laughed at that one. <Don't worry,> Maia added, <I'm only saying this to you because we know her so well. I understand that I have to be discreet.>

<And she's an important Ship,> the other agreed, <though still learning the ropes. I wonder what her first assignment will be?>

<Perhaps she'll be sent to New Roma? I'd like to go there, even though I won't see much of the land except the coast.>

<I haven't been that far yet, though I like the Med. The Greek islands are beautiful. I can see Mount Vesuvius from here, you know. Would you like to see?>

Maia was instantly enthusiastic. <I'll have to ask *Blossom*. I can't remote-view on my own yet.>

She relayed her request and felt the Ship's indulgent smile.

<Good idea. I can show you which linkage to open for the relay. It will be nice to see something other than a grey sky, a grey sea and the incessant rain!>

Suddenly, it was if a window opened up in her mind's eye. She could see her surroundings, but overlaid was another scene, bright and sunny even though it was the beginning of winter. Maia marvelled at the huge bay, ringed with clusters of buildings. *Patience* obligingly focused in on objects in the far distance, including the great brooding volcano that loomed over the entire area.

<It's been quiet lately,> *Patience* informed her <but you can see the devastation it's wreaked in the past. Only the Gods know what's buried beneath all the current buildings.>

Maia eyed it with awe. <Is it controlled by Vulcan?> she asked.

<You'd have to ask a Priest,> her friend said.

<It all looks lovely,> Maia sighed. <Can you see the weather here?>

<Ah, Britannic grey,> *Patience* said with a laugh. <I'm glad I can't feel the cold any more. I should be hanging around here for a while, but I'll let you know when I'm on my way back.>

<Please do> Maia said. <Maybe I'll see you before I go for initiation?>

Her friend fell silent and Maia could sense her unease.

<I would like that. Just...take care, Maia. I have a premonition that something's out there in the darkness, very old and vicious...>

The Ship's voice trailed off and Maia felt a cold shiver travel up her spine. She knew to take her friend's warning seriously as she was descended from Apollo and his lines often had a touch of foresight.

<I'll do my best to stay out of trouble,> she sighed, <but you know how it likes to find me. Security here's beefed up, so I

should be safe enough, I hope. If anything does come, we'll set Cap'n Felix on it and he can swear it to death!>

Her friend laughed, but Maia knew that the vision had frightened her.

<Still, you must be extra vigilant, please?>

<I will. I promise.>

Blossom's gentle mental nudge told her that their time was up.

<I've got to go. We'll talk soon!>

<Soon!>

The connection broke and her friend's warm presence faded. It was a consolation that they'd be able to talk directly when, if, Maia passed her initiation and got a vessel of her own. Then they truly would be sisters together, for a very long time.

*

A few days later, the *Blossom* was making her way up the eastern coast of Britannia and braving heavy weather, when they received another communication.

<It's the *Augusta*!> *Blossom* was clearly surprised. <She wants to talk to you, Maia.>

If she'd been in her body, Maia knew that her mouth would have fallen open. She hadn't a clue why the Navy's Flagship would want to talk to her. Perhaps Admiral Pendragon had ordered her to Send a message? *Blossom* was naturally filtering all the Ship's communications, as some wouldn't be for a trainee's ears.

Maia braced herself and took over the link. <This is Maia Abella, Ship-in-training aboard the *Blossom*, ma'am.>

The presence at the other end of the link was strong, weighted with centuries of experience.

<Greetings, Maia Abella. This is the *Augusta*. I wished to speak with you.>

There was a pause and Maia was reminded of a very old lady gathering her thoughts before she spoke.

<I knew your father. He was a good man and a good Captain. He didn't deserve what happened to him.>

<Thank you, ma'am. I didn't think that anyone knew.> She sensed amusement from the ancient Ship.

<Those that need to always do. My Admiral told me. I feel there is more, but he has remained silent.>

Maia could feel the deep bond that existed between the *Augusta* and Admiral Pendragon. They had been together for many years, though he was the latest in a very long line of commanders. Did she still remember them, or had their faces and voices faded from memory over the centuries?

<You will be a young Ship, just beginning your years of service to Britannia and the Empire. You will see things come to pass that weren't dreamed of when I first set sail and you will be travelling the world long after I am gone. I know that you have already sacrificed much. Remember this, child. Passion is the enemy of duty and duty must always come first. I wish you success in your journey.>

<Thank you ma'am. I will heed your advice.>

The *Augusta* Sent her approval. <Now I must go. Admiral Titus calls. Farewell and may Fortuna smile on you!>

<Farewell, ma'am.>

Maia was puzzled as the Flagship broke the link. She hadn't heard of an Admiral Titus and she'd studied the Navy lists extensively, memorising names and Ships.

<*Blossom*, who's Admiral Titus?>

The Ship was uneasy at her innocent question.

<It was just a slip. She meant Admiral Pendragon, of course. She's so old that these things happen.> She seemed unwilling to elaborate, so Maia left it there.

Had the *Augusta* really forgotten her Admiral's name?

Later, in her quarters, after she'd recovered from the stasis spell, she pulled out a book she hadn't read yet.

'*Famous Britannic Sea Battles*'. The *Augusta* featured prominently and she spent the time before dinner flicking through to check for the name. Admiral Titus – not to be confused with the Emperor of the same name. She knew about him already.

She was about half way through when she came upon him. Admiral Titus had lived over four hundred years ago and had commanded the *Augusta* during the Battle of the Mare Germanicus.

Maia shut the book with a snap, meaning to read the rest later. It was just a slip, as *Blossom* had said. After such a long time it was easy to get people mixed up.

Wasn't it?

*

The Britannic Ocean in early December was as rough as its reputation said it would be. The calm waters and fair weather of her earlier voyages were just a memory, as the *Blossom* forged her way through the wind and lashing rain that carried the icy breath of winter from the lands to the east.

Maia was still with *Blossom,* observing the Ship's every move as she battled the precipitous waves and hoping that her body would stay securely in its bed. She checked on it, then opened up a conversation with Heron, while still following the action aboard the vessel.

Robin had departed to promote his new device in Londin and she missed him already. Heron did too, though he wouldn't admit it.

"I can't stand those idiots at the Admiralty," he told her, steadying himself as the vessel's movement slowly increased. "Now Robin can get his words out, he's the one to do all the demonstrations and such. I'd rather be here working on this."

He gestured to several unfinished contraptions that littered the Mage quarters.

"Will you be training a new apprentice?" she asked, while noting that the storm was increasing in power.

"Possibly, if they can find anybody mechanically minded. I'm afraid that magic is slowly dwindling into light shows and the odd fireball. Nothing like it used to be." His face fell. "Most of the really powerful Mages are dead and gone, no matter what the Collegium says. There'll never be another Merlin. Raven's the last and even he doesn't use much Potentia these days. More and more youngsters are choosing to branch out into other disciplines to complement what Potentia they've got – healing and such. In time, there won't be any of us left."

"Heron, you are needed." *Blossom*'s voice broke in.

"Ah, the wind is building," Heron said. "Time to earn my keep and finally show you what a Ship's Mage can do."

Maia watched as he threw an oilskin over his robes and headed up on deck. She followed the Ship's instructions to keep their course steady. The coast was barely visible through the rain and the vessel heeled to the left as she battled the huge waves. Everything that could be fastened down already had been and the vessel creaked and groaned under the strain.

The Captain and Lieutenant were hanging on to the rail as Heron approached.

<*Blossom*, tell him to raise the shield now,> Plinius ordered. <Keep propulsion steady, minimum speed until you're settled, then we can get going again.>

<Aye, Captain.>

Heron swung himself up to them with an agility that belied his age and Maia could see the faint purple glow that was surrounding him. He'd already put up a personal shield to mitigate the worst of the weather – no wonder he could move so easily.

He gestured and muttered a few words, his eyes fixed as he concentrated. Maia felt the Mage's Potentia flare, dovetailing neatly with an answering surge from *Blossom* as she drew on her innate power. Maia stayed quiet as she had been instructed, feeling the energy mesh together to form a solid sphere of Potentia that swelled like a huge bubble, expanding rapidly outwards to encircle the whole vessel in a dancing purple halo.

Instantly the shriek of the wind fell away and the Ship righted herself, secure once more under the magical protections. Enormous waves clawed in vain on the sides of the shield like invaders trying to breach a castle wall, rising up almost as high as the topmost spars.

Blossom looked satisfied. "That'll hold," she said.

"It will," Heron said. "Good job, too, as we can't put into port soon."

"Why not?" Maia asked. Her voice came from *Blossom*'s mouth.

"We're off the Isle of the Dead," Plinius replied. "All the land there is sacred. It's where the old Chiefs and Kings are buried since time immemorial. No-one's allowed to set foot there without permission. We have to round the point, then we can head west for the mouth of the Thamesis."

Maia strained her vision, but couldn't make out anything through the foul weather.

"How long can you maintain the shield?" she asked. Heron answered her.

"The record is five days out in the open ocean, but both Ship and Mage were severely strained and everyone was running out of breathable air. The shield allows a small amount to pass, but it's not wise to keep it up for long periods. This should tide us through until either the storm abates or we reach calmer waters, whichever comes first."

The Potentia thrummed through the vessel, guided by *Blossom*'s sure mental touch. Maia examined the link with Heron and saw that the power was running both ways in a steady stream, constantly reinforcing the spell with each part feeding off the other. It was an elaborate and elegant magical construction.

Jupiter had told her that she would have enough Potentia to fulfil her duties as a Ship, even though nothing had manifested and, as yet, she didn't have a clue how to draw it forth from wherever it was hiding. Perhaps it would be made clear during the initiation ceremony?

<*Blossom*. How can I use my Potentia like you do? Does it come naturally?>

<No, you have to practise. It isn't always something you can switch on and off at first and many candidates have little or no control over it anyway. Some do. It's much easier to use when you're installed because of the living wood. Having a Shipbody makes all the difference.>

The Ship didn't sound worried at all. Maia realised that she would just have to trust Jupiter's word on this, though the little nagging voice that told her she was unworthy still persisted.

"That's better," *Blossom* said aloud. She increased speed on the Captain's orders and they were soon making good time, safe in their magical bubble.

"Why do some Ships wreck, if you can protect yourself like this?" Maia asked the Captain.

"All sorts of reasons," Plinius replied. "Hidden shoals, sudden squalls, bad timing, or, more often than not, overconfidence. It's too late when you're capsizing or impaled on rocks. Always remember, it's better to be safe than sorry. New Ships spend most of their first months drilling, so that when the time comes everything's automatic."

"You all know what to do."

"After so many years, I should hope so!" Plinius replied. "Still, it's good practice. Overconfidence, remember? Prayers and sacrifices to Neptune help, but you can't always rely on Divine intervention when you need it!"

Maia remembered that Plinius had found the Sea God terrifying, unlike friendly Mercury. She knew from listening to the crew that Neptune occasionally manifested in physical form. That would probably be even scarier than if he took possession of someone else. Maia had to agree with Plinius; it was always wiser not to rely on his goodwill.

A few hours later, they rounded the headland and the great Thamesis estuary came into sight. The wind finally slackened and the waves fell, so *Blossom* and Heron released the Potentia. The bubble stretched thin, before vanishing with a loud pop, allowing the fresher air in once more. It didn't affect *Blossom* and Maia, but the crew looked relieved, taking deep breaths of the cold, salty breeze.

"Much better," Durus said. He raised his telescope to his eye. "Civilisation ahoy! Captain, should we anchor for the night?"

"Certainly. There are treacherous sandbanks," he explained to Maia. "We'll stay near the mouth of the river for now and make our way upstream in the morning with the tide." He nodded at his Lieutenant who went to oversee the crew. *Blossom* talked Maia through the procedures and told her what she knew of the river.

<I've passed this way more times than I can recall,> she said. <You must always remember that things often change from one season to the next. Big storms can move the sea bed, making once safe channels perilous. Mapping and taking soundings are important to keep us all from running aground.>

Maia absorbed the information, storing it in her capacious memory and watching everything with fascination. She was pleased when *Blossom* let her operate the anchors, controlling the heavy chains carefully.

As she did so, she thought she glimpsed a silvery wisp of something fly past the vessel, like a piece of gauze caught in a breeze. She tried to get a better look, but, no sooner had it had appeared, it was gone.

*

Londin was its usual bustling self, even more now as the capital made its preparations for the winter festival of Saturnalia. *Blossom* had been assigned a mooring in the Royal Dockyards, alongside several of her friends who also had the good fortune to be in port at this time of year.

There was a sense of anticipation amongst the crew and officers alike, as this would be an opportunity for everyone to have a thoroughly good time.

"Only two more days!" Plinius said, cheerfully. "I'm going home to spend the time with Fausta and as many of the family as can get there. I've a new grandson to greet as well."

His eldest son's wife had given birth two weeks before and he was clearly overjoyed.

"Another little Plinius," *Blossom* teased. "How many's that, now?"

"That makes four between them all. I think that Justinia was hoping for a girl second time around, but you know that boys run in the family. She might have another baby. Still, we take whatever the Gods give. As long as they're healthy I don't care what gender they are."

"Quite right too," his Ship agreed. "Maia, you and I will spend a happy Saturnalia together and you can eat all the things I can't."

"Make the most of it," Plinius said. "This time next year you should be settled into a vessel of your own."

"I can't think that far ahead," Maia said, feeling the familiar stab of fear.

They laughed.

"Initiation will be on you in a few months," *Blossom* told her. "There isn't much more that I can teach you like this. You're almost ready."

Maia didn't feel ready. She was back in her body now, though she could still chat to *Blossom* through her earring. She'd also be able to talk to Captain Plinius, which cheered her up. Distance was no barrier to the Ship link.

"I need to go shopping," she said. She'd like to purchase some gifts for her friends, as was the custom.

"Yes and you can get me some things too," the Ship said.

"I'll arrange an escort for you," Plinius said. "Meanwhile, I'm off to the Club."

Its full name was the Royal Naval Officers' Club, but everyone just called it the Club.

"Have fun," *Blossom* called after him. "Don't forget to pop back before you set off for Portus."

"I won't."

Maia watched as the Captain disembarked and hailed a carriage. The vessel was operating with a skeleton crew now, as many of the men had headed into Londin, either to see family or to catch up with old acquaintances in the many waterfront taverns. All the businesses that catered for sailors would be doing a roaring trade as the city began to gear up ready to celebrate.

"I didn't see the *Regina*," she remarked.

"No, she's in Portus," *Blossom* told her. Maia was secretly glad that she didn't have to pay another courtesy call to her old Academy classmate. She was looking forward instead to having time to relax and catch up on her reading, while stuffing her face with as many delicious things as she could coax out of the Ship's cook.

She'd just settled down in her cabin for a quiet time, when *Blossom* alerted her.

"Master Mage Raven is here to see you. I've told him to go to the day room."

Maia groaned. What did he want? Maybe it was just a courtesy call to see how she was doing. She hauled herself up, brushing down her skirts to knock off the cake crumbs and adjusted her cap in the little mirror. She'd become used to her scarring now and her hair had grown longer on top so that she could brush it forward and hide the shiny bald patches where it had been burned away. At least it didn't hurt any more, not since Mercury's present of cakes. She still thanked him on a regular basis, placing her offerings on the Ship's altar.

"I'm on my way."

*

Raven was just settling himself into a chair, when Maia entered the cabin.

"Greetings, Maia."

"Greetings to you too, Master Mage. May I offer you some refreshment?"

"I won't say no," the ancient Mage replied. "It's chilly out there so a cup of mulled wine would be most welcome. Maia?"

"Chai for me, please."

The Ship's servant, who had escorted him down, bowed and exited. They exchanged pleasantries while they waited, though Maia knew that she had to guard her tongue as *Blossom* would be listening in.

"So, how are you finding things?" Raven asked.

"Fine," Maia said. "We had some rough weather off the Isle of the Dead and I finally got to see a shield raised."

"Won't be for the last time," he said. "Especially as now we're well into winter. It will probably get worse from here on in. An easterly is the worst as it can bring freezing winds and snow from the continent, so watch out for that. Ah, thank you, Philo, I'm much obliged."

The servant smiled, pleased that the Mage had remembered his name and Maia approved of his consideration. She'd become used to being addressed as 'girl' over the years, or simply being ignored.

When Philo had left, Raven took a long, appreciative sip of the steaming liquid.

"That's better." He cocked his head as Maia prepared the chai, carefully spooning out the dried leaves into the pot.

"I could never see the point of that stuff," he remarked.

"It's very fashionable."

"And expensive!"

"That too," Maia admitted. "I like it. I used to drink the dregs from my old master's cup at my first place, when I could get to them. Now I can have a whole pot to myself."

"Within reason, I expect."

"Every day, as long as we have enough and it hasn't run out yet!"

She lifted the pot lid and gave the brown liquid a stir, before allowing it to settle once more.

"This isn't just a social call," Raven told her. "Have you got plans for the festival?"

Maia was on alert immediately.

"I'm spending it here, with *Blossom*," she said. "Captain Plinius invited me down to Portus to stay with his family, but I couldn't face the journey."

Or a house full of gawking strangers.

"I have another proposition for you," he said. "You have been formally invited to spend Saturnalia at the home of Senator Madoc Britannicus Rufus, just outside Londin. I offered to be the messenger. Have you heard of him?"

Maia's heart sank. "Yes. Matrona mentioned him." She took the little silver strainer and poured her chai to hide her confusion and annoyance.

"He's the leader of the Imperial faction, which wants closer ties with Roma. He was high in the favour of the old King and still wields a lot of influence in the Senate."

She frowned. "Why would he bother to notice me?"

"You're quite the heroine in certain circles," Raven pointed out, "and the only Ship-in-training we have. That gives you status in the eyes of the nation. I won't lie, it's probably to increase his standing with certain groups."

"You mean, I'm about to be trotted out like a prize mare, whether I want to be or not," Maia groaned.

"It helps to have powerful friends," he said, "and you are of a noble family, after all. He probably got some intimation of it."

That was a possibility. Word could have leaked out about the *Livia* and the Senator would have his own sources of information. She wouldn't be claiming any of her inheritance as nothing was official but, as the *Augusta* had told her, there were always people who knew.

"As long as he didn't get any other information," she muttered. Raven raised his eyebrow and quickly shook his head.

"He won't know the whole story," he said carefully.

"What if I refuse? I'd rather stay here."

Raven pursed his lips. "That would be unwise. I fear that you're caught up in politics now, whether you want it or not."

"A tabula piece to be moved about as the players wish it," she said bitterly. "No change there then!"

"I am truly sorry." He sounded like he meant it. "If it's any consolation, the Senator is a good man and a friend of mine. You'll be treated very well. Don't you fancy a whole week in the lap of luxury?"

"Not really. I don't want to be stared at by the Senator's house guests."

To her surprise, Raven chuckled. "Believe me, they wouldn't dare. Being a Ship-in-training means that you have Potentia. One frown from you and they'll wet themselves!"

Maia burst out laughing. "Me? I still don't believe that I have any Potentia at all."

Raven raised an eyebrow. "Do you doubt the King of the Gods?"

"No," she said hastily, "but there've been no signs. Will you look for me, please? Perhaps there's been a change from last time."

"Very well," the Master Mage agreed. "Now be still while I concentrate."

Maia felt the atmosphere in the cabin start to thicken as he extended his awareness. A sensation like cobwebs brushing against her skin made her grit her teeth as he used his Potentia to check to the heart of her. The seconds passed as he worked and when he spoke, his whispery voice made her jump.

"You're different somehow, but I can't pin it down. Give me your hand."

She reached out, but as soon as their fingers touched it was if a door suddenly burst open…

…*and the summer sun* was slanting obliquely across a quadrangle surrounded by ancient, two storey buildings, the colonnades at their base filled with noisy young men hurrying back and forth, grey robes flapping as they hurried to their next lessons.

He was in a rush, threading his way through his fellow students with a growing sense of urgency. His first assignment and he was going to be late for the briefing. Damn Jay and his mad idea to drink in every tavern between the Collegium and the Temple of Apollo! It had been an excellent night, but he'd lost track of time in the subsequent stupor.

He put on a final burst of speed, nearly crashing into a couple of younger boys whose yells of indignation followed him to the large double doors that led to the inner quad. A muttered password triggered them to swing open, too slowly for his liking and he squeezed through as soon as he was able…

…and Maia was back aboard the *Blossom*, disorientated and gasping like a landed fish. Where had she just been? Everything had been so vivid; she could feel the sun and the young man's hangover as if it had happened to her, but it was somewhere she had never been and it wasn't her body, either. *Who* had she been?

Raven had snatched his hand away and was bent forward, as if in pain. She was just wondering whether to call for help when *Blossom* rose through the floor like a spirit from the deep.

"What in the Gods' name is going on, Maia? Raven, are you all right? Do you need an Adept?"

He raised a hand to forestall her and shook his head.

"Maia?" *Blossom* looked from one to the other, demanding an explanation. "I felt the Potentia run through the vessel, first Raven's, then yours."

"Mine?" Maia could scarce believe it. "I was…somewhere else," she said, knowing that it sounded lame but unable to come up with an alternative explanation.

"*Blossom*, would you leave us, please?" Raven said, faintly. "Feel free to monitor, but I need to speak to Maia alone."

The Ship looked worried. "Her Potentia's just manifested, hasn't it? You must tell me if her ability might affect my functions."

"I will," he promised her. The Ship gave Maia a last concerned glance, before sinking back into her vessel.

Raven lifted his head. If anything he looked older and more time-worn than before.

"You were in the Collegium of Mages in Londinium, a very long time ago." She looked at him, bewildered. "The young man, who was still rather drunk and very late for a meeting, was me." She felt her mouth fall open and she swallowed convulsively. How?

"You took a dormant memory straight from my head and translated it into an inner reality, so that we both relived it as it happened. It was correct in every detail. Has anything like this happened before?"

Maia was dumbfounded. "Never!"

"You remember what a *certain person* said?"

Jupiter. He'd seen something when she'd been under his scrutiny. What had the *Livia* done to her in those last, desperate moments?

The undead Ship's words echoed in her brain.

"My last gifts to you...fire and mind!"

She hadn't realised that she'd spoken them aloud.

<You didn't.>

She jerked at the voice in her head, looking around. It had been a man's, deep and edged with amusement.

<I'm in front of you,> he added. She stared in shock at the Master Mage, who nodded.

"Something has activated in your brain," he said in his regular voice. Now she could see how time had changed him. When she'd been part of his memory, he'd been young and strong, full of the certainty that he could talk his way out of anything life could throw at him.

Now, he was a scarred and shrivelled husk. What had happened to him?

"I was a handsome lad," he said, "black of hair and blue of eye. I could run like the wind and study all night – when I wasn't carousing with my friends. I felt I could do anything and I had Potentia to spare. I still have the Potentia, but little else." He shrugged in resignation. "It's the way of things."

Maia reached out. It was like using invisible muscles she never knew she had.

<But why can we hear each other?>

<Like I said. You have forged a link between us. It was the *Livia*'s strength and one which she has passed on to you.>

Again, she marvelled at the contrast between his physical and mental voices.

<Can anyone else hear us?>

<No. This is a private link. We can speak freely in our heads. It may come in useful, though I don't expect you to be chattering away at me at all times of the day and night!> he added, warningly.

<I'll keep it for emergencies,> she assured him.

He grinned. "Just when I thought I was incapable of surprise. You've just taught an old dog a new trick, so you have. And now I'm forgetting what we were talking about."

Maia was tempted to say 'hangovers' but decided not to push her luck.

"The Senator's invitation. I'm not going for the whole week, but I might stay a couple of nights. How about that?"

"It's a reasonable compromise," he agreed. "See how it goes. You may want to stay longer."

"Or not."

"I know you're glaring at me," he said. It was her turn to grin.

"I'll tell *Blossom* that I'm to be put on show again, with the other curiosities."

"You and me both," he replied, enigmatically. "We'll be curiosities together."

III

The first day of Saturnalia arrived before Maia felt ready for it, sweeping through the capital like a drunken sailor on a rampage after months at sea.

She'd spent the previous days preparing for the festivities by helping *Blossom*'s remaining crew to decorate the vessel with the traditional greenery and coloured lanterns. She was glad that she'd had a little time to pay some unobtrusive visits to the nearby shops for the Ship and herself, to buy the traditional presents. These were just small tokens of affection, some of which would enable *Blossom* to play practical jokes on her friends.

"I love these," the Ship confided to Maia, gazing with undisguised glee at the pile of packages. "Last year I got a load of fake beards and made my officers wear them. They looked like Northmen. We weren't in port, so they were all at my mercy!"

She grinned wickedly. Maia had already admired the Ship's new hair style. She'd foregone the little plaits and formed her tight black curls into a high tower, adorned with multi-coloured blooms that complemented her dark complexion.

"They've escaped you this year," Maia said.

"It only gives me more time to plan some extra special joke for next season," *Blossom* sighed. "Saturnalia seems to come around every five minutes these days."

"I'm sorry I won't be here for the whole time."

"It's all right. You might even enjoy yourself."

Maia pulled a face.

"Stuck in a house full of drunken revellers? I don't think so! Maybe he's got a good library and I can hide out there."

She'd packed her bag with her uniform, stubbornly refusing to wear anything gaudy as most people did. She would be there under sufferance as it was.

"Tell me if anyone interesting turns up," *Blossom* said. Maia shrugged.

"I won't know who anyone is. I'm not looking forward to this."

"Remember to smile!" the Ship told her and was rewarded with a scowl. "Oh, I can see Raven approaching. It seems he's going to escort you himself."

The sound of oars in the water drew her attention and Maia's eyes widened at the sight of a very splendid barge. A carved and gilded bear decorated the prow and Maia remembered Matrona telling her about the bridge they'd passed underneath. This craft alone was a prominent statement of the Senator's wealth and influence.

The lone passenger was sitting to the rear under an all-weather canopy, looking more like a bundle of blankets dumped carelessly on the bench than a powerful Mage. Maia said her farewells to *Blossom* and the remaining crew and left the vessel, walking to the steps that led down to the wharf. Philo followed her carrying her luggage, which he handed down to the rowers. She hopped aboard and made her way aft to sit with the Master Mage.

"Nice boat," she said.

"Isn't it just? The house has a private landing, so I thought a river trip was in order. Have you seen the streets lately?"

"I have," she said. The decorations had been impressive, but the city was packed to bursting with shoppers and revellers who had already started their celebrations in earnest. This way would be quicker.

She waved as the *Blossom* retreated into the distance and caught curious glances and calls from the other Ships as she passed. They were all decked out for Saturnalia too, flags and banners flying and she suspected that there was a little competition to see who could look the most festive. She had got to know some of them while she was training, so gave them a friendly wave back.

"They're impressed with your transport," Raven said. "Have you made a lot of friends?"

"A few. They were very kind after I was injured."

"Well, settle back and enjoy the ride. It won't take too long. Are you warm enough?"

He'd woven a spell around them both to keep out the cold, just as he had, belatedly, whilst crossing the harbour in Portus. That seemed an age ago now.

"Yes, thank you."

She watched the river flow past in the December sunshine and wondered what awaited her in the house of the Senator.

*

The barge took them as far as it could, eventually pulling up at a private landing on the riverbank. Huge ornamental gardens stretched almost as far as she could see, with a gravelled drive cutting through them in the direction of the villa.

A small carriage was waiting to take them the remaining distance, pulled by a pair of matched grey ponies with plaited and decorated manes. Maia thought it funny that the Senator needed a carriage just to cross his garden.

"It's a large spread," Raven agreed. "Wait till you see the house."

The entrance to the Senator's villa was as impressive as the riverside gardens had promised, with a spacious portico running along the façade and a fine glass fanlight over the doorway beyond. Several liveried servants were in attendance, and one, a large burly fellow, hastened to open the carriage door to help them alight. She glanced to her left, seeing carefully pruned topiary and statues. Further away, a gentle splashing told of fountains playing and, even now in the winter time, flowering bushes and evergreen shrubs added colour and life. The air was full of the sharp smells of winter, tinged with a hint of wood smoke. She followed Raven as they climbed up the wide front steps, to where a huge bear of a man with a shock of fiery red hair, greying at the temples, was standing ready to greet them.

He clasped the Master Mage's arm in the gesture of friendship.

"Greetings, friends! I freely offer you the hospitality of my house!"

"My thanks, Senator." Raven replied, smiling. Maia thought he looked more relaxed now they had arrived. "May I introduce Miss Maia Abella, Ship-in-training?"

Maia saluted smartly, arm across the breast in the old Roman fashion.

"At your service, Senator."

"You are most welcome here!" the Senator replied, his voice booming out over the assemblage of guests and servants. "Delighted to meet you, Miss Maia!"

His pale blue eyes twinkled in the torchlight as he held out his hand to shake hers and Maia liked him immediately. He seemed genuinely pleased to see her, though something told her that to hold his position in court he must be shrewd as well as amiable. The fact that he had come out to meet them in person showed that he held the Master Mage in high esteem.

She also wondered what advantage to himself he saw in her.

"My wife, Drusilla Camilla."

The senator's wife was a slender, dark-haired aristocratic woman dressed in the latest fashion, a high-waisted silk gown, embroidered with delicate golden flowers. Her jewellery was expensive and tasteful. She smiled and inclined her head, her slender frame contrasting sharply against her husband's bulk.

"Please do come inside. You must be exhausted after your journey," she said. Her Britannic was accented and Maia reflected that she was probably from elsewhere in the Empire, possibly even Roma itself, and was more used to speaking proper Latin. It was still the official language of the country, but most people spoke Britannic nowadays. She signalled to the man who had opened the carriage door.

"Petrus, please show our guests to their chambers."

"This is our steward," Rufus explained.

"All is prepared, master," Petrus said. He was wearing a slave's chain and Maia guessed that he was one of the Senator's most trusted servants.

"Excellent!" Rufus turned to his guests. "Perhaps you would both care to join me, after bathing of course? Get some of the stiffness out, eh?"

"That would be splendid, Senator," Raven said.

"My servants will attend you and I will meet you again shortly."

Petrus stepped forward to direct the men, whilst Drusilla guided Maia into a large atrium that was covered by a glass skylight to keep out the worst of the weather. It was dominated by a large statue of the Goddess Minerva, realistically painted and dressed in full armour. Her stern grey eyes sparkled in the light and Maia saw that they had been inset with little specks of mica. She admired the fine craftsmanship, wondering whether it had been created from life.

"Athena Minerva is the patron of our family," Drusilla explained. A small altar stood before the statue, ready for offerings of incense, while, to one side stood the usual shrine to the Lares and Penates, the household Gods. This looked like a little house, made of gilded wood, complete with miniature columns and doors. Drusilla looked on as both Maia and Raven made the customary offerings, then gave a signal. A tall blonde girl wearing a delicate slave collar stepped forward.

"Xenia will be your personal servant whilst you are here with us, Miss Abella," Drusilla said. "Just ask her if you need anything. I'll see you shortly."

"This way please, ma'am," Xenia said, eyes downcast.

Maia thanked Drusilla and followed the slave into a corridor. She steeled herself to explain that she wasn't yet ready to have a full bathing experience, as Campion had warned her to avoid extremes of heat and cold. She'd just have to come out with it.

"Xenia."

The girl looked round, an inquiring look on her face. "I can't use the baths. I was badly burned." She hadn't wanted to whip off her veil in front of her, remembering the *Regina*'s response.

"Oh yes, ma'am. I've been told to give you a private wash and massage."

Maia breathed a quiet sigh of relief. Someone had explained things and everyone must know that she was still recovering.

Of course, the Senator had his own household bath suite, as only the very rich could afford. Each room was lined with precious marble from every part of the Empire and Maia had to stop herself from gaping at the gorgeous decoration. The anteroom was painted in the latest fashion from the faraway land of Chin, with pagodas and dragons swirling across the walls, but the other rooms were more traditional, showing Gods and heroes together with scenes of lush gardens and flowering trees. It was a far cry from the overcrowded public baths in Portus with their sharp smell of cleanser.

Xenia paused to allow her to admire the effect, then led her on to a smaller suite of rooms.

"These are private, ma'am," she assured her. They were no less luxurious and Maia sat quietly while the girl sponged her down and gently rubbed perfumed oils into her skin, only using a strigil on her undamaged areas to remove the dirt and residue of the day's travel. She could really get used to this, she decided.

The room had a large mirror along one wall, but Maia found herself avoiding the sight of her own reflection. The change was still too startling and unsettling; not that she'd ever had much time to use a looking glass other than to check that her hair was tidy. She could have happily dozed off, but her stomach was reminding her in no uncertain terms that she'd not eaten for a while.

Xenia produced clean clothes – her own she was glad to note – and helped her to dress, before light footsteps sounded on the heated floor and Lady Drusilla entered the room.

"I do hope that you are feeling better now, Maia?"

If she was startled by the sight of Maia's injuries, she displayed nothing in her manner. Xenia had been matter-of-fact as well, too well trained to show anything but polite attentiveness.

"I am, thank you my lady."

Drusilla regarded her hair, which she'd brushed forward to cover the worst of the burnt skin.

"I have come to offer my help. You must feel self-conscious about your injuries, yes?"

"I wear my veil when I'm away from the *Blossom*," Maia said. Drusilla nodded.

"I don't suppose that anyone has suggested a hairpiece, or cosmetics?" she asked, frankly.

Maia blinked in astonishment. Nobody had.

"I thought not. You are in a very masculine domain, my dear. I expect that everyone is saying, 'you'll be fine when you're a Ship!' Am I not correct?"

Maia had to smile. "Yes."

"And in the meantime, here you are, hiding yourself. You should bear your wounds with pride, but there are ways to ameliorate them."

She cocked her head on one side, pursing her lips.

"What do you think, Xenia? Have we something that will do?"

"Oh yes, Domina. Perhaps another hair colour, or something complementary?"

"Which colour would you like, Maia? I have all sorts of wigs and hairpieces."

She nodded to Xenia, who hurried off.

"I don't really know," Maia admitted. She hadn't even thought about it, though she'd seen plenty of women wearing them. Marcia Blandina, her late and unlamented mistress, had had several, one for every occasion.

"Well, it is Saturnalia, so you can be as bold as you wish. We will be wearing masks some of the time too, so you can be whoever you want."

Xenia and another girl appeared, each carrying a wooden stand with three wigs pinned to fake heads. They ranged in colour from jet black to blonde and even a golden one with cunningly wrought ivy leaves twining through it.

Drusilla looked at her expectantly. "So," she smiled. "Which one do you like? I know!" she added, seeing Maia's confusion. "Why don't you try them all?"

In the end, Maia settled for a pale silvery blonde that didn't contrast too sharply with her skin. She also allowed Xenia to apply some sort of concealing cream to her face and neck and found that she was pleased with the result. The scars didn't stand out too much and she could always decide to wear a mask for the festivities.

She stared in the mirror and linked to *Blossom,* activating her visual relays to allow the Ship to see through her eyes.

<Hello! What do you think?>

<Ooh, what a difference!> the Ship replied, adding, with regret, <I should have thought of that.>

<Don't worry,> Maia told her. <It doesn't matter when I'm on board and you mostly see me from the inside out anyway.>

<You're always lovely,> *Blossom* said, loyally. <Keep your head held high!>

Maia broke the connection and turned to thank the three women.

"I was just showing the *Blossom* my new look," she explained. The slaves' eyes widened and Drusilla nodded respectfully.

"Please give her my compliments."

"I will."

For a moment, Maia felt strange. She'd become so used to the Ship link that talking mind-to-mind was second nature to her now. Raven had been right about the awe Potentia was held in by regular humans.

"You must be hungry. My husband and I have arranged a small, private meal for you, then you can rest before this evening's events. I will see you soon."

After Drusilla had left to attend her other guests, Maia followed Xenia through the villa, past delicately painted statues and rows of busts that depicted the Senator's illustrious ancestors, all men and women of high rank. The marble felt warm under her shoes and she wondered if the new underfloor gas heating was used here instead of having slaves keeping the fires going in the hypocaust. However it was done, it certainly took the chill off the December day.

"The Senator is using the small dining room, not the larger one," Xenia explained. "He's just had it refurbished."

She opened a panelled mahogany door and stood back to allow Maia to enter first. Raven was already occupying the couch opposite the Senator's, but she still felt a little self-conscious until the latter rose to meet her and lead her to a place. It was all she could do not to gape at the opulent surroundings. Three of the walls were papered in the new style, with artfully painted scenes of fruit and flowers spilling from luscious cornucopia. Realistic looking birds fluttered and soared in a blue sky and, above them all, winged putti danced and played in rose-tinted clouds. One wall was draped with curtains of embroidered silk that matched the elegantly upholstered couches arranged on three sides around a low central table. Clearly the Senator favoured the old Roman style of dining in a triclinium, unlike many who preferred to sit upright on chairs.

Lady Drusilla gestured her to recline at her side. Maia noticed that she had changed her gown and now wore a necklace of large, lustrous rubies interspersed with brilliant-cut diamonds that flashed against her olive skin. Her hair was piled high, with jewelled ribbons twisted through it.

"Well, I'm hungry," Rufus remarked. "Let's not stand on formalities. We thank Minerva and all the Gods for their bounty and protection!" he announced, pouring the ritual libation onto a small, portable altar. He then signalled to Petrus who in turn waved in several servants, carrying platters. The aromas rising from the food made Maia's mouth water and Rufus gave her a surreptitious wink.

"This all looks delicious, Senator," she said.

Rufus laughed. "All the more reason to enjoy it now. Most of it is from my own farms and I have glasshouses for the grapes, oranges and pineapples. It's a shame we can't grow them outside in this climate, though my gardeners have managed to find some hardy fig bushes. I fear that productive olive trees are beyond them."

"Ah, the wonderful Britannic weather," Raven said. "I like a good tart apple myself."

"We stock up when we're in port," Maia said, "though the *Blossom* hasn't been too far lately."

"Training fine young Ships." The Senator raised a glass in salute to Maia. Meanwhile the servants busied themselves pouring scented water over the guests' hands then drying them on fine linen cloths. Maia watched carefully and copied what the others were doing. The evening was turning out to be a lesson in the lifestyles of the rich and powerful, but she remembered *Blossom*'s words and held her head high.

"So important to the security of our country," the Master Mage observed. He had already located the pickled fish sauce and was helping himself, his blindness no obstacle. Maia was offered a dish of quail on sippets of bread, which she was glad to accept. She noticed that Drusilla was using a dainty silver fourchette to pick at her food. A quick glance told her that she had been given one too, so she used it, enjoying the novelty.

One course followed another and by the time the cheese and fruit were served Maia's stomach was signalling a warning. She'd never eaten such fine foods in her life. The wine had tasted good too, though she didn't know enough about it to make a proper judgement, so had drunk sparingly as it wouldn't do to end up befuddled. Most of the conversation was about current affairs, mentioning people in the government about whom she knew nothing and the state of trade throughout the Empire. She listened attentively, picking up information as the others talked and filing it away for future reference.

"And how is life at Court?" Raven asked. Rufus raised his eyebrows.

"Interesting. Our new King is finally listening to his advisors, but as you know, there are certain parties who want Britannia to pull away from outside influences and build an Empire of her own," the Senator said, "starting with the New Continent. They don't want to share."

"Tensions are rising," Raven agreed, "and I personally hope that everything will be settled amicably. We've enough with the Northern Alliance breathing down our necks without the Empire squabbling with itself."

"Quite," Rufus agreed. "More and more of their Ships are coming into port. There's even talk of them setting up temples to their own Gods." He shuddered. "Big savage hairy men carrying axes. Ugh! And don't get me started on the women."

"Why?" Maia asked him.

"Worse than the men," he said, giving her a meaningful look. "As some of our more unwise citizens are finding out. No blushing maidens there!" He gave a great laugh. "Annoy them at your peril!"

Maia thought that it served the men right, trying to take advantage of foreign women. It wouldn't be a mistake they made twice.

"Their ambassadors are quite cultured and knowledgeable," Rufus continued. "I think they appreciate the benefits of good roads and decent baths, though we don't have much snow for them to roll about in afterwards. It's cold where they come from."

"Peace is always preferable to war," Raven said, drily.

"True. Too many young idiots read the heroic tales and think it's a glorious thing. We know better eh? Still, things will be as the Gods will it. Look at Troy."

"And dozens since."

"Alas. But let us talk of happier things! I hope you enjoy the entertainments I've got planned, Miss Maia."

Maia perked up. She hoped so too. Maybe she'd stay more than a couple of nights after all.

*

The Senator's guests started arriving in the early evening. The winter's night had already fallen and the villa and grounds were lit with torches and coloured lights that gave the whole place an air of joyous festivity.

Maia stared at herself in the mirror, wondering whether to keep the same wig, or exchange it for another. The one with the black curls reminded her of her friend, the *Patience*, who would be celebrating with her crew far away. Unconsciously, her hand moved to the little necklace Briseis had given her back at the Academy, before she had left her flesh body behind to go into the wood. The pearls and little gems were smooth against her roughened fingertips as she remembered the happy times they'd spent together.

She gazed appreciatively around the chamber she'd been given. The furniture and colourful rugs were made of the finest materials, many imported and the best that money could buy. The dressing table alone was covered with enough bottles and jars of cosmetics to please a whole salon full of ladies and the spacious bed was draped with fine gauze, embroidered with flowers and butterflies. Xenia had shown her where everything was, including her own personal washroom.

"This was Lady Rufilla's room, the Senator's daughter," Xenia had told her. "She was married last year. Lady Drusilla hopes you like it."

Maia certainly did. These must have been the sort of luxurious surroundings Tullia had grown up in. Moving to the Academy must have been a whole new experience for the spoiled Admiral's daughter, even though the rooms had been very comfortable by anybody else's standards.

A voice broke into her thoughts.

"Ma'am? A parcel has arrived for you."

Xenia stood in the doorway to her room, a small gift-wrapped box in her hand.

"For me?"

"Yes, ma'am. It has your name on it."

Maia took the parcel and unwrapped it, to reveal a flat oval box made of some exotic wood. There was a little gold clasp securing the two parts. When she undid it and lifted the lid she could hardly believe her eyes. Behind her, she heard Xenia sigh in admiration.

Lying amid the black velvet interior was the most gorgeous necklace of pale stones, set in silvery metal.

"It's exquisite!" she breathed. She searched in vain for a note or card, to tell her who had sent such an expensive present, but found no clue.

"They're moonstones, ma'am," Xenia told her, her wide eyes fixed on the shimmering jewels.

"Do you know who sent it?" Maia asked.

The girl shook her head. "No, ma'am. It was left on the table in the atrium and the card only had your name on it. Would you like to wear it now?"

Maia looked longingly at the shimmering stones, but thought that the necklace looked quite heavy. She could wear her pearls for short periods, but this looked as though it would chafe her neck and she didn't want to have to take it off half way through the meal. It might be construed as an insult if the anonymous donor was watching.

"No, I'll leave it off for tonight," she decided, "but I'll mention the gift and be sure to wear it later."

She still thought it strange that it was without a donor. "Perhaps the tag fell off, or there was another card that was mislaid?"

"I'll check again with the doorkeeper, ma'am," Xenia said.

"I'd better get ready," Maia told her. "Will there be many guests?"

"Oh yes, ma'am. Senator Rufus has lots of friends and most of them will be here for the first night."

Maia looked out of the large windows into the gardens beyond. The night was bitterly cold and the wind had dropped, so there would be a frost before morning.

"Could you fetch me my blue shawl please, Xenia?" she asked. She probably wouldn't need it during the meal because the room would be heated and full of people besides. But it was best to have it with her just in case.

Xenia looked sheepish.

"Oh, I'm sorry ma'am. It was stained, so I took it to the laundry."

Maia shrugged.

"Thank you, Xenia, I didn't realise. Oh well, it's a good job I've got another. I'll wear the white one instead."

*

The villa was transformed, full of crowds of excited guests milling about and sampling the various delicacies on offer. The banquet had been splendid, with toasts and speeches, but now that was over, the main theme of the evening was entertainment. Maia had been so overawed by everything that she realised she had quite forgotten to mention her gift. No matter, she could ask Lady Drusilla about it later. She'd worn the silver wig, though she'd insisted on wearing her uniform, to Xenia's evident disappointment. She'd been aware of glances in her direction throughout the meal, but nobody had been rude enough to stare.

Now, the Senator was outside, demonstrating the workings of his new steam carriage to a crowd of interested onlookers. Their breath hung in plumes in the frigid air while jugglers and acrobats mingled with the partygoers, performing tricks for their amusement. Maia watched from the side lines; her face was hidden behind a bland silver mask though her uniform proclaimed her identity to all. Looking around, she was certainly one of the more demurely dressed women. Tonight was a time for excess and most of the guests were already well into their cups.

"It's bad form to be sober, you know," a quiet voice whispered in her ear. She turned and looked into the Master Mage's clouded blue eyes.

"So, we're both breaking tradition," she replied, tartly. "I don't think it would do me good to get drunk."

Raven looked disgruntled. "You're right unfortunately, though the odd glass of fine wine can have medicinal value. I fear that the maxim 'everything in moderation' flies out of the window at this time of year. So, what have you seen so far, apart from happy drunks?"

"I didn't like the mechanical doll," Maia said. The Senator was proud of his growing collection of automata, but the clockwork figure had unnerved her.

"The shape of things to come," Raven told her. "Devices are becoming more sophisticated. Of course, mechanical servants are mentioned in the Odyssey, but the secret of making them was lost to mortals long ago. Now it seems that the Artificers are re-discovering it."

He didn't sound thrilled.

"They are remarkable," she admitted, "but I preferred the singing bird. Oh, and the silver swan that bent its neck. That was beautiful!"

"I wish I had the sight to appreciate them more fully," he said. "These devices don't worry me – it's the uses to which this technology may eventually be put. I often think that this was the main reason that Jupiter banned Divine offspring. They caused enough chaos with swords and spears. Imagine what a son of Mars could do with cannon and muskets!"

"That would be frightening," she agreed. Mercury had mentioned that some of the Gods hankered for the old days of simple shepherds and goat herders. There were still plenty of those around, but just as many cunning Artificers and factories churning out more and more new machines. She had the feeling that the older Gods didn't like change.

The Senator moved on, his entourage following behind him like a brood of obedient ducklings and leaving some of the younger men eyeing up the steam carriage. Maia could feel a joy-ride coming on and said as much.

Raven grinned. "Once upon a time, I would have been the first up on there, trying to get it to work," he admitted. Shall we go in and see what's happening? You mustn't get cold."

"I'm fine," she told him. "I'll be in soon. I just want to watch the fire eaters."

"All right, but remember. We curiosities should stick together."

"Ha, ha."

"Very well, Miss Sarcasm. I'm going for another drink. See you shortly."

The Master Mage disappeared indoors to where the refreshment tables were laid out, leaving Maia alone. She'd noticed that, while she was greeted respectfully by the other guests, few of them had any inclination to strike up a conversation. She watched the entertainers for a while, before a high-pitched shriek nearly made her jump out of her skin. The youths had found the carriage's whistle. One was in the driving seat, yelling and encouraging the others to clamber aboard, wreaths askew and togas hanging in disarray as the gleaming machine began to lumber forward, steam hissing from joints and moving pistons.

A few unwary revellers were forced to leap out of the way as the great metal engine wheezed and clanked its way across the gravel, picking up speed and leaving deep ruts beneath its iron shod wheels. The whistle screamed again, echoed by raucous cheering and shouts. One man lost his grip and fell off the back, arms pinwheeling, to land with a thud on the ground. Maia gasped, but he seemed uninjured.

They were all having a wonderful time, but the noise and frenetic activity were becoming a little too much. She turned to see if she could see Raven in the atrium, but her view was blocked by staggering guests, whose glazed eyes and flushed faces showed that inhibitions were melting away as the alcohol took hold. Maia found that she was slightly disgusted by it all. Maybe if she could have got drunk herself it wouldn't have mattered and she could have joined in with the songs and dancing, but she wasn't in the mood.

She drew the shawl around herself and slipped away into the darkness, hoping to find a quiet spot away from all the pandemonium, where she could muster her thoughts in peace.

*

The uninvited guest crouched in the shadows of the trees, hissing softly to herself, feeling the newfound strength in her muscular coils and hope burning in her withered heart.

The Olympian had returned.

Now it was time to fulfil her end of the bargain. One small death was all it would take for a chance to be free again.

At first, she was unwilling to leave the cave that had been her sanctuary for so long, but the offering the Goddess brought her restored life to her sluggish limbs and put an edge on her hunger. Even now, she could feel the digestive juices working in her shrunken belly as they absorbed the essence of the prey and she felt more alive than she had for centuries. The Olympian spoke, then a harsh light had taken her somewhere else. The spell left her disorientated. Where was this place? She tasted the air, shuddering at the cold, searching for the scent of the mortal that lingered on the cloth the Goddess had wrapped around her upper arm.

She didn't like it here. Her desire was for the heat of prey and the sweet taste of hot blood in her throat, not this wintry wasteland.

There. Something large and powerful was approaching, roaring like a creature of old resurrected from the ashes of the past. She uncurled and moved to meet it eagerly, her desire rising at the thought of a potential mate. Hadn't she been promised lovers? The terrible, enticing noise grew closer and she reared to her full height in anticipation.

The stink of hot metal flooded over her, of deadly iron and hardened steel. The memories made her recoil in horror and an almost physical pain stabbed into her gut, as if the swords and spears she had fled from long ago were assailing her once more. This was no monstrous mate, but a dead, unnatural thing born of mortal cunning! Sorrow and rage filled her breast as she shrank back, watching the infernal device chug past. Smoke and sparks wrapped it in a bitter shroud that polluted the calm of the night.

Where had it come from? After a while, she tasted the air once more. There! Beyond the cold and the brittle, leafless branches, was a place full of deliciously warm prey that called to her and woke her hunger. She could sense the wavering outlines of the fires and the fluttering heartbeats of many mortals.

It was time to feed. Once her strength was returned and her appetite sated, then and only then, would she do the Olympian's bidding.

She set off eagerly towards the warmth and life, ready to devour the world.

IV

It was too cold to stay out long. The temperature had dropped even further and Maia was beginning to feel chilled to the bone. She should have nipped back to her room and grabbed a thick coat, but it was too late now. The best thing would be to head back to the warmth of the house and slip quietly away to her room to try and get some rest, if that was possible with all the noise. When she'd been a skivvy, she'd been able to snatch sleep at a moment's notice, but now it was sometimes harder to entice Morpheus to grant her his blessing.

Giggles from quiet corners told their own tales of what was happening under the cover of darkness. Hopefully, the amorous revellers wouldn't pass out and freeze to death before dawn. Maia picked up her pace and returned to the villa, grateful for the warmth if not the company.

There was still no sign of Raven. She debated whether to open up their private link and see what he was doing, before deciding against it. She hadn't dared disturb him so far and he might have even retired to bed himself. No, she would head back to her room and try on her new necklace. It would match her mask perfectly.

Dishes of cakes and sweets were set out on little tables along the corridor and she grabbed a couple as she trotted past, hiding them guiltily under her shawl before laughing to herself. There was no need to hide them now, but habits ingrained from childhood died hard and the magnificence of the villa brought back some unpleasant memories. At least she wouldn't be required to scrub these floors. It was also just as well that she was going to be a Ship, or she'd have no teeth left by the time she got to twenty-five.

She was still smiling to herself as she entered her room, placing her booty on a table and throwing off her shawl.

Her maid was sitting at the dressing table, staring into the mirror.

"Xenia?" Something about the girl's unmoving form made Maia's heart beat faster and her senses sharpen. "Are you all right?"

There was no answer. Maia approached her carefully, seeing the locked muscles and rigid limbs, as if the slave was straining against invisible bindings. Xenia's swollen lips were parted in a silent scream, her face masked by runnels of blood that dripped steadily from her eyes, nose and mouth to soak the front of her dress in a great crimson stain. Around her neck, the moonstone necklace winked evilly in the lamplight.

An inarticulate noise burst from Maia's throat and she staggered back in horror. It was clear that there was nothing she could do for Xenia now. A part of Maia's brain observed dispassionately that the maid hadn't been dead long, as the blood was still wet. She must have tried on the jewels just after Maia had left for the banquet, meaning to enjoy herself before joining the other slaves. Maia knew that if their positions had been reversed, she would have done exactly the same.

She looked wildly around the room, before opening the link to Raven.

<Raven! It's Maia! Can you hear me?>

The reply was immediate.

<Yes I can. Please don't shout, I like my brain the way it is, thank you.>

Something must have leaked through the link as, abruptly, his tone changed. <What's wrong?>

<My maid's dead! She tried on a necklace someone sent me and now she's dead!>

<Where are you?> he asked, urgently.

<In my room!> Maia could feel the panic rising, just as it had when Blandina had been crushed.

<Stay put!> Raven shot back. <Lock the door and admit no-one until I get there. Don't raise the alarm or contact anyone else. I don't know whom we can trust.>

<Yes, please hurry!>

<I'm coming.>

A few moments later there was a stealthy knock and she knew that he was outside. She opened the door a crack to check, then opened it enough for him to slip inside. He put a hand on her shoulder.

"Where?"

"Over there, at the dressing table," Maia whispered. She clutched at the Master Mage's sleeve as he went to examine the body, only releasing it as they approached. Raven didn't touch the corpse directly, but moved his hands around it in a fluid motion.

"Poisoned," he confirmed. "Do you know who sent it?"

"No. It came this afternoon. Xenia said that it had been left on the table in the atrium with my name on it."

Raven frowned.

"Nasty and unsubtle. I'm afraid that it took some time for her to die, but the paralysis must have been almost instantaneous, trapping her in place."

Maia felt numb. Unlike Marcia Blandina, the maid had been innocent. It was a cruel twist that her envy had caused her death.

"But her envy saved your life." Raven finished her thought. "I fear that this is the only positive at the moment."

The ancient Mage's head cocked abruptly, listening. "Did you hear that?"

"What?"

It was a couple of seconds before she heard the sounds of the party replaced by distant screams, growing louder and more frantic.

"What in the name of all the Gods is happening?" Raven muttered, just as every lamp in the room flickered in a sudden draught. Maia caught a brief glimpse of a silvery flash, before the window shutters slammed shut, locking themselves and a heavy table flew across the room to crash against the door.

"Is that you?" Raven demanded.

"No! There's something here! In the air."

"It can't be your mother."

<*Sister!*>

Maia started. The tiny voice was in her head.

<*Stay here!*>

Raven raised a hand, ready to cast a defensive spell.

"It's my sister," Maia told him. "I can only see a sort of light in the air."

She turned quickly, trying to spot the tell-tale shimmer.

"She has the form of a Tempestas," Raven said, as if confirming something he had already expected, "a spirit of air. Jupiter said that she had no human flesh. What did she tell you?"

"To stay here."

The screams and yells of terror were outside now, combined with running footsteps, fading into the distance as the guests fled past along the corridor.

Raven seemed torn between his desire to protect her and the need for information.

"Go!" she urged him. "I can hide here." She grabbed an ornate iron lampstand. "I'll defend myself."

He hesitated, until a whirling mass of air shifted the table away from the door, encouraging him to leave.

"You're needed," she insisted.

He blew out a breath in frustration, then addressed the air.

"Guard your sister! I will return."

After he left, the door locked and the table slammed back into place. Maia strained her eyes, but could see nothing.

"Where are you?"

An idea came to her. She picked up her discarded shawl and threw it into the air like a cloak over the place where she thought the draught was thickest. The material twisted and writhed like a living thing, before stretching out horizontally. As she watched, an imprint began to form through the cloth; nose, chin, cheeks, indistinct but recognisably human and female. A bulge resolved itself into a hand, fingers outstretched like a glove.

Maia stepped forward and took it in her own, feeling the shock of connection.

<*I am Pearl. Stay here!*> the voice said in her mind.

"Hello, Pearl," Maia replied. Despite the circumstances, a feeling of happiness stole over her. "You saved me from Blandina."

<*Yes and I was bound to the gull as punishment for interfering. I did what I could to stop the Revenant, but I wasn't strong enough.*> Pearl's unearthly voice was filled with pain. <*I'm so sorry!*>

"Don't be," Maia said, firmly, keeping an ear open for any signs of trouble outside. She clasped her sister's hand tightly through the cloth. "If it wasn't for you I'd be dead anyway. I think that the Thunderer only spared me because of my injuries."

<Maybe,> her sister agreed. *<I have been permitted to come here now to tell you that you are being hunted. Stay here and stay quiet. Fortunately, the Mother of Monsters has been distracted.>*

Maia's mouth dropped open. What in Hades?

She released her sister's hand and gripped the lampstand tightly, hoping that Raven would be back soon before she needed to use it.

*

How to gain entry? The walls were solid and when she tried the door it was securely barred. She hissed in frustration, her long claws scoring deep grooves in the wood as she scratched in vain.

There had to be another way in. A plume of hot, steamy air somewhere near her carried the scent of mortals to her questing tongue. She tasted the sweet fragrance, breathing it in and luxuriating for a few moments in the sense of well-being that flooded her body. Following the trail, she found another opening higher off the ground, with panels of some clear substance that allowed the light to shine through. This was not so well secured; a small crack widened and splintered as she dug her claws into the surround and pulled. The whole structure cracked and shattered. She threw the remnants to one side, plucking out the shards that had lodged in her scaly hide and peered into the space beyond.

It was some sort of passage, lined with smooth, tiny stones arranged in patterns. She couldn't see anybody, but there was a lot of noise coming from another door opposite and she knew that was where she needed to go.

The opening was small, but she compressed herself and wriggled through the rectangular gap, counterbalancing herself with her lower body until she reached the floor inside. After that, it was a simple thing to slide the rest of herself through. She was so thin, she thought, sadly. When she'd been in her prime, she would never have fitted through such a tiny space but, for once, her emaciated body worked in her favour.

She paused, listening. She could detect the vibrations through the ground, tiny movements that told her where her prey was located. Most were coming from straight ahead. It only took a moment to raise herself up and approach the wooden door. This time, she could see there was no lock to bar her way.

She rammed into the door, slamming it against the wall inside with the force of her blow. A gust of steam bathed her body in welcome moisture, hot and invigorating, filling her senses with a cornucopia of tastes; mortal sweat and desire, lust and satiation, all rampant and displayed openly before her.

"Oi! Shut the damn door!" A man bellowed. "You're letting in the cold!"

She lunged at him first, her fangs extended in a lightning strike that pierced his flesh, paralysing him instantly. He collapsed to the floor, helpless. His female companion was next to feel her deadly bite, before she turned on the others. One tried to escape, but she had wedged the door shut with her muscular tail and he couldn't open it. She turned her attention to him and he collapsed, gurgling in pain and shock.

She couldn't believe how easy it was. There was no cold metal here, no warriors eager to prove themselves, just soft, naked flesh ready for her kisses and the loving embrace of her twining coils. Their bodies would become part of her, lying in the warm darkness of her belly as she drew forth every last drop of life-giving sustenance. A feeling of bliss washed over her as she seized another screaming mortal and stretched her jaws wide.

*

The Master Mage moved quickly but cautiously through the deserted corridors of the villa, noting the scattered items of clothing and other belongings hastily discarded by the fleeing guests. A man's head poked out of one of the rooms, regarding him with bleary eyes.

"I say, what's going on?"

"Go back inside, lock the door and hope a God owes you a favour," Raven replied tersely, just as the guest realised whom he was addressing and hastily withdrew.

He crossed through the main rooms, stepping carefully to avoid detritus and spilt wine, his sightsense stretched to its limit. Still no-one around, though he detected movement to the rear of the building where the private baths were situated.

Raven frowned as he tried to grasp the situation. It was clear that somebody wanted Maia dead, but why the attack on the villa? Was this nothing to do with her personally, but an attempt to kill or discredit the Senator? The fact that a candidate was attacked under his roof would be a blow to his ambition and his political party.

"Master Mage! Thank the Gods!"

It was Petrus, the steward, followed by two others, all armed with muskets.

"The Senator sent us to find you and make sure you were safe. The rest of the men are outside the bath house. There's a monster in the sudatorium."

Raven barely had time to wonder what sort of monster would end up in the steam room of a private house before he was following the frightened men through the rear corridor towards the Senator's suite.

Rufus was standing in front of a line of heavily armed retainers who were busy loading muskets with powder and ball. His face sagged into lines of relief as soon as he saw the Master Mage.

"What are we dealing with?" Raven asked him tersely.

"Take a look for yourself," Rufus said, "though it's hard to make anything out through the steam. We've turned off the valves so it should start to dissipate soon. I have my suspicions, but I'd like confirmation before we go in."

He moved to a small observation panel in the wall and slid it aside to reveal a window. He was right, the room was obscured, blocking Raven's sightsense.

"I can't tell," he said in frustration. "Describe it to me."

Rufus squinted through the glass. "It appears to be vaguely female from the waist up, but with a cowled head, like a king cobra. Its lower half is a bloody great snake."

"What's it doing?" They purposely kept their voices low, so as not to provoke the thing inside.

"Eating. We don't know how many victims it's already consumed."

Raven considered for a moment. His sightsense wasn't working, but there was nothing wrong with his nose. The humid air stank like a nest of reptiles.

"Aim for the head," he whispered. "The lower body will be armoured with scales. Is there anyone else in there?"

"We can glimpse bodies, but they're either dead or paralysed."

"Then make ready. This is a job for mortal weapons, not Potentia."

Rufus stepped away and went to give the order. There were a few quiet affirmations and the sound of ramrods being used and replaced, before the men hefted their muskets. One man stood by, ready to open the door on command.

"Form up for salvo," Rufus commanded, checking his own weapon. Raven knew that he wouldn't hang back when his men were in danger, though secretly he wished the Senator would be more circumspect.

"Minerva, strengthen our aim," the Senator prayed, then he gave the nod.

The men formed into ranks, three deep, as the retainer pulled the door open, releasing a blast of steam mixed with a foul miasma of reptilian musk.

Immediately, the men at the front stepped through the doorway and dropped to their knees, sighting along their cocked weapons. The others closed up behind, muskets pointed in the direction of the horror that lay before them. The steam was starting to clear now, revealing the full extent of the carnage.

The creature was lying supine in a heap of massive, serpentine coils. A man's legs were disappearing into the distorted jaws, which pulsed rhythmically as it gulped its prey, swallowing it whole. The entire scene was like a vision from the darkest depths of Tartarus. Glowing, lidless eyes swivelled to focus on the creatures that dared to interrupt its meal.

"Aim for the head! Prepare to fire!" All muskets cocked simultaneously.

"Give fire!"

The Senator's order was drowned out by the deafening report as a dozen lead balls smashed into the nightmare. Some pocked the wall behind, scattering shards of tile, but most hit their target. Gouts of clear, slimy ichor erupted from gaping wounds and the creature writhed in agony, hissing like a thousand steam kettles, even as its last victim disappeared into its cavernous throat. Its body uncoiled, thrashing wildly as it raised its arms in a vain effort to protect itself.

"Reload!"

It seemed an age before the flintlocks fired again, but the men could see that the thing was becoming weaker.

"Fire!"

The villa shook as the guns fired once more. Bits of flesh and bone exploded outwards, red blood mixing with the creature's as predator and prey died together.

Finally, the shattered torso collapsed to the tiled floor with a meaty thud, though the thick, scaly coils continued to twitch and twist.

The men backed out of the room, coughing and choking in the sulphurous air. The Senator wiped his face with a towel.

"Well done, men," he said, hoarsely. Raven heard a few of them rush past him, probably to find a corner to bring up their dinner in private. It had been grisly work.

It was time for him to be of some assistance. The steam was almost gone and the room was cooling rapidly, helped by the draught from one of the open exterior doors. The freezing air was welcome, as it carried away some of the stink.

He stepped carefully into the sudatorium; once a peaceful place of cleansing and relaxation, it now resembled nothing less than an abattoir.

The creature took up most of the space, sprawled inelegantly in death and surrounded by bodies bearing savage puncture wounds. She had used her venomous bite to incapacitate them, ensuring that she could devour them at her leisure. Some had been crushed by her death throes, but maybe one or two could be saved.

"Senator!" he ordered. "Get these people out and call for your Adept!"

Several men, who clearly had stronger stomachs than their fellows, rushed in and carried out the people he indicated, two men and a woman. He could tell that the others had already succumbed. Several had been caught in the constricting coils and crushed, ready to follow their friends into the monster's cavernous maw.

He extended his Potentia and approached the creature cautiously, but it was clear that all life was gone. She had probably died after the first volley, but autonomic muscle reactions had continued to operate and made it seem as if she were yet living. He had formed a theory from Rufus' description and, as he examined the broken corpse, he realised he'd been right.

The Senator joined him, still shaken but determined to find out just what had invaded his house.

"Echidna," Raven told him. "The Mother of Monsters herself."

"I thought she'd died years ago," Rufus said grimly. "How in the Gods' name did she get here?"

"I've no idea, though to look at her she wasn't in great shape. That's probably why she headed straight for food and warmth, in that order."

The Senator regarded the corpse with distaste. It was true that the legendary monster had seen better days. Her torso was skeletal, withered breasts hanging limply over the smashed ribcage and long, curved fangs extended from what remained of her upper jaw. Even her mottled, scaly body looked wasted and flaky, as if she hadn't fed in a long time. Several lumps along its length told of her recent feasting.

"I don't suppose they're still alive in there?" he said.

Raven shook his head. "Alas, no. Unlike a normal serpent, she was equipped to deal with large amounts of food very quickly, plus she would crush them first. They'll be mostly digested by now."

"I'm not even sure who was in here," Rufus admitted. "I'll have to organise a roll call." His blue eyes scanned the length of the body, before spotting something incongruous.

"Wait a minute. What's this?"

He leaned forward and tugged at a length of blue material wrapped around Echidna's scrawny arm. After a vigorous jerk, it came free and he shook it out to inspect it.

"It looks like a woman's shawl."

Raven took it from him, running the cloth through his fingers, before turning it to show his friend the little gold anchor embroidered in the corner.

"This belongs to Maia." The Senator's eyes widened in alarm.

"I take it she's safe?"

"She is now, but just before this happened somebody tried to poison her. I'm afraid that your maid died instead."

Rufus groaned, horrified at the destruction visited upon his household at what should have been a happy time.

"Great Gods," he muttered, running a hand over his face. "I must go and see to the welfare of my guests and try to ascertain which ones are missing. Could you look to Maia?"

Raven nodded.

"As to that thing," the Senator continued, jerking his head towards the bloody corpse, "I think I'll have her stuffed, mounted and gifted to the temple of whichever God is responsible for this outrage. She didn't get here of her own accord, that much is clear!"

"I wouldn't do that," Raven advised.

Rufus grimaced. "Damn it! I know, I'll give it to the temple of my patroness, Athena Minerva. She can add it to her collection. She already has the Gorgon's head, so this thing should fit right in."

Raven leaned closer. "I suspect that this is the Huntress' doing," he whispered. "You were just in the way and no, I can't go into details, but I think it imperative that I move Maia back to the *Blossom* as soon as dawn breaks. She's safer on the water."

Rufus could only agree. "The Gods are playing games again," he said, bitterly.

Raven jerked his head in agreement. He could sense the Senator grinding his teeth in frustration.

"Could you see to it? I'll have guards put on all the entrances and outside her door too, good people I can trust."

Raven snorted. "Be careful. Some may have higher loyalties. That shawl didn't walk to Echidna by itself and who was better placed to purloin it than Maia's body servant?"

He left Rufus with a lot to do and more to think about. It was time that he updated Maia.

<I'm on my way back,> he Sent. <You can stand down.>

<What happened?>

<There was a monster, but we shot it,> he replied. <I won't be long.>

*

Maia's arm was stiff from clutching the lamp stand and she released it with a groan, though she knew that she couldn't afford to relax. This monster, whatever it was, had come here for her. The *Patience*'s warning still rang in her head and she felt slightly sick.

<*They killed her. She wasn't proof against mortal weapons.*>

Pearl's voice whispered in her head.

"Who?"

<*Echidna, Mother of Monsters, she who birthed Cerberus, the Hydra and Scylla. She got into the bath house.*>

"How do you know?"

<*Our mother has told me. She watches, though she can do nothing and her heart is forever broken.*>

"You can talk to her?"

<*Yes. She held you in her arms when you were born, but I issued forth like this. She could never hold me.*>

"But she can't hold me, or even talk to me."

<*No. It is her eternal punishment. I comfort her in her grief as best I can.*>

Maia couldn't help herself. All her bitterness seemed to surface at once.

"She shouldn't have broken Jupiter's law then, should she? She brought all this on herself and condemned us both, as well as causing our father's murder!"

Pearl fell silent. She probably didn't have an answer, Maia thought. She refused to feel sympathy for her mother.

<She named you Gemma. Her little jewel.>
Pearl and Gemma. Maia's hand flew to her necklace. Briseis' instincts had been right. She would have made an excellent Priestess.
<You are safe for now, so I must go. Farewell, sister. Please don't be too hard on our mother. For a brief time she had a human body with all its desires and frailties. She is suffering more than you can know.>
There was a sudden swirl of air then Pearl was gone. Maia sank down into a chair, feeling exhausted and wishing that she could magic herself back to her cabin aboard the *Blossom* as soon as possible. She hadn't contacted the Ship before as there was nothing she could have done, but now she needed that reassurance.
<Maia to *Blossom*.>
<*Blossom* here, Maia! I hope you're having a lovely time!>
Maia sighed.
<You won't believe what's just happened.>

*

This time, no sunlight poured through the windows at the Collegium; only the noisy scatter of hail rattled the glass. The winter weather had turned savage.

Milo had been summoned once again, fresh from his mission to keep a watchful eye in the north. Over the years, he had spent time building up a useful undercover identity as a cloth merchant, which had enabled him to pick up some valuable information, but this time, in the main, everything had been quiet and relatively well-ordered.

Now, his old Master needed him once more. There weren't many Collegium-trained Agents about; even if he hadn't had the chance to finish his studies, he had enough Potentia to give him added options when needed.

Raven was sitting, huddled into his robes as usual. At least one thing in his life remained consistent Milo observed, taking in the gnarled fingers and milky eyes.

"How was your trip up north?" the Master Mage inquired.

"Useful," Milo replied. "Everyone seems to be getting along and trade is good. Mostly, people just want to keep up the flow of merchandise and make as much money as they can. There are even new settlements springing up, as well as temples to the Northern Gods."

Raven sniffed.

"As long as they don't start performing human sacrifices here, they can do as they like, though the Olympians won't be pleased. It won't be long before all these newcomers regard this land as their own, just like everyone else. We all end up as Britons of one sort or another."

"True," Milo agreed. "So far, the peace seems to be lasting. Whether we'll get trouble spilling over from the New Continent, who can say? People only want to mind their own business interests and get on with their lives."

The Master Mage nodded. "I hear that the Northern Gods are as capricious as the Olympians, so we'll just have more of them to choose from. Odin and Jupiter can sort things out between themselves. I dare say they'll come to an arrangement eventually. It might make the Twelve try a bit harder to attract worshippers."

"I thought it best to propitiate the Allfather, as he's a God of Information. I could do with all the help I can get sometimes."

Raven grinned. "Couldn't we all? Speaking of information, I need you to keep a close eye on a certain young lady, currently our only Ship-in-training."

"Really? Is someone trying to scupper our candidates?"

"I can't tell you why," Raven told him. He was losing count of the number of times he was being forced to obfuscate the truth. It was becoming annoying, though he understood the reasoning all too well. "It appears to be a personal grudge and there have been several attempts on her life. She's currently aboard HMS *Blossom,* moored at the Royal Dockyards in Londinium."

Milo noted that the old man still called the capital by its full name. He supposed that old habits died hard.

"I'd rather she was out at sea, but the weather is foul and the Admiralty has decided that it's better to proceed with her initiation before we lose her altogether. It's a risk, as always, but it appears to be the only option. Her enemy is too powerful and it's only a matter of time before an attempt succeeds."

"What did she do?" Milo asked.

"Oh, *she* is blameless. It was her antecedents who transgressed."

"And the blame has passed to her. Poor girl," Milo said, with feeling. He had never known his father and could barely remember his mother. He had been taken from her at a very young age and placed in a Foundling Home, before being taken to the Collegium. Then they'd kicked him out, for reasons they never specified. He felt a lot of sympathy for her already.

"You've dealt with her case before," Raven informed him. "Her name is Maia Abella."

Milo's eyes widened. She was the foundling he had been sent to ask after in Portus. Pieces of a puzzle began to click together in his mind.

"I gather that this isn't her birth name?"

"No," Raven allowed.

"Someone set that Revenant on her, didn't they? I heard that it was born of the *Livia*. Funny how it vanished when I burnt Valerius' corpse. Is she related?"

"I can neither confirm nor deny that rumour," Raven said flatly.

"And she has Mercury's support. Which God is against her?"

Raven paused for a few moments before answering.

"The Huntress, but keep that to yourself."

Milo's jaw dropped.

"What? This is bad. Suppose she doesn't make it through initiation?"

Raven spread his hands. "She isn't without allies. In the meantime, we must do all we can to watch over her until she has her chance. She's visiting the Shipyards tomorrow to take a look at a new vessel. The Navy think it's lucky and will help her to transition. His Majesty's keen for more to be built as we expand the trade routes, but they'll end up as inanimates if we can't get the candidates and I don't have to tell you how it would damage Britannia's standing if it leaked that we had no other candidates in the pipeline."

That was true enough. There were many foreign powers who would love for the supply of living Ships to end. Sacred oak boughs from Dodona were all well and good, but they didn't have the Potentia and mind of a trained human and still relied on crews to carry out operations. Nor did they have the battle capabilities of a powerful Ship, being only able to relay certain messages and give cryptic warnings of danger ahead. The rest of the Empire looked on with envious eyes, as Britannia sacrificed gifted women to the cause of her defence and expansion.

"Many of the Ships are getting older," Milo observed. "The Navy needs to replenish the stock."

"Exactly. And that is only one reason why we need to keep Maia alive."

"You like her, don't you?" Milo observed.

To his surprise, the wrinkled face broke into a smile.

"We have a lot in common. She's a survivor, too."

"I can't argue with that. I'll do my best," Milo said. He'd stop by the temple on his way and offer up a quick prayer to Mercury. This girl needed all the help she could get.

He might even be able to persuade the Navy to fork out for another ram.

V

The remainder of Saturnalia was a muted affair. *Blossom* and her crew tried to make it as festive as they could, but for Maia all the joy had gone, to be replaced with a looming sense of dread.

"I never totally understood the story of the Sword of Damocles until now," she told *Blossom*. The Ship had joined her in her cabin, as Maia was reluctant to move from below decks. Word had somehow filtered out that the Huntress was responsible for the attack.

"She might resort to a sniper," she continued, miserably. "One shot and that would be the end of me."

"That wouldn't be sporting enough for her," *Blossom* replied in disgust. "She's trying to make an impression on someone. Why else would she transport a creature everyone thought was long dead and gone, purely to kill you? It doesn't make sense. And why is she obsessed, anyway?"

Maia shrugged. "Half the world seems to be obsessed with something at the moment, so why should she be any different?"

"Hmm." The Ship pressed her lips together. "We're still not getting the whole picture."

"Perhaps it's because I haven't been an easy target?" Maia suggested. "Maybe she's caught up in the thrill of the chase and doesn't know when to stop."

"Could be," *Blossom* admitted. The normal working noises of the docks had been replaced by sounds of celebration from the other Ships and crews. There were even going to be fireworks later, a rare treat. *Blossom*'s crew had already been augmented by marines, both on board and around the dock, probably together with other eyes and ears she wasn't aware of. The other Ships were keeping watch as well, which cheered her a little. They had closed ranks around their potential sister.

"All Ships have been ordered to sacrifice to the Huntress," *Blossom* said, "in the hope of deflecting her intent."

"Won't that make her stronger?"

"It may pacify her. You'll have to be present and make your own petition."

Maia shuddered at the thought. "I don't think it will work."

"We can but try. I wish she could be as easily diverted as Echidna was, though it was horrible how all those poor people died."

The death toll had risen to eight, but it could have been a lot worse if one of the guests hadn't been late to the party and seen what was happening. Echidna had managed to unlatch a window and slither in, heading straight for the warmest place.

"The Huntress must be spitting feathers," the Ship agreed. "The necklace was an added touch. You would have been incapacitated, allowing Echidna to finish you off at her leisure."

"Except nothing went to plan. Raven thinks that Xenia stole my shawl. I thought she looked shifty when I asked her about it, but I assumed she'd taken it for herself."

"Well, she paid for her disloyalty many times over," *Blossom* said.

"Yes. It was a terrible way to die." Maia stared at the wooden planks of her cabin floor. "What happens now?"

She'd already had a long conversation with Plinius. He'd wanted to rush back immediately, but she'd insisted that he spend the festival with his family. She would see him in a few days when he returned to duty and it wasn't fair to make him miss precious time with his wife, children and grandsons. In the meantime, she was holed up here, trying to dismiss the vision of Xenia's glazed eyes and bloody corpse.

"Would you like to talk to the *Patience*?" *Blossom* offered.

"I don't want to spoil her Saturnalia too," Maia said, miserably. She hadn't mentioned her sister to the Ship, on Raven's advice. It was yet another secret she was being forced to keep. She would have loved to tell her friend that her intuition was right.

"I think you should," *Blossom* said firmly. "She's worried about you enough as it is and at least you can tell her that the danger is over for now."

"She knew something was coming for me," Maia said. "She definitely has Apollo's gift. The Navy should have left her to be a Priestess."

"She's exactly where she needs to be," *Blossom* chided her. "We need Ships and she's a good one. It wouldn't surprise me if they give her an upgrade when she changes vessels."

"But that won't be for years," Maia pointed out. *Blossom* shrugged.

"It will be as the Gods decree. I think the shortest time anyone's had a vessel is just under two weeks."

"Really?"

"Yes. Let me see, it was the *Emerald,* just under a hundred years ago. An enormous kraken rose up and smashed her to smithereens. The poor girl lost half her crew. It took her a long time to recover from the shock, but she got over it eventually. These things happen."

"We haven't spoken to her, have we?"

"No. She's a quiet one, though she listens in. She's away to the south, patrolling the waters off Africa."

"I bet she'd like the kraken detector."

"Oh yes," *Blossom* agreed. "She hates the creatures with a passion, though there's rarely any malice in them and, when there is, they're acting on the orders of Neptune. They're just big animals. She was unlucky that this one was hungry and stupid enough to mistake her for dinner."

"How did she survive?"

"She was forced to detach, though she had the wit to launch her boats so that some of her crew could get aboard. They were picked up after a couple of days."

Maia digested this information.

"Have you ever had to detach?"

Blossom shook her head. "Not in a crisis situation thank the Gods, only when I've changed vessels. It's a traumatic experience and only done when there's no other way of saving yourself. The sad fact is that sailors are more easily replaced than Ships, though we always try to save our crews." Her eyes became distant as she remembered the thousands of men who had served aboard her over the years. Most would be dead now. Maia still found it hard to grasp just how old she was.

What would she be like in three hundred years' time? She dismissed the thought, hoping instead that she'd make it through the next few days without ending up dead herself.

"What happened to the Ships before the *Augusta*?" she asked, curiously. "She's the oldest, isn't she?"

"Yes, she is now, but even Ships don't last forever. They lose their personalities and stop speaking," *Blossom* said, sadly. "It usually happens in port, as if the land calls to us and one day the Ship is gone and there's just an inanimate left. If the crew's lucky, there's usually some warning. Me, now, I'm going to retire to be a rich lady and eat toasted cheese off silver plates!"

They laughed, but Maia had her doubts. It wouldn't be easy going back to a frail flesh body with limited senses and, after several hundred years, the only family you'd have left would be those you'd served with at sea. Perhaps some Ships did get to stay with their Captains after all? She thought of the *Livia* and shuddered. It was best not to even think of it.

"I'm calling the *Patience*," the Ship informed her. "You need to talk to somebody other than me, so I'll open the link and leave you to it. I'm going to go over the new security arrangements with Phrixus."

Maia had already met the Sergeant of Marines. He was a grizzled, older man with sharp eyes and a capable manner who'd done his best to reassure her. It was no comfort that she was up against an immortal who was presumably immune to mortal weapons, though they'd finished off Echidna without any trouble. It must be different for monsters than Gods. She could only hope that Mercury was still looking out for her.

<This is *Patience*. Maia, can you hear me?>

<Maia here.>

<*Blossom* just told me what happened. How awful for you! I'm so sorry.>

<I was supposed to be poisoned and eaten,> Maia told her. She felt her friend's horror through the link. <You were right. Something was coming for me.>

<You'll be glad to know that I haven't had any more premonitions,> *Patience* said consolingly.

<Well, that's something. You must let me know if you do, as you've been spot on so far. I'm just waiting for the next attempt.>

<Is this something to do with the Huntress? I'm only asking because it's unusual for a mass sacrifice to be made by the Navy, unless it's to Jupiter or Neptune.>

<She wants me dead,> Maia said flatly. She could tell her friend this much, at least. <It's because of my parents' actions. I know where I came from now, though I can't tell you as it would put you in danger.>

<That isn't fair on you!> the Ship said indignantly. <You've a lot on your shoulders and it's not your fault!>

<It is what it is and I can't change that. I just want to thank you for being such a good friend, just in case I don't get the chance again.>

<Keep fighting, Maia. If she does harm you, I swear I'll tell everyone that she's attacked an innocent maiden who did her no wrong. I'll send a message to the Daily Journal and they can plaster it all over the Empire! She'd never recover from the bad publicity!>

Maia almost laughed at her normally placid friend threatening to take on the powerful Goddess on her behalf. She'd be capable of it, too.

<I wish I could tell the papers,> she said ruefully, <but it's complicated. This goes back years and years and I'm just at the tail end of it. Hopefully it will all blow over and she'll find something else to occupy her.>

<I hope so,> *Patience* agreed, <but I mean every word.>

<Thank you.> Maia decided to change the subject. <What are you doing for Saturnalia?>

<Oh, my officers are away attending diplomatic parties onshore and my crew are getting very, very drunk in Neapolis,> she said, wryly. <I'm getting some peace and quiet for once, though there was a good joke last night.>

<What happened?>

<Some of the lads asked to borrow my boat and dressed up as women. I sailed them around the harbour while they propositioned all the other crews. Luckily nobody fell in. I insisted that at least two of them were sober so they could fish out the others if they had to. It was very funny, especially when they started singing.> She sighed. <I suppose you had to be there. Are your lot up to anything?>

<Not really. Cap'n Flint keeps coming out with a really obscene rhyme. It's worse than usual, but Scribo swears he didn't teach him it.>

<That parrot!> *Patience* laughed. <He's legendary! You'll have to tie his beak shut if you get anybody important on board.>

<*Blossom's* already threatened to do it,> Maia remarked. <Scribo's convinced that the bird's in love with me.>

<Lucky you. One of my crew has a monkey. It gets into everything and craps everywhere to boot. I'm thinking of copying the *Augusta* and banning the creatures completely.>

<Doesn't she like them? I think they're sweet.>

<No, she can't stand them. The rumour is that one bit her when she was human and she's hated them ever since.>

<Or maybe it's because of the mess?>

<Nothing worse than a dirty vessel. Talking of vessels, I'm anchored near some Imperial Ships. They're very different.>

Maia was intrigued. <How so?>

<It's strange talking to an oak branch. There's no personality behind it. They use their Priests, you know, to impart the will of the Gods, though some Captains can hear them. I think they find us just as strange because we're human, though we have the wood in common. You'll understand when you're initiated.>

<What happens then?>Maia asked, daringly. *Patience* thought for a moment.

<It isn't easy and I think it's different for everybody. Words can't describe it. Think of it as another test you have to pass. Your determination will see you through and I know you have tons of that.>

<Tullia managed it and if she could, I can,> Maia agreed.

<Exactly. Oh! I'm being hailed. I think some of my men are returning and they've found some friends. It's going to be a noisy party on board tonight! Good job I don't need to sleep. Goodnight, Maia.>

<Have fun! Goodnight, *Patience*.>

She signalled to *Blossom* to break the link and settled back on to her bed. She felt better for talking to her friend, though the pit of her stomach still felt like it was full of stones.

Hopefully things would look better in the morning.

*

The next day brought unexpected news.

"I'm getting a message," *Blossom* announced.

She opened the link to Maia, who listened with interest.

<*Admiralty to* Blossom. *New orders. Proceed to Durobrivis Docks with all speed. The candidate is to inspect the new vessel that awaits her, should she pass initiation. Captain Plinius has been informed. Favonius, on behalf of Admiral Pendragon. End of Sending.*>

All Maia felt was relief. They would be travelling down the Thamesis and out into the estuary, away from the capital. At last, she would be able to come up on deck and see something other than constantly patrolling marines.

"This is unexpected," *Blossom* said to her, thoughtfully. "I wouldn't have thought that you were ready for the next stage right now, even if you have learned most of the ropes. I thought we'd get longer together."

"What do you mean?"

"This is the last step before initiation. The Navy likes their candidates to see their vessel. They think it's lucky and an incentive to pass the test. Just a superstition, really."

"What happens if I don't pass, or something happens to me?" Maia asked.

She could sense that *Blossom* was deciding what to tell her.

"Not everybody comes back," she confessed. "There was a girl I trained once, a few years back, when the supply of candidates began to peter out. She fought against her training every step of the way and I tried to have her dismissed as unsuitable. She was virtually dragged off to her initiation, and that was the last I ever heard of her. I don't want to lie to you, Maia. Nothing's certain about any of this, but if anyone can succeed, you can."

"*Patience* has threatened to go to the Daily Journal if I'm killed."

Blossom snorted. "The Navy won't let her. Ships are used for political ends, but not allowed to get personally involved. We're symbols of Britannia's power, but not seen as people in our own right anymore. They'd be too afraid to print it, especially as it involves Olympus."

It had been a nice thought.

"I'll just have to survive, then," Maia said. "Have we enough crew to get to Durobrivis, or do we have to wait?"

"Some are returning," *Blossom* said. "And I can manage, as it's not far, though this is unusual. It's the tradition that crews lucky enough to be in port get Saturnalia off, but they know that they can be summoned at a moment's notice. It's a good job that the Northmen are busy celebrating too at this time of year. Hopefully, Heron will have got the message. He's been off seeing some Mage friends to talk shop."

Blossom turned her attention to preparations for departure, much to the surprise of the other Ships, who had settled in for the party season.

<It's for the best,> the *Fortuna* said, to a chorus of agreement from the other Ships. <Have a good trip. Let us know about the new vessel!>

Ships always liked to know what was in the wind. Maia had decided that most started a wish list for their next vessel almost as soon as they had a new one and built on it over the years.

"Won't it take time for the Captain to arrive from Portus?"

"No. They're portalling him in, which goes to show that the Navy is ranking this as an emergency. I think that they want this sorted out whilst everyone is diverted by the festivities. The docks will be quiet, so we can sneak in and out relatively unnoticed. I wonder what your new vessel will be like?"

Privately, Maia hoped that it would be as impressive as the *Regina*. She'd suffered too much for it to be some tiny little thing, though she would never say so. Her friends' vessels were decent enough. Perhaps if it was smaller, she could be fast and outrun anything that dogged her? If she made it through initiation, was that even a guarantee that the vengeful Goddess would leave her alone? She couldn't bear the thought of putting her crew in danger. She would have to ask Raven when she saw him.

A carriage clattered along the waterfront. Maia peered through her window, trying to see who it was through the thick, rippled glass, but the image was too distorted for her to make much out.

<Hello ladies! Did you miss me?>

Captain Plinius' familiar voice sounded in their heads.

<Welcome back! We didn't miss you at all,> *Blossom* replied teasingly.

<Hah! Well, here I am. Somewhat unexpectedly, but to tell the truth, I've been on pins ever since I heard about…you know.>

<I'm glad you're back, Captain,> Maia Sent. <How are your family?>

<Oh, they're fine. It was good to see them and I was sorry to have to cut my visit short, but that's the way things are. It's not like I'm gone for months or years, like some officers. We'll be back in Portus soon, no doubt.>

She could sense him boarding and moving down to his cabin, where his servant, Victor, was laying out his belongings.

<*Blossom*, status?>

<We're just waiting for a couple of crewmen, plus Heron, Durus and Campion. I'm not sure if Danuco will be joining us, though. They should be along shortly, then we can sail with the tide.>

<Good. Make ready.>

<Aye, sir.>

<Can I partner with you?> Maia asked.

<I don't see why not,> the Ship replied. <You could do with the practise in negotiating the Thamesis and the estuary. River travel can be even trickier than sailing the ocean as there are more dangers, unless you're hugging the coast. You don't want to get stuck on a sandbank.>

The rest of the crew straggled in over the next hour and Maia felt like the vessel was waking up after a restful nap. Voices and the sound of footsteps broke the silence as the Ship prepared to slip her moorings and depart.

Heron finally appeared, rubbing his hands and seemingly unbothered that he'd been dragged back to duty.

"I'm glad to see that you're unharmed, Maia. Raven told me about the nasty business at the Senator's villa. Echidna, eh? Did you get to see her?"

"Hello, Heron. No, I was whisked away," she replied.

He looked disappointed for a moment. "Pity. I'm trying to get an accurate description. I hope they preserved her venom sacs as it would be useful if we could replicate the substance."

"I'm glad I didn't get close to her, or she would have finished me off," Maia told him. He looked startled. Sometimes she felt that he was so busy looking at the whys and wherefores, he forgot about the people involved. It seemed to be a failing among Mages.

"Er, yes. Of course." He looked abashed, for once. "Forgive me. I have the tendency to regard events as academic puzzles to be dissected. I understand that people died."

She nodded.

"But, let's look on the bright side," he continued, his smile returning. "You weren't one of them! Now, what can I do for you?"

"I'd like to partner with *Blossom*, please."

"Excellent idea. No point in being idle. River navigation, eh?" He waggled his bushy eyebrows at her. "That'll keep you occupied. I'll put you in stasis and, just for extra security, I'll put a ward around your body too. The whole place is crawling with marines, you know."

"Yes. Phrixus is like a cat on hot coals," she agreed. "I know I'll be happier when we're out on the river."

"Me too. I was coming back anyway to finish my work. I wish Robin was here to give me a hand. By the way, the kraken detector was approved!"

Maia was delighted. "That's wonderful news. I hope the *Emerald* gets one."

"*Blossom* told you, did she? Yes, that Ship'll be one of the first," Heron agreed. "I've never known anyone panic over the beasties quite so much. It's become a phobia with her. Right, young lady, let's get you sorted, shall we?"

The vessel opened up to Maia, like a mother's arms.

*

The trip down the Thamesis took all of her concentration and skill, with *Blossom* giving her helpful nudges here and there as needed. It was indeed different to sailing on the open ocean and Maia was relieved that the crew were used to the occasional awkwardness.

<You can't be expected to get everything right,> the Ship pointed out, after a clumsy manoeuvre with the sails spilled the wind.

<I know, but I need to improve quickly if I'm to get my own vessel,> Maia wailed in frustration. <You won't be there to help me. It's hard to concentrate on several things at once. I can do them one at a time, no problem!>

<Relax!> *Blossom* ordered. <New Ships aren't thrown in at the deep end. There are a lot of drills and trials before you even go on your shakedown cruise. You have to get used to working with your Captain and crew, all the while making sure that everything operates as it should. I know every inch of my vessel and the machinery has become smooth with use. I can tell if anything's off by even the smallest amount, or when something's stretched to its limit. You'll have to learn all these things. Each vessel has its particular foibles as well, like any device. Slow and steady, that's the proper way. Now, try that again.>

The next time was easier and the sails responded better to her touch.

<Excellent!>

Maia's mind remained occupied until Durobrivis came in sight. The original Roman fort had expanded over the years to become a thriving city. The docks and shipyards were nearby, like a town in their own right and it was one of the places where vessels were built for the Royal Navy. Maia could see the buildings stretching along the coast, together with the great dry docks containing the hulls of what were to become homes for new and existing Ships.

<Will these be allotted as upgrades, as there are no more candidates at present?> she asked Plinius.

<Yes,> he replied, scanning ahead. <Many of these vessels will have improvements that the older ones could do with. It's amazing, the rate technology is advancing, mostly down to clever chaps like Heron and Robin. We can't afford to lag behind.>

The short winter's day was fading into night and lamps were winking on like little beacons in the gloom. At a word from *Blossom*, Maia activated her lights in answer, before anchoring in the estuary.

The next morning, Maia, the Captain and a boatload of marines led by Phrixus made their way across the water to the jetty in front of the Dock Offices. Normally the area would be bustling, but most of the workers were enjoying the holiday, so the place was nearly deserted.

Maia put on her veil. She had worn it away from her face on the journey over to get the benefit of the weak sunshine that was filtering through patches of grey and silver cloud. The temperature had risen over the past day and the cutting wind had dropped, so it was almost pleasant to be out. It beat being cooped up in a stuffy cabin.

Vessels of all shapes and sizes were berthed in the docks, being built or re-fitted. There didn't appear to be an empty one, which backed up what she'd heard about the new King wanting to expand the Navy. She tried to make out the names of the vessels being refitted.

"There's the *Justicia*," Plinius observed. "I heard she wants a brand-new vessel, but she'll have to wait in line, despite being a Royal. She needs replacement masts, so she's stuck here and her crew are on leave."

"I'm sorry that everyone had to come back on my account," Maia said, contritely. Plinius smiled at her.

"It's our duty to protect you, just as you will, if the Gods permit, spend your life protecting us and our descendants in return. Besides which, we'll have a party on the way back, just you wait and see." He leaned over to her and whispered," I fear that my dear Ship is planning one of her famous practical jokes. Did she tell you what she had us doing last year?"

"The beards," Maia giggled.

"Yes." Plinius pulled a face. "Mine itched abominably. I've threatened to grow my own ever since, just to annoy her." He looked at her hopefully. "I don't suppose you know what she's up to?"

Maia shook her head. "She hadn't planned anything much this year with everyone being ashore, but I wouldn't put it past her to have something up her sleeve, just in case."

Plinius let out a breath. "Me neither. We'll have to wait and see. I swear that she enjoys tormenting us!"

Maia laughed. Ahead of them, great ribs of oak clutched at the sky like skeletal fingers.

"I see that they've started yet another brand new vessel," the Captain remarked. "It's a wonder there are enough suitable oaks."

"Do they replant immediately?"

He nodded. "Yes, but they're using more and more and with these trees you have to plan ahead. It's no good using imported timber either. If it's for a Ship, they have to be grown in Britannia. That's why the foreign powers can't do what we do – some quirk of the land. Quite remarkable, really."

Maia counted at least six vessels in the process of being built from scratch and several more being re-fitted or upgraded. The *Justicia* loomed over the rest; even without her masts she was a formidable sight. The dock next to her contained a much smaller vessel and Maia wished she could magnify her vision, like she could when linked to the *Blossom*.

"Ah, I see that the *Jasper* is in. Have you come across her yet?"

"No," Maia said.

"I'm surprised. She's the biggest gossip in the fleet. Don't tell her anything that you wouldn't want the world to know!"

That was probably why *Blossom* had kept her at arm's length.

"Thanks for the warning."

They were approaching the main offices now. Statues of the Imperial Eagle and the Britannic Dragon stared out from above the door, paint fresh despite their obvious age and standing like giant sentinels protecting the dignity of His Majesty's Navy. They mounted the steps and passed under their shadows, glad to get out of the crisp air.

Inside, while not crowded, there was still a lot of activity despite the time of year. Clerks in their familiar Naval uniforms were manning the desks, overlooked by more scenes of the Empire's triumphs adorning the walls. She remembered how overawed she'd been as a ragged waif, dragged into the Admiralty Offices in Portus. It seemed like a very long time ago now.

They were shown through to an office immediately. A fire crackled merrily in a large marble fireplace, the flames casting a cheery glow into the room. Ensconced before it, in an armchair, was a figure she recognised immediately, his wispy hair surrounding his wrinkled face like thistledown.

"Hello, Raven."

The ancient Mage waved a hand.

"Greetings, Captain, Maia. Do come and take a seat. I thought we'd be better meeting up here where it's warm before heading out to tramp around a cold, unfinished vessel. I'm also waiting for the Chief Architect to join us, but apparently he's been delayed."

Plinius raised his eyebrows. "So, Master Pholus is coming? We are honoured."

"Indeed." Raven replied. "He can't wait to show Maia his new designs. You know how he loves his work and he might not have the opportunity to impress another candidate for a while."

The Captain grunted in agreement. "Yes, he lives for his work all right. I imagine he's being kept busy at the moment. I can't remember seeing as many new vessels in the docks."

"True, but we need every one." The Master Mage tilted his head. "Here he comes now."

Maia listened for the sound of footsteps, but could only hear a horse passing outside. No, it wasn't outside, it was in the corridor. She was just about to ask why somebody was leading a horse through the building, when the door opened and a head thrust through, ducking under the lintel.

"Greetings, Master Pholus!" the Captain said.

Pholus was a glossy chestnut from the waist down and a dark-skinned man from the waist up. A neatly combed mane of thick black hair flowed from his head down his back and he was wearing a fashionable tricorn hat, which he swept off in a bow. A Naval sash across one broad shoulder completed the look.

"Hail and well met!" he boomed, showing blocky teeth in a smile. "Sorry I'm late. The workers have the festival off, but I'm not so lucky. Happy Saturnalia!"

Maia felt her jaw drop a little. She'd seen centaurs before, of course, but they weren't common at this end of the Empire, usually choosing to remain nearer to their ancestral lands of

Hellas and Kypros. She could tell that he was from Hellas originally, as he didn't have horns.

She'd never imagined that one was responsible for designing vessels for the Royal Navy.

"May I present Maia Abella, our latest candidate?" Plinius said. She saluted smartly and he responded, turning his gaze to her. His eyes were liquid and very dark, with long eyelashes like a horse.

"Delighted to meet you, ma'am. I can't wait to show you the vessel. I hope you approve!"

His voice still held a trace of accent, though she could tell that he'd lived in Britannia for a very long time.

"Likewise, sir. I can't wait to see it."

He beamed. "It will have all the latest improvements, though naturally it isn't finished as yet. I pray to the Gods for a successful installation, then we can add the final touches."

"As do we all," Raven remarked. He turned to Pholus. "I suppose you want me to leave this nice cosy fire and head out into the cold. Oh well. Needs must."

The centaur laughed, clearly used to Raven's sense of humour.

"You can stay here if you like, but we're off sightseeing, right Captain?"

"Absolutely."

"And how is the luscious *Blossom*? I must pop over and pay my respects to your Ship while you're here. I don't get to see either of you often enough these days."

Maia imagined that Pholus must be used to sailing, though it seemed an odd thing for a centaur to do. He'd have good balance, at least, though the ladders would be beyond him.

"I know she'd love to see you, too," Plinius replied. "She sends her regards and a standing invitation."

They both laughed and Maia realised that it was an old joke. Pholus would have to stay above decks, as there was no way that he would fit into one of the cabins, or sit down for that matter.

"Tell her that I'll be seeing her soon," the Architect said. "In the meantime, shall we head out? I've arranged for lunch to be served here afterwards, though I must apologise that I can't offer all the usual pomp and circumstance."

"That's understandable," Raven said. "And I know you won't stint on the wine."

"As long as you don't expect me to touch the stuff!" Pholus said. Centaurs had no tolerance for alcohol.

"More for the rest of us, then," Raven fired back. "Let's go."

Outside, the clouds had thinned and the temperature had dropped. Ice rimed the cobbles and salt had been strewn to aid footing. Maia huddled into her cloak, though Pholus didn't seem affected. The steady clopping of his hooves accompanied their footsteps as he guided them past a skeletal vessel and towards one that was much more complete.

"Here we are!" he announced.

Maia felt her heart skip and her breath catch in her throat.

Even without masts, the vessel was glorious.

The morning sun glinted off new wood, painted in the Naval colours of black and yellow. The line of the hull shone with bright copper plating and Maia could see one of the massive anchors secured to the cathead at the bow. The vessel towered above them as they approached and more features appeared but it wasn't until they were standing at the edge of the dock that she could see everything in detail.

"Well Maia, isn't it a beauty?" Pride in a job well done shone through Pholus' words. "Do you approve?"

Maia could only stare, entranced, her eyes touching every part of the huge vessel that would be her Shipbody, if the Fates were kind.

"It's very big," she said, in wonder.

"Why, are you disappointed?" Raven inquired with a straight face.

"Oh no," Maia said hurriedly, "it's just that I thought…after the *Regina*..."

"I was ordered to design something spectacular," Pholus smiled. "The King has ambitions to expand the Navy and this will be his first commission. He wants nothing but the best, so a first-rate it is. We've made good progress, so hopefully it will be ready for you when you pass your initiation, Gods willing."

The thought of that final hurdle made Maia's stomach lurch again, but she quelled her doubts.

"Thank you. It's truly splendid." Privately, she opened a channel to the *Blossom*.

<Can you see this?>

<Gods of Olympus! It's *enormous,* girl! You'll be spending the first six months working out all the controls!>

<I know,> Maia said, satisfied, adding. <I think it's better than the *Regina's,* don't you?>

<Meow!>

She felt *Blossom*'s chuckle. So what if she was being catty?

<I just didn't want to end up with a smaller vessel and have to spend the rest of my career being sneered at by Tullia 'I'm a queen' Albana!>

This would wipe the smile off the *Regina*'s face. Again. It was almost worth all the mess she'd had to wade through to get here.

<Well, don't get carried away yet,> *Blossom* warned her.

<I know. I have to pass my initiation first.>

Surely it couldn't be that difficult?

She realised that Pholus was leading them aboard, across a wide gangplank that could accommodate his not-inconsiderable bulk. She could smell the freshly-applied preservative and tar over the scent of cut wood. Everything was shiny and new, untarnished by weather and salt spray that would eat into a vessel's fittings and rot them from the outside in. It all felt raw and undiscovered, birthed from the inventive mind of the person before her. Pholus ran a loving hand over the rail as she absorbed all the details.

"Go below," he urged her. "The main cabins are nearly finished, so you'll have a good idea of the general standard."

Maia needed no further prompting, so the Captain, Raven and herself headed off to explore. She could feel *Blossom* in her head, looking out from her eyes. It was strange to have their positions reversed, for once.

They moved through the vessel, the Captain commenting on things that caught his eye and discussing the more technical aspects of the build.

"I must ask Master Pholus about the kraken detector," Maia said. "I know Heron's working on something else, too, but I don't know what it does yet."

"I just nod and smile," Plinius told her. "He'll expound at length when he's ready. Let's have a look in the Captain's cabin."

It was the largest one, panelled in light oak and painted with little scenes of nymphs and sea creatures. She admired the artistry and knew they would be appreciated, by her at least. The windows at the stern were of thick glass surrounded by carved decoration of fruit and flowers, also freshly painted, with crossed tridents and leaping dolphins in and among them. A shiver ran through her when she thought of her new Captain.

She gazed around at the space. He would work at his desk and sleep in his hanging bed, like the one she had aboard *Blossom*. These were things he would bring with him, along with his sea-chests of possessions. A part of her wanted him to be young and handsome, but she knew that such a large and imposing vessel would mean she would begin her career with an experienced Commander, who would be older and well-connected. She would be satisfied with a good Captain, fair but firm with her crew and sure of his position.

The Mage quarters reminded her of Heron, though as yet there was none of the clutter she associated with him. It was all bare bones without the objects humans used to flesh out their private spaces. He would surely have his own collections and curiosities, though she hoped he wasn't as untidy as Heron. Robin had always complained about not being able to find things without a good rummage and constantly tried in vain to keep his Master's disorder in check.

"This is excellent," Raven was saying, his voice filled with approval. Maia noticed that his head was moving as though he could see. She knew that the old Mage possessed another means of visualising his surroundings despite his ruined eyes.

"Truly, no expense has been spared," Plinius said, raising his eyebrows at the opulence.

"Jealous?" she teased him.

He grinned. "I'll stay where I am, thank you. It might not be as splendid, but it's home."

<I'm glad to hear it,> *Blossom* said, over their link. <I don't want you tempted away by a newly painted hussy!>

<Hey, who are you calling a hussy?>

She could almost hear *Blossom*'s uproarious laughter across the water.

The two men fell to talking practicalities as Maia walked about the cabin. The shipwrights were doing an excellent job. She knew that there would have been upwards of two hundred at a time working on her vessel, not counting the specialist construction Mages who bound everything together magically as every nail and joint was put in place. They would then add mystical defences to the conventional ones, ensuring that the Ship would have every chance to operate to the best of her ability.

Part of her felt daunted at the challenge. A large vessel meant a large crew and complicated operations and she didn't feel ready. She could only hope that she wouldn't be pushed straight into initiation without further training. The niggling fear took some of the joy out of the situation but, then again, she told herself, she'd worry about that if she managed to be installed in the first place. One step at a time.

She ran her hand over the smooth wooden panels, knowing that she would be seeing the vessel very differently after installation, moving through this same wood that would become part of her for years and years. It was an unsettling thought. It wasn't the same aboard the *Blossom,* as she knew that she could always return to her body, disfigured as it was. What must it really be like to be lodged inside a vessel forever?

A cold shiver ran up her spine and she hugged her body unconsciously, as if unwilling to leave it. Her movement didn't go unnoticed by Plinius, who stepped over and put his arm around her in concern.

"It's a lot to take in, isn't it?" he said, quietly. Of course, he'd shown many a candidate around a vessel and would know something of what was going through her mind.

She nodded. "Yes. I'm not ready for this."

"Not yet," he reminded her. "You've still got a lot to learn, but you'll get there. There'll be plenty of support, too."

"If I don't end up dead first," she said, the bitterness in her voice surprising even her.

"We'll protect you as much as we can," Plinius said. "I know you wouldn't want me to lie and say that it's going to be a walk in the park, but once you're installed, *she* touches you at her peril. You'll belong to higher powers then."

"More Gods. How wonderful."

His calm brown eyes looked sympathetically into hers. "I think it's time to go," he said. "Raven, is there anything else you want to take note of?"

The ancient had been poking around in the Mage quarters, checking out the storage.

"It all seems adequate," he remarked. "If anything, there's too much space. I hope you aren't assigned a pack rat, or it would take him a year to gather all his things together."

"That settles it. You're not getting Heron," Plinius said.

Maia rolled her eyes. "No, I'll leave him to you." She liked Heron, but often wondered how *Blossom* tolerated his eccentricities.

"That will all be arranged later," Raven said. "I shall doubtless be consulted. I'll have to find you somebody suitable, who's not too irritating."

"Find me a Mage who isn't. Present company excepted, naturally," the Captain said, winking at Maia.

"Oh dear. That will be a problem then," Raven said, deadpan. "Now, let's go and tell Pholus what a wonderful job he's doing, shall we? That will make his day."

VI

Milo watched as the little group made its way back from inspecting the new vessel, the Chief Architect's distinctive figure towering above the humans. He'd been on duty for several hours, sheltering in the lee of the ropewalk and he'd long since begun to lose the feeling in his fingers and toes.

Raven had decided against putting him aboard the *Blossom* immediately. He didn't want to alarm the Ship and it was harder to dissemble among such a small and tight-knit crew, so Milo was tasked with keeping an eye out for anything untoward on shore.

"Besides which," the Master Mage said, "It's unlikely that anything will attack them at sea. I've a feeling that the Goddess will be drawing Potentia from the land, so the threat will probably come from there."

Milo agreed, which was why he was trying to think warm thoughts and envying everyone who was enjoying their Saturnalia. The group of marines who'd come ashore looked as cold as he did, which was some small consolation. They'd taken up position along the route but hadn't spotted him; he knew how to cast a spell of cloaking as well as any Mage.

While the marines were looking for physical threats, he was alert to supernormal ones. Echidna and a poisoned necklace had been overkill in his opinion and the Huntress would be enraged that her plan had failed so spectacularly. He didn't think that the Navy's sacrifice would sway her one little bit; they could offer up animals from now until the end of all things but Diana would be implacable. She had taken on her Artemis aspect and that was always unpredictable and dangerous.

Personally, he thought that the girl didn't stand a chance and they were only prolonging the inevitable. He'd seen her walking across the docks, the scars on her face invisible at this distance and he pitied her with all his heart. Showing her this grand new vessel seemed like an added cruelty, even if it was normal protocol. He fingered the butt of his pistol, the wood and metal of the grip a tangible reassurance. Powder and shot had done for

Echidna, which only went to show how the power of mortals was growing. No wonder the Gods were getting nervous.

None of them wanted to be overthrown, as they had overthrown their progenitors.

He relaxed slightly when the inspection party disappeared inside, to be wined and dined. The river was beautiful in the late afternoon light, the low sun turning the ripples to gold and he wondered how long it would be before Maia Abella's story would end, like all the others, in fear, blood and death.

*

Milo had only just got back to Londin, when the summons came. Raven wanted to see him without delay. That meant trailing across the city in the cold, all the while resenting the fact that talking by speechstone wasn't secure enough for the Master Mage. Surely he was becoming paranoid in his dotage.

"Help yourself to a drink," the old man said, when he arrived. Milo poured himself a large glass of brandy.

"I've nothing to report, though there's plenty of gossip floating about. I can't do much from back here, you know. Are you sure you don't want me aboard the Ship?"

Raven pursed his lips. "Not at the moment. I've improved the *Blossom*'s security as much as I can and Heron is very capable."

"They couldn't stop the Revenant," Milo pointed out.

Raven sighed. "First the undead, then a legendary monster. I'm beginning to think that Maia has a charmed life."

"She wasn't unharmed."

"No, but she isn't dead, mostly because of her own actions, I hasten to add. We'll just have to hope that whichever Gods favour her continue to work on her behalf. She's got a few more weeks partnered with the *Blossom* before she undergoes initiation. The Admiralty wanted her to go immediately, but I persuaded them to give her a little more time. There's no way that she could cope with a vessel like that without further training."

"They should have given her a third or fourth-rate, then," Milo pointed out, not unreasonably.

Raven scowled.

"The King wants bigger and better Ships and this is his only chance for the foreseeable future."

"You've been at the palace a lot, recently."

Raven raised an eyebrow.

"A little dog has been telling tales, I see. Yes. The King has charged me with tutoring his sister and finishing her education before she's married off. They've just opened up negotiations with the Gauls."

"She's what, twenty-one now?"

"Just."

"Bright?"

"Very. It's a shame that she wasn't born male."

Milo snorted. He knew his old Master's opinion of young King Artorius, but the lad was only nineteen. He'd settle after a few years in the job.

"They need to get him married off, or we'll end up with Marcus."

Milo knew his friend and fellow Agent Caniculus' low opinion of the Prince and hoped that Artorius would do his duty and produce an heir before too long. There were plenty of willing candidates among the Britannic aristocracy, or even further afield if he decided to import some new blood.

"It'll happen before too long, but that's not our sphere, thank the Gods. Returning to our current problem, there's not much we can do for Miss Maia now. Keep your ear to the ground for as long as you can, but I suspect that you're about to be posted to the south-west. There are rumours of weapons being smuggled to separatist groups."

Milo groaned.

"Not more lunatics rambling on about Britannia's former glory, before the evil Empire came and conquered us all."

"That's right," Raven said, far too cheerfully for Milo's liking. "It's the right of every Briton to wage tribal warfare, sacrifice humans and run in terror from the Fae."

"No thanks," Milo said, with feeling. "Times have moved on."

"Speaking of Major Fae, be alert. I've heard rumours that they're stirring again and there are always those who are stupid enough to think that they can strike a bargain with them."

"May the Gods protect us!" The deities they had were bad enough, but the Major Fae regarded humans as animals put on the Earth for their own use and amusement. "They can stay in Hibernia. We don't want them here."

"Quite. Keep me updated."

As Milo let himself out, he wondered which Gods he'd annoyed to be sent to the back of beyond on such a crappy mission. Until then, he was determined to enjoy himself in the capital while he still could and make the most of the last days of the festival.

He'd also heard a rumour that the fabled Echidna was going to be put on show at the Temple of Minerva and he wasn't going to miss that for a gold clock, even if he did have to queue.

Maybe he could salvage some entertainment after all?

*

For once, the Mare Germanicus was relatively calm as the *Blossom* made her way up the north-east coast of Britannia, stopping at various ports along the way. Maia's head was stuffed full of facts about tides and treacherous sandbanks that lurked off the flat coastline and she knew that both Captain Plinius and the Ship were trying to equip her with as much information as they could before she was called to undergo initiation.

"I can understand their reasoning, but I don't agree with it," Plinius grumbled to *Blossom*. Maia was resting below, so he could speak freely. "How can they possibly expect her to be ready yet?"

"She's already picked up more than most in the time she's been with us," his Ship pointed out. "She can sort the rest out later with some short trips up and down the coast. An experienced Captain will guide her."

In her Captain's opinion, *Blossom* was far too sanguine about the whole thing.

"I don't like it." He scanned the grey skies, as if expecting an attack any minute.

"She's safer here than on land," his Ship pointed out. "Maybe the big sacrifice to *her* worked?"

"Maybe. Maia wasn't happy about taking part."

"Can you blame her? She did it, though. It's funny how the Priests have been quiet."

"They're probably embarrassed. The Gods can be vengeful, but this is extreme."

Blossom shrugged. "Who can fathom them out? Not me, that's for sure, though I swear if anything else happens to her, I'll never sacrifice to *her* again and nor will any other Ship. An attack on one is an attack on all."

Plinius raised an eyebrow. His normally placid partner was ready for a fight, her face set in angry lines.

"All we can do is support her," he said.

"And we shall. Maybe we should petition Neptune and ask him to intervene? She's going to be offered to him as much as to the Mother, so he has a stake in this."

"Good idea," her Captain said. "Call Danuco and arrange it. We'll need the whole crew on standby. Do we have any gold on board?"

Blossom frowned. "Not much, only a few items for real emergencies. Perhaps he'll be happy enough with an animal."

Plinius sighed. "We'll do that, then, but add some gold as well, to be sure. I'll make it up myself, later."

Neither of them wanted to admit that they were running out of options.

*

The crew was assembled, sacrifice was duly made and the animal went calmly, much to everyone's relief. This feeling only lasted until Danuco began to read the entrails. Plinius, standing next to him, could smell the putridity wafting up from the carcass and watched as the Priest blanched.

"What do I say?" Danuco hissed.

"The God warns of trials ahead," Plinius muttered quickly, while keeping a bland expression. The Priest composed himself before announcing the result of the oracle. There were a few glances exchanged among the crew, but nobody demurred.

Plinius could hear *Blossom* cursing quietly in his head.

<It's not good, is it?> Maia asked him.

<The entrails are rotten,> Plinius told her reluctantly.

Maia stared out to sea. What had she expected? At least the God hadn't sugar-coated the warning. She was still in danger, though the fact that the animal hadn't struggled meant that Neptune himself wasn't unhappy with them. All she could hope for was that she would be well away from the Ship when whatever was going to happen, happened.

"We must thank the God for his warning," she said, formally, not meeting his eyes, watching instead as a few gold pieces were cast into the sea in supplication.

Later, she was partnered with *Blossom* on the night watch when the order to return to Londin came through.

<I had to report the result of the oracle,>*Blossom* told her, sadly.

<I know. To tell the truth, I don't mind. I'm ready to go for initiation and see what happens. I've a feeling that I'm putting you all in danger by staying here. Could you do one thing for me?>

<Of course!>

<I didn't tell Matrona and Branwen about Echidna, or the necklace. They think I had a good Saturnalia. If I don't come back, will you give them some letters I've written? There are ones for the Captain and *Patience* as well.>

The Ship was silent for a moment and Maia could sense *Blossom*'s sudden apprehension through the link.

<Yes. *If* anything happens to you, I'll pass them on.>

<You know I can't thank you enough. I never knew my mother, but you and Matrona have more than made up for that.>

Blossom felt as though her oaken heart was about to crack with sorrow. She enfolded Maia's consciousness in a mental hug, wanting to be as close as possible to this girl who had suffered so much.

Maia felt the Ship draw closer and...

...*the shack was old*, built of wooden planks with a beaten earth floor. One window, partially blocked by a crude shutter, let in a little light, just enough to make out the meagre contents. A stench of sickness, decay and death hung in the sticky, humid air. Outside, insects chirped and scratched in an unceasing litany.

The man lay on a rough wooden bed, a tattered blanket drawn up over him, features slack and grey. Two women were finishing their work on his corpse and arranging his flaccid, wasted limbs as best they could, to try and give him some semblance of dignity. They tutted and muttered between themselves, their haggard faces and shabby, worn clothing testament to their own sufferings.

"Ifede, say goodbye to your Pa," one of them said, not without sympathy. Maia realised that the woman was looking right at her. She looked down at unfamiliar hands clasping thin knees through the threadbare cotton skirt and knew that she was a small child in a land far away.

She shook her head, dumbly. The thing in the bed wasn't her Pa, the tall man with the flashing smile who carried her on his shoulders, his strong hands swinging her up and over his head, laughing as she squealed in delight. The one who had held her, comforting her as they watched Ma die, both of them crying together knowing that they only had each other. The one who had promised that he would never leave her, but he had, just like her mother, wasting away day by day even as he fought the disease that was killing him, trying to sing and smile to ease her pain. Now she had nobody left, only the charity of neighbours who themselves had nothing but hungry mouths to feed. Alone in the darkness of an empty hut, with everything sold to pay for food.

"Child, come now." The woman beckoned, her face creased in both encouragement and misery, extending a hand to where she crouched shivering in the corner.

She couldn't, wouldn't. A pressure began to build inside her, swelling and growing, a hot rage that pounded and battered inside her head like an angry beast clawing to be set free. She ran outside into the hot night air, heedless of the woman's cries and opened her mouth wide then wider, screaming her grief into the dark. Suddenly, the pressure burst like an over- ripe fruit, its contents erupting outwards in a blast that rushed through her like a hurricane.

The ground answered her screams, shaking and heaving like a bucking horse. Objects were hurled into the air, twisting in a maddened maelstrom that mirrored her pain and despair. All she could feel was her body shaking, hair crackling with sparks, muscles taut and rigid as the world fell to pieces around her…

*

"…*Maia, Maia!*"

"Maia! Can you hear me?"

There were voices, far away but coming closer. She struggled to focus on them, recognising their familiarity.

What had happened? Slowly, her other senses returned and she knew she was lying down, with a pillow under her head and covered by a soft blanket. Wood creaked around her as the vessel swayed and the noise of the men filtered through the decks to where she lay. Maia opened her eyes. Three worried faces loomed over her; Captain Plinius was peering over Heron's shoulder, whilst *Blossom* was directly above her on the ceiling, worry etched into her features. She blinked in confusion.

"Thank the Gods, she's awake," Heron said, gently wiping her face with a cool, herbal-smelling cloth. "Thank you, Campion. It seems to have done the trick." The Adept's round face appeared briefly in the gap as he took the cloth from the Mage, before being replaced again by the Captain. "Now, can you tell me your name?"

Maia struggled to form the words. "Maia…Abella," she whispered, the effort exhausting her.

"Good!" He sounded relieved. "Can you sit up?"

Heron helped her into a sitting position and gave her something spicy to drink.

"This should help you regain your wits."

"Is she well?" Plinius interjected.

"Aye, sir. Just gave us all a fright." The gangly Mage gazed up at *Blossom*. "We'll have to talk, ma'am. I need to know exactly what happened. Now, we'll let this young lady rest a while."

He gathered up a few items and exited, followed by the Captain. That just left the Ship, who glided down the wall so that she was facing the end of Maia's bed.

"How are you feeling?" she asked softly.

"Confused," Maia answered, fighting her way through the fog inside her brain. "What happened?"

The Ship looked apologetic. "You really got inside my head, girl. That's not supposed to happen. You know there's a filter so we don't get everything the other's thinking and feeling."

Maia was shocked. A stab of panic ran through her. "I'm sorry. I didn't mean to. It just happened and I couldn't stop it!"

"I know, I know," *Blossom* quickly soothed her. "I don't understand it either, but there I was and it was like it was happening to me all over again. We both passed out for a few seconds."

"The vessel…" began Maia, appalled that it might have been in danger.

"All fine. I came to quite quickly but there was a bit of panic from the crew. They were running round like headless roosters!"

There was a discreet knock on the door.

"Soup and bread, ma'am."

"Thank you, Philo," The servant laid the tray on the bedside table, bowed briefly and left as silently as he had come.

It smelled good and Maia was hungry. She caught a brief flash of envy from *Blossom* as she set the tray on her lap.

"You eat and rest. I'll be back later."

The Ship rippled backwards, merging seamlessly with the wood until the wall closed over her and smoothed out after her passing. Off to talk to the Captain and Heron, Maia thought.

She wondered whether to confess that it had happened before, with Raven. It had been the same, as if she was catapulted into another's body, feeling what they had felt down to the last detail. Now she knew why *Blossom* didn't talk about her past. She wasn't sure where she'd been, but it wasn't Britannia. The air was too hot and filled with moisture, like the steam room at the baths. The insect and frog noises were unfamiliar to her too.

A conversation she'd once had with Briseis returned to her. *Blossom* had been born on the New Continent, like her friend, so she must have returned there, to a pivotal point in her life. At least there was no damage to the Ship or her vessel.

Maia put her head in her hands. She feared that she was becoming a liability. It was a good job that they were returning to port, or she would have insisted that she be put off at the earliest opportunity.

She wouldn't preserve her own life at the cost of her friends'.

*

"She shouldn't have been able to do that."

Blossom's voice was firm. Both Captain and Mage regarded her steadily. They were seated at the Captain's table in his day room, where they could speak in private. It was essential to understand what had just happened.

"Read your thoughts, you mean?" Heron asked.

"Not just that," *Blossom* insisted. "The memories were pulled out of me and I was forced to relive them whether I willed it or not. It was as if it was happening all over again." She shuddered, unable to hide her distress. "You know I don't dwell on that part of my life, Plinius."

Her Captain nodded.

"I do know that, my dear. You told me about what happened and I must confess that I can't see you letting your guard down. The filter should have prevented it."

Heron steepled his fingers before him, his green eyes hooded in thought.

"I think it's her Potentia manifesting. She must have power of mind."

Plinius and *Blossom* both stared at him.

"We must ask her if this has happened before. I have a feeling that it has."

"She can't control it," the Captain said. "That might be a problem. She couldn't help herself."

"I agree that this needs dealing with," Heron replied, "but I don't think we'll have time. It takes a lot of mental discipline to erect a barrier at will." He paused. "You know that this was the *Livia*'s strength?"

"I wasn't sure," Plinius replied. *Blossom* looked worried.

"I'll ask her about it," she said. "It's strange that her Potentia is only manifesting now. There's still a lot we don't know. I've asked for more information, but the higher-ups are tight lipped.

Even Matrona was evasive. What happened at the Temple of Jupiter?"

Heron shrugged. "It must be following on from Valerius and the *Livia*. I've a horrible suspicion that the Huntress is involved, or why would everyone be ordered to sacrifice to her, of all the Gods?"

"My head is aching, just thinking about it," Plinius said. "I know that Maia knows more than she's saying and I also think that she's under orders to keep quiet." He and *Blossom* had had a secret communication warning them that Maia was in danger and it didn't take much to put two and two together.

"That doesn't help us," *Blossom* objected. "How can we act if we don't know the full story?"

"It's fruitless to speculate without data," Plinius replied. "I suggest you have a word with her, *Blossom*, and learn what you can. In the meantime, we'll make the best speed possible for Londin. I think that Maia had better be kept separate for now."

"Aye, Captain."

"And I'll inform Raven," Heron said. "He'll want to know about this."

As she headed for Maia's cabin, *Blossom* wondered what on earth she was going to say to her.

*

Maia felt bad about being unable to reply to *Blossom*'s questions, but it couldn't be helped. She was tempted to tell her everything, but Jupiter's warning echoed in her head and she knew that she didn't dare. The Ship would just have to trust her.

"It's for your own safety," she insisted.

"This is all to do with Valerius and the *Livia,* isn't it?"

Maia gave her a slight nod.

"I knew it!" *Blossom* said. "It's so unfair that you must pay for her crime."

"It's just the way it goes," Maia replied, in resignation. "How long will it be before we get to Londin?"

Blossom knew that she'd changed the subject deliberately.

"Another ten hours."

"This is the worst part," Maia told her. "It'll be better when I can actually do something. I think I'll come up on deck and take the air."

"It's cold," *Blossom* warned her. "You'll need to wrap up."

"I know. See you up there."

Durus smiled at her as she emerged on to the quarterdeck. The sun was already setting, though it was only late afternoon, and dusk was falling. The water was choppy, but the wind was in their favour and the vessel was forging through the waves at a steady speed. To her right, the Ship was standing on watch, her senses scanning the way ahead through the growing darkness.

Overhead, a gull called and Maia looked up to see if she could spot a flash of white wings against the clouds. Instead, she glimpsed a silvery wisp, twisting in the air like a ribbon twirled by an unseen hand.

"Pearl?"

<*Greetings, sister! I am near.*>

"I can see you. We're heading for Londin so that I can go for my initiation."

<*Yes. I am permitted to watch, but I cannot interfere.*>

"I understand. Thank you."

<*I am praying for you,*> her sister replied, before vanishing into the freezing air.

"Who were you talking to?"

Danuco's voice made her jump.

"Er, a Tempestas," Maia said, guiltily.

"In the air?"

"Yes."

"A friendly Tempestas, then. Does she often talk to you?"

"Sometimes."

The Priest gave her a sharp look. "A Tempestas and the Lady of Storms, eh? You seem, shall we say, well-connected?"

Maia stared him down. "I don't know what you mean."

Danuco nodded, slowly, then relaxed, as if she'd passed a test. He was quite an unremarkable looking man, she thought, as she'd been unremarkable before her injuries marked her out. Brown hair, brown eyes, medium height with regular features. Just the sort to be posted unobtrusively to keep a watchful eye on someone with a secret.

"I once heard tell of a woman that fell in love with a Mer Lord," he said, conversationally. "She gave birth to a child and took him to live on land with her family, telling no-one of his parentage. Jupiter quietly made an exception to his decree: after all, it wasn't as if the lad was about to disrupt the natural order of things, though he has become an excellent Captain. He can swim like a fish, too."

He smiled, as if at a secret joke.

"Is he still in the Navy?"

"Yes, but I can't tell you his name of course. It was only because of unusual circumstances that I know about it at all. These things have to be kept quiet, don't they?"

She stared at his profile as he looked out at the water. So, she and Pearl weren't the first.

"Yes," she agreed. "They have to be kept very quiet."

He turned to her, his face shadowed. "You've done well, Maia. Don't give up hope."

There was a faint, deep echo to his words, as if another was speaking almost at the same time and Maia's eyes widened.

Then the Ship's bell rang out for the change of watch and the moment passed.

"Time for dinner," Danuco said, cheerfully. He sounded quite normal. "Shall we go down?"

He seemed unaware that anything had happened at all.

*

They slipped into the Londin Docks with the tide. The city was its usual bustling, noisy self, though not as frenetic as the last time she had been there during the festival. Normal work had resumed and the river was crowded with vessels and cargo being hauled upstream. New factories and warehouses were springing up along the riverbank like weeds and smoke billowed from an ever-increasing number of chimneys. Maia could taste the soot in the air. *Blossom* shook her head.

"I can't believe how much the city's changed from when I first came here. There was hardly anything on the south side of the river and it was a lot wider too. These new embankments have really made a difference to the channels."

Maia remembered the terrified and angry girl whose mind she'd entered, if only for a short time.

"How old were you when you saw Londin for the first time?"

"Fifteen. I stayed in Portus for more than six years, whilst I was trained. I was sixteen when I was installed."

Sixteen? Maia was shocked. "You had no life at all!"

The Ship shrugged. "The Navy needed Ships. The Navy always needs Ships. Technically, we have to give consent. What else was there for me? I wasn't cut out to be a Priestess and my Potentia took a dangerous form. I lost count of the stuff I smashed in those first years."

Maia remembered Tullia's temper tantrum and the whirling chaos of her room. She'd been punished for it as well.

"Were you the only candidate?"

"No. There were three other girls and we all became Ships, one after the other. We're all still going, as well."

"Who are they?"

"The *Justicia* was one, but we didn't get on. That's why we don't communicate unless we have to. I once threw a vase at her head without lifting a finger and she's never forgiven me. She was a high-ranking general's daughter and a total cow."

Maia tried not to laugh. Tullia hadn't been that bad.

"Did you hit her?"

"Oh yes!"

"So that's why she didn't say anything in Durobrivis?"

"Yup. Still sulking after three hundred years." *Blossom* grinned. "It warms my heart every time I remember the look on her face. Of course I was punished, but it was worth it. She was terrified of me ever after. She may be a Royal, but not many of us like her very much."

"Who were the others?"

"The *Persistence* and the *Cameo*. As you see, we stay in touch more than some of the others. We're getting to be some of the older ones now, though the *Augusta* is the oldest of us by far. She started out as a trireme, with oarsmen."

"I read about her in '*Famous Britannic Ships*' and '*Famous Britannic Sea Battles.*'"

"Famous everything," *Blossom* agreed. "After five hundred years, she deserves it."

"She was in the Battle of the Mare Germanicus," Maia said.

"Yes. That was a bad one. We had to beat the Northmen back and at that time we only had a handful of Ships. They hadn't brought in all the improvements from the Arab and Chin lands then, so everything was in the old Roman style. No lateen sails or cannon then."

Maia was still amazed that the ancient Ship had deigned to speak to her and said as much.

"Oh she's very gracious. A real lady, unlike some of the others who put on airs without real cause. She's the last of her kind."

"What was her name?"

Blossom shrugged.

"I don't think anyone living remembers who she was before and, to tell the truth, it doesn't matter. It'll be in the records, somewhere. That's just the way it is. She's outlasted all the others from her time." She seemed to be about to say something else, but changed the subject instead.

"We won't be together for much longer, Maia. I think you'll be leaving me very soon, possibly within the next couple of days. The Admirals are terrified they'll lose you."

"I just want to get it over with, one way or another," Maia said, firmly.

"Listen," *Blossom* said, urgently. "You can do it. Keep your mind on the prize and focus on that gorgeous new vessel that's waiting for you. Don't let anything stand in your way, get it?"

Maia knew that the Ship was trying to help her as much as possible.

"I'll do my best."

"Now go and get some sleep and eat those sweets you've squirrelled away!"

As Maia made her way below, *Blossom* stared out over the smoky city, feeling every minute of her two hundred and ninety-six years.

She sighed and opened a link to the only people who could understand.

<*Blossom* to *Persistence* and *Cameo*.>

Time to catch up on the latest gossip.

*

There was a very long queue in front of the Temple of Minerva. Milo had had to wait weeks, kicking his heels in the capital, expecting to be posted to some Godsforsaken corner of Britannia, but, to his surprise, the summons hadn't come. Another poor sucker must have been given the assignment. Part of him was glad, while the rest grumbled that he'd been overlooked. Now he was sitting with Caniculus in a smoky tavern, not far from the Forum.

"Stop complaining," his friend said. "Honestly! Would you rather be holed up in some flea-ridden inn waiting for a bunch of tossers to give themselves away so you could arrest them, or here sampling the delights of the capital?"

Milo scowled. "I'm bored."

Caniculus took a swig of his ale. "No pleasing you, is there, Ferret? Hey, have you seen it?"

He indicated the line of people waiting patiently in the cold.

"Not yet. You can't get near and I'm not standing freezing my bits off in this weather."

His friend grinned so widely that Milo wouldn't have been surprised to see the top of his head fall off.

"You're in luck, old son. I can get us in."

Milo stared at him, sceptically.

"Oh yes?"

"You'd better believe it. My family was charged with moving the body. Personally, I think it was just in case the old girl came back to life. You can never tell with these original monsters."

Milo knew that Caniculus' family sourced and kept exotic animals for the various Games that took place up and down the country. They'd be the natural people to go to when you had a dubious creature to transport, dead or alive.

"So, you have a pass?"

"I do indeed!"

Caniculus produced a pasteboard card from an inside pocket with a flourish worthy of the most gifted Mage in Britannia.

"When do you want to go?"

"No time like the present. Sup up! We've a monster to gawk at."

Milo grinned back, his spirits lifted. "Come on, then. Let's marvel at the taxidermist's art, shall we?"

They opted to approach the Temple by a side door, the habits of secrecy and concealment too ingrained to allow them to flaunt their good fortune, though Milo would have enjoyed strolling past the long line of eager faces.

Caniculus handed the card over for scrutiny, not to a Priest, but a City polisman. He exchanged a glance with Milo; they must have drafted in reinforcements to help with the crowds.

"This seems in order. In you go, gents," the man said.

"Thank you, Officer," Milo said, politely. "Got your hands full?"

The polisman nodded. "They're queueing morning, noon and night to see 'er. Who'd 'ave thought it? It used to be that you needed some sort of Godly weapon to deal with the likes of 'er. 'Ow the mighty 'ave fallen, eh?"

"And the Goddess is all right with it?"

The man shrugged. "Must be. She's Senator Rufus's patron, so she wouldn't 'ave been too pleased about the attack. We're all wondering who the guilty party is."

He raised his eyes heavenward.

"Who can tell?" Milo said, diplomatically. "There can't be many of these things left in the world."

"Not around 'ere, anyway," the polisman replied, with an air of satisfaction. "And if any more show up, we'll give 'em what we gave 'er!"

"Too right!" Caniculus said with feeling. "My Dad wanted her for the arena. Imagine the crowds!"

"Don't 'ave to. They're 'ere."

They nodded in agreement.

"It would have been better if they could have caught her alive," Caniculus said, wistfully, once they were inside. Milo shot him a look.

"How many people did she kill and eat? Seven? Eight? I hope they paid the taxidermist extra."

"Now that doesn't bear thinking about," his friend agreed, with a grimace.

They paid for the customary incense and joined the lines for the altars to make their offerings to the Goddess. Her impassive marble face stared down at her devotees, grey eyes surveying each one and Milo felt a chill run up his spine. This many worshippers would benefit Minerva, or Athena, or whatever you wanted to call her, the smoke rising to add to her large store of Potentia.

A frieze of carved and painted Gorgon heads ran round the walls, reminding everyone that Minerva kept the head of Medusa. Another reason why the Olympians were pre-eminent in the Empire.

The corpse was being displayed in an antechamber. The queue shuffled forward, bit by bit, slowly enough to read the information boards that had been set up, as well as the various pictures showing Echidna in her prime.

"Good old Minerva," Caniculus muttered. "A lesson as well as a spectacle."

"What do you expect from the Goddess of Wisdom?" Milo hissed back. "Is it me, or do you get the feeling that she's making a point?"

His friend glanced around at the throng. "Definitely. Tell me, are there any supernormal beings left in Chin?"

"What?"

"Or have they killed all theirs off with gunpowder?"

"I think they use special prayers. Don't know about the rest, though their dragons are supposed to be beneficial."

"Lucky them. Makes you wonder, doesn't it? If gunpowder did for Echidna, what else could it kill?"

"I wouldn't wonder too loudly."

"You're probably right."

They concentrated on the first board, which gave a potted history of the creature in Latin and Britannic, together with pictures for those who couldn't read.

"Blood and sand! She had a lot of kids."

Milo looked at the list. "They're mostly dead now. Except for the Hound of Hades and the various Hydrae and Scyllae, though I suppose they should be classed as grandchildren."

"That's a point. I hope that Senator Rufus doesn't end up facing her son at the Gates of the Underworld. Would you want to admit that you had his old Mum stuffed and put on display? Cerberus can be touchy at the best of times."

"He'll just blame the Adepts. Don't forget, it was done with the Goddess' permission."

The next panel showed Echidna giving birth to the Lernaean Hydra. The woman in front was assuring her son that no, there were no hydras in Britannia and if any showed up, they'd be shot too. The small child, about seven, Milo reckoned, was staring at the picture with eyes like saucers.

"I bet they'll be running school trips soon," Caniculus said.

"Good idea. It isn't supernormal monsters that they should be scared of, but the ones that walk on two legs. Ask any polisman."

Caniculus nodded. "Alas! Still, I think he's a bit little. I hope he doesn't have nightmares."

The woman had moved ahead and a quiet shuffling from behind them urged them to catch up.

The last panel showed an artist's rendition of the final battle in the bathhouse. Senator Rufus and his men were facing the monster, plumes of fire spurting from their muskets, while Echidna, fangs bared, threw back her head in agony. One arm was clasped dramatically to a gaping wound in her breast, whilst the other was upraised in a last, desperate appeal. The viewers murmured in awe that was tinged with anticipation.

Finally, they entered the chamber. The line formed three sides of a square, to give everyone the maximum time to have a good look at what was arranged on a platform in the middle, artfully lit and posed with care.

The Adepts hadn't quite managed to remove the smell and Caniculus wasn't the only one to wrinkle his nose.

Echidna was over twenty feet long, her thick serpentine tail coiled beneath her, tapering to end in a point like a regular snake's. Her scales appeared to have been oiled and Milo suspected that there had been some restoration, as some patches looked newer than others. Maybe she'd been about to shed her skin? Her upper body was raised, the skin pale and unwholesome looking, like a frog's belly and her breasts looked like they'd been padded internally to make them more prominent. Sinewy arms ended in human-like fingers, tipped with long, yellowed claws and her jaws were stretched unnaturally wide, displaying her fangs and serrated teeth. Behind her head and neck, a scaled hood spread out in a cowl. Blank, lidless eyeballs gazed into space; they'd probably replaced them with glass, or crystal.

She was both fascinating and repellent. Milo pitied the poor souls whose last moments had been a vision of her open throat as she struck.

The eager chatter ceased. Everyone went past in silence, eyes fixed on the mother of horrors that had preyed on humans for centuries.

As they left, they passed a small shrine and memorial to her victims. Milo saw that the names of the three slaves that had died had been added alongside the free victims and approved. When it had come down to it, Echidna had made no distinction. All were food to her, male and female, free and enslaved.

The mood of excitement had dissipated into grief and there were a few tears, as people left small offerings to petition the Gods to see the victims' souls safely to Elysium. Milo was relieved when they emerged into the Forum once more.

"Well, that was both interesting and horrible," he remarked.

"Naturally, but the real question is, how did she get to the Senator's villa? There are all sorts of rumours."

"The official line is that it was the Separatists who smuggled her in. Do you believe that?"

"It seems strange," Caniculus admitted. "Why not just shoot him? There's more to this than meets the eye, but I couldn't tell you what it is."

Milo resisted the temptation to say any more.

"True. I don't know about you, but I need a drink."

They escaped the early February gloom and found a table in a nearby tavern.

"So, how's life at the palace?" Milo asked.

Caniculus sniffed. "Fairly quiet, though the King's advisors are having fits every time he announces that he's going on another hunt. I'm surprised there are any animals left in the Royal forests the way he's going. I'm spending my life trailing along behind, trying to keep up."

"Any news on marriages?"

"Ha! You sound like an old woman."

Milo dug him in the ribs.

"Hey! Watch my drink. This isn't the cheap stuff!"

"I know. I bought it!"

Caniculus rolled his eyes. "All right. There are various names being bandied about for Artorius, but they want Julia to marry old King Parisius."

"It's always useful to have an alliance with Gaul and, if she gives him an heir, that will strengthen the ties as well."

"They could send her north to bolster the new peace with the Alliance," Caniculus reflected. "I know that some are pushing for that."

Milo pulled a face. "They'd probably have to hog-tie her and shove her in a sack."

His friend sputtered into his beer. "They would. I get the feeling that she's the brains of the family, apart from old Pendragon, but he's away on the *Augusta* most of the time. You know how he hates the Court."

"I've heard. How's the Prince?"

"Oh, him? Marcus is busy keeping in his cousin's good graces, while probably hoping that he'll fall off his horse and break his neck like his father did."

Milo raised an eyebrow.

"Well, wouldn't you?"

"No. I'd rather be a Prince and free to play around, than a King with all that responsibility."

Caniculus looked sceptical.

"Suppose so. Anyway, the negotiations for the Princess are down to squabbling about the dowry. To tell you the truth, I think that the fault must lie with Parisius. Two wives and no kids? Something's wrong in that department. The Emperor will end up having to pick a new King from his nephews. If it goes ahead, I bet she's back on the market in a year or two. Anyhow, have you got any work in the offing?"

Milo shrugged.

"Regular surveillance."

"Lovely. Sniffing out Separatists, eh? Could be worse. Foxy got sent to Kernow."

"Rather him than me."

As they toasted each other and the absent Foxy, Milo couldn't help but wonder if Kernow might have been the better option.

Just why had the Huntress sent Echidna to the Senator's villa? And what had she got against Maia Abella?

VII

The order came the next day, just after breakfast.

"You're to report to the Admiralty immediately to go through the formalities," *Blossom* told Maia.

"What sort of formalities?"

"Paperwork, what else? You need to sign a consent form."

"Probably in triplicate," Maia sighed. "They must have stacks and stacks of the stuff somewhere."

"They do," the Ship agreed. "The Empire couldn't run without it."

Maia thought for a moment. "Do I need to take anything?"

"No," *Blossom* admitted, "but you are allowed a keepsake."

Maia's hand flew to her necklace. She couldn't have borne to leave it behind.

"Can I take this with me?"

Blossom nodded. "Yes, but I have to warn you, it will remain with your flesh body. You won't be needing anything else."

That was true. The Navy didn't encourage their Ships to have many possessions other than their vessels, as they were thought to engender negative thoughts. They wanted their gazes firmly fixed on the future, not the past.

"At least I'll know that I still have it, somewhere," she said, wistfully.

Now that the time had finally arrived, Maia just felt sick. It was one thing to know what was theoretically about to happen, but another to actually go through with it. Only the knowledge that her Academy classmates had undergone the same trial gave her any relief.

"It'll be fine," *Blossom* insisted. Remember -,"

"Keep my mind on the prize, yes." Maia smiled to take the sting out of her words.

"All the other Ships are Sending you best wishes."

Maia had been in the link the night before, receiving the customary encouragement from those whom she hoped would be her sisters before too long. She wished she could tell *Blossom* and the Captain about her real sister, but knew that it was out of the question. Maybe one day, if things changed, she could tell them everything but for now she had to keep her lips firmly sealed.

"Heron will take your earring," *Blossom* said. "Just think, you won't need one to talk to me and I'll always be here for you, anytime, until you don't need me anymore."

Maia's face crumpled. "I'll always need you," she said, her voice cracking and her eyes misting.

"Don't cry, you'll start us all off!" the Ship said. Maia gave her a hug, her ordeal at the hands of the *Livia* pushed aside for once. If all went well, soon she would have her own wooden flesh, supple yet unyielding, impervious to rot and the ravages of time until the moment her *anima* left it.

"Now then. What's all this?"

Captain Plinius' voice came from behind her. "No tears, young lady. This is the start of a new and exciting life for you!"

Or the end of this one, she thought. All she wanted was to stay with him and *Blossom,* sailing the seas far away from those who wished her harm. Still, in a way she could. If all went to plan. Diana didn't have any sway over the waves.

"I'll be accompanying you for the first stage anyway," he told her. She smiled at him and went to get ready.

It was time to depart. She looked at the familiar faces lined up to say goodbye, most smiling at the thought that they were getting another powerful Ship to add to their Navy.

Old Hyacinthus clasped her hand and wished her luck, while Scribo and the others gave her a resounding cheer. Cap'n Felix regarded her solemnly.

"Damned monsters!" he shrieked. "Kill 'em all!"

Scribo rolled his eyes. "What are yer on about? What monsters? Stupid addled featherbrain! No yer don't!" he added, as the bird started on its obscene rhyme. Cap'n Felix looked disappointed, but subsided.

"Not the words you want to go out on," Heron observed.

"I don't know," Maia shot back. "Why should today be any different?"

Everyone laughed. She had already said farewell to Campion, who was attending training onshore. Durus saluted her and wished her well. He would be leaving soon himself, to take up another post as Captain of the *Farsight*, a neat little fourth-rate. The Ship's cheerful outlook would counterbalance his calm stoicism and she knew that he would do well.

"New horizons for both of us," he said. Maia thanked him for his kindness.

"*Farsight* is a lucky Ship," she told him.

"I agree," *Blossom* added, smiling.

She handed her little ivory dog back to Big Ajax. She valued the present he'd carved for her when she was injured and hated the thought of losing it. "Will you keep him for me?" she asked. "I'd like him back, later."

The huge man blushed and bobbed his head, shyly. One by one, the rest of the crew said their own words of farewell.

It was time. Heron removed her earring with a muttered word and she felt the link break and vanish. Suddenly, her head and body felt too small and empty. It took all her courage to follow Plinius down the gangplank, to where a carriage waited to take them into Londin and the perils that awaited.

*

The drive in was uneventful, though the Captain insisted that the blinds be drawn down on the carriage, so she couldn't see much of the city. She could certainly hear it over the noise of the horses. The streets were congested as usual, so their progress was slow and she wondered why they hadn't gone by river.

"Not much point," Plinius had said, when she asked, "and there's someone we need to pick up first."

That someone turned out to be Raven.

"I don't intend to miss your important day," he said, somewhat grumpily she thought. "Let's see what the Admirals have to say, shall we? I believe the Lord High Admiral himself will be attending. The *Augusta*'s back in port."

"It might be a good idea if she were to stay here," Plinius said meaningfully.

Maia gave him a quizzical look, but he didn't elaborate further and, before she could ask him what he meant, the carriage pulled up.

They were shown through immediately. This time, Maia didn't even bother with her veil, staring boldly around her. Plinius gave her a nod of approval and she knew that he was talking to *Blossom*.

The nine members of the Admiralty Board were sitting at a long rectangular table, waiting for them. Maia knew that they were the most senior officers in His Majesty's Navy, responsible for its day-to-day running. They were the ones who controlled the appointments of personnel, including Ships, and they also oversaw operations both at home and abroad. There was also another Mage present and she felt Raven stiffen slightly.

"Master Mage Raven, Captain Plinius, Miss Maia Abella, do take a seat."

She recognised Admiral Pendragon immediately. He was presiding at the head of the table, a thin-faced, grey haired man with the weathered cheeks of a true sailor. He gestured to the three empty chairs. Maia made sure that Raven was sitting before saluting and taking the seat next to him, her hands clasped before her. The only other face she recognised was Admiral Albanus, the *Regina*'s father, sitting next to Pendragon and smiling at her with an air of benevolence. She acknowledged him with a polite nod. As usual, a clerk was at a desk to one side, taking notes and Maia had a flash of memory. It was so like the first time in Portus, except that now there were more people. Introductions were made and Maia committed each name to her prodigious memory. Some were familiar to her and it was interesting matching them to faces.

<I believe you've already met the King's uncle,> Raven's voice whispered in her head. <The others are all senior members of the aristocracy, save Florus Helvius and Blasius Cadogus who've worked their way up from more humble beginnings.>

<Who's the Mage?> she Sent back.

<Bullfinch, Prime Mage and Head of the Collegium.>

Maia was going to ask why he was here when it was a Naval matter, but he was being introduced and she had to concentrate. There was something about his smug expression she didn't like, nor the way his beady eyes bored into her. She knew without asking that there was no love lost between him and Raven.

"Delighted to meet you at last, Miss Abella," Bullfinch said, with an ingratiating smile.

And what do you want? She didn't trust him and something told her that he had his own agenda.

The Lord High Admiral was speaking again.

"Gentlemen, we are meeting here today to confirm that Maia Abella has been appointed to the new vessel currently being completed. I know that you aware of this, but it gives me great pleasure to formally announce that, if the Gods permit, not only will she be a first-rate Ship-of-the-Line, but His Majesty has designated her a Royal Ship."

Maia could not hide her surprise, quickly followed by a burst of triumph. Beside her, she heard the Captain's sudden breath and knew that he was delighted for her. It was a great honour, though she knew that it was mostly for propaganda purposes.

The Admirals were smiling, including Albanus.

"If you are willing, you will be signed on for a trial period of six months, during which time you will be expected to grasp all the essentials of your craft. After this period expires there will be another meeting to assess your performance and suitability."

Maia nodded. This was standard procedure. She also doubted that they would ever dismiss her.

"All here present know of your family line. His Majesty has also been informed, but this will not be released as general information. I am told that you have been discreet."

"Yes, my lord."

<I take it they mean my father?> she Sent to Raven.

<Yes. Only that side of your family,> he replied.

"Excellent." Pendragon's eyes raked her thoughtfully. "Then there is simply the matter of signing the final contract and you'll be ready for your initiation. On behalf of the Board, may I wish you success and I hope to greet you on board your new vessel soon."

Suddenly the clerk was at her elbow and Maia saw that, for her, the meeting was over. She was glad to make her exit and hoped there would be a chance to eat something before she was taken away to wherever the rituals were going to take place.

*

Raven's sightsense skimmed over the men sitting before him. He was pleased with Maia's performance and attitude. She'd given the Board no reason to be suspicious of her, even though most of them didn't know the full story of her birth. Pendragon certainly did, but there was a man who could keep a secret. He had the feeling that if they'd had any other candidates, they might have let her go rather than risk the Huntress' wrath, but, as the stuffed corpse of Echidna showed, times were changing. Both he and the Captain gave their reports on her progress and conduct.

"She is an obedient and sober young woman," Plinius finished, "and both the *Blossom* and I believe that her talents can be put to good use in His Majesty's and the Empire's service."

"The signs are favourable, despite the attempts on her life," one of the younger men agreed. It was Aeron Silius Fortus, head of the Admiralty's Supernormal Liaison Section, or SLS. His department kept tabs on all encounters with the Divine, unusual or just downright bizarre that were reported by crews on their travels. It was essential to know what might be encountered, especially as Ships ranged further afield into unknown territory. He was rumoured to have some immortal blood himself from many generations back.

"It seems that the Gods are of two minds about her," Pendragon said. "Still, she is an unknown quantity and I don't want to draw any further attention."

"Hopefully that will abate when she's installed and put to work," Raven commented.

Glances and nods were exchanged up and down the table.

"Have we had any word from the Huntress or her Priests? Fortus, that's more your department."

The younger man peered through his round spectacles and riffled through some papers.

"Apparently the Goddess was gracious enough to receive the offerings, but whether that means that she is appeased or not is unknown. Word has somehow got out that she was responsible for transporting Echidna, though why she would target the Senator is also unknown. Footfall to her main temple has reduced as a consequence. The people aren't pleased and the word in the city is that she's out to cause trouble and raise her standing. I doubt that this is true, but you know that rumour moves faster than a greased pig."

"It's a worrying development, nonetheless," Bullfinch stated.

"The Gods will move as they will. All we can do is batten down the hatches and weather the storms that they bring," Pendragon said. "We've done our duty and I hope that we hear no more of the matter once Miss Abella goes through the initiation process, for good or ill. I hope that she is successful, as His Majesty is very keen to have his own Royal Ship. He's announced that he will launch her personally."

"Interesting," Helvius muttered. "There hasn't been a new one for fifty years or more. She'd better make it, or we'll have to draft in someone else."

"The King has chosen to act on his prerogative and the Navy needs to expand," Pendragon said briskly. "Don't forget that we're fortunate to find a suitable candidate. You know that they're becoming harder to find as the blood thins."

"She's got enough, it seems," Helvius said. "Let's hope that she has the wit to match. What was she – a foundling scullery maid? A Valerius, too. It doesn't bear thinking about."

There were murmurs of agreement around the room.

"How is her control? Master Mage, you know her better than most."

"She's adjusted well to her new situation," Raven said. "Considering all that she has suffered, she's able to keep her temper and experience has taught her patience and resilience in equal measure."

"On behalf of the Royal Navy, I would like to offer a vote of thanks to the Master Mage for his help in this matter," Pendragon said. Hands rose around the table, some slower than others, Raven noticed.

Pendragon nodded at the clerk, who scribbled away industriously.

"Thank you, my lord. It was a duty and an honour to serve," Raven replied.

Bullfinch cleared his throat. "Thank you, Master Mage. We won't keep you from your duties any longer."

Raven inclined his head. *Officious little toad. At least you're good at paperwork.*

He paid his respects and left, determined to be present when the subject of the new Ship's Mage was discussed.

Maia was waiting for him in a side room.

"Oh, hello, Raven. I saved you a cake."

He smiled at her. "It's all right, my dear. You eat it."

*

"Well, that's it," Heron said, as he and *Blossom* watched the carriage disappear along the wharf. "Either she'll succeed or she won't. We've done all we can for now."

"It doesn't get any easier," the Ship replied. "I thought it would, but it hasn't. I have to tell you that I'm even more worried than usual with this one."

Heron raised an eyebrow. "Why?"

"It's in the nature of the testing," *Blossom* said. "And I'm not convinced that *she* has given up yet." The Ship jerked her head to the heavens, grimacing.

"I pray that Maia will end up safely in the arms of the Mother," Heron said.

"Yes," *Blossom* sighed.

"By the way, I believe Maia hasn't been the only one you've been mentoring, lately," Heron said, gazing at her reprovingly.

"I don't know what you mean," *Blossom* said, her generous mouth twitching.

"I have to congratulate you on your cunning Saturnalia prank. It's been driving everyone mad for weeks. Please could you teach that damned parrot something else, before he ends up in the sea with a weight around his neck? Just saying."

Lieutenant Durus, walking past, wondered what the joke was.

*

Maia had expected to be taken back to the Naval accommodation she'd been put in previously, but Raven led her instead to an area she hadn't been to before.

"I'm going to send you directly to the Temple of the Mother," he told her. "The Priestesses will take it from there and prepare you for your ordeal."

Ordinarily, Maia would have been thrilled to have the chance to travel by portal.

"Will you be coming with me?"

"No," he told her, gently. "You'll be passing beyond the mortal realm now. I'm afraid we won't be able to talk, either, as there's a barrier around the whole complex. You'll be travelling to the ancient heart of Albion."

"Have you been there?"

He smiled. "Yes. All Mages go there at least once, some more often. Be strong. I know you can do this."

She shivered. "Can it really be worse than what I've already been through?"

"I can't answer that, but you of all people understand hardship and pain."

"You know, I'm looking forward to a time when there isn't any," Maia told him. "A day of sunshine, good company and hope for the future. It would be nice."

He nodded. "Yes. It would, wouldn't it?"

The room they entered was set aside for far transportation. The circle in the centre was permanent, with symbols inlaid into the floor. Raven gestured for her to enter it and she was about to obey, when, suddenly, an impulse made her reach around her neck and unclasp her little necklace.

"Please, I want you to have this."

He tilted his head. "Don't you want it to stay with you?"

Maia thought about it for a second. "I did, but I think you should have it to remember me by, you know, just in case."

A strange expression crossed the withered face. His mouth opened, but no sound emerged. Instead, his voice, deep and strong, echoed in her head.

<Thank you. I'll treasure it.>

She dropped it into his gnarled hand, her burned skin brushing his wrinkled palm and his fingers closed over hers. A surge of emotion passed between them, like a glimpse of age-old suffering that she couldn't understand, before he broke the contact and it vanished.

He slipped the jewels into a pocket and waited for her to settle herself in the smaller circle within the larger working.

"Are you ready?"

"As I'll ever be."

"May Fortuna smile on you! See you on the other side."

His blind eyes closed and he raised his arms. Maia felt his Potentia surge, like a million insects running across the surface of her skin and she gasped at the sensation.

Then a swirl of light exploded into her eyes and Raven vanished.

*

She wasn't actually physically sick, but it was a close thing. It felt as though she'd been turned inside out, then back again in the blink of an eye. She staggered a little and felt arms hold her up on either side.

A voice was talking and she concentrated on that, while waiting for her vision to return. A cool breeze brushed her cheek and she knew that she was outdoors, far away from the smoky city she'd been in only seconds before.

"That's it, move your legs and we'll get you out of the circle."

The woman's voice guided her as she stumbled on, blinking to try and clear the mist from her eyes. Then, the back of her knees touched a wooden bench and she sat, grateful for the support and keeping her head down until the blood stopped thundering in her ears.

"Take deep breaths and the dizziness will pass," the unseen woman advised her and she did as she was told, filling her lungs and exhaling slowly until she felt better.

Colour bled back into the world and Maia found herself staring at grass that was dotted with tiny wildflowers. She raised her head and looked about her, still amazed that she could be in another place so quickly. She appeared to have emerged in the middle of a forest.

"Welcome to the Temple of the Mother," another voice said. An older woman, her black hair streaked with white, was approaching her. She was simply dressed in a woollen robe of green and brown. Maia couldn't help staring at the blue patterns that snaked up her neck and across her forehead. Was she a Pict? She sounded quite ordinary.

"I am her Priestess. Call me Ceridwen. You have been brought here to be admitted to the Mother's Mysteries, so that you may become part of the living wood. Do you consent to this?"

Maia bit back a sarcastic reply.

"Yes." She knew that she sounded less than enthusiastic. The Priestess raised an eyebrow, her dark eyes glittering.

"Then come."

She led Maia towards a clearing that contained a cluster of small, round buildings with conical thatched roofs that almost touched the ground. They surrounded a larger dwelling that sat in the centre, like a hen guarding her chicks. Behind the little settlement, a hill loomed, crowned with a small wood of tall trees. The wintry afternoon sun slanted through their branches, outlining their starkness with a fiery glow.

Ceridwen ducked inside the nearest hut and Maia followed her apprehensively. This wasn't at all what she thought it would be. It seemed ancient and primitive, untouched by time, as if it had been like this for thousands of years, whilst outside Empires rose and fell, armies marched and cities grew. She had no idea where she was, but it had to be very far from anything people called civilisation.

The interior was dark, smelling of earth and the wood smoke from a small fire burning in a ring of hearth stones. Lazy coils rose sinuously, drifting upwards into the darkness of the roof space. There were no fine marbles or intricate mosaics here and Maia wondered what sort of Goddess dwelt in such a place. Ceridwen seated herself on a bench and added a few sticks of wood to the fire from a nearby pile. The flames lapped greedily at the fresh fuel and Maia felt a little warmer.

"This is where you will stay for the next few days, until you are ready," she said.

The woman's dark eyes fixed on Maia's own and she felt a tiny shiver of Potentia creep into the air as the Priestess sent out a subtle probe. This would be the first test. Whatever she saw, it seemed to satisfy her, as she nodded once.

"Your robes are on the bed. When you have changed, come to the great house for some food and to meet the other Priestesses and acolytes. Have you any questions?"

Maia felt that she had about a million, but didn't dare ask more than one.

"What is the name of the Goddess you serve?"

Ceridwen's teeth shone white in the semi-darkness. "She has as many names as the peoples of the world, some so ancient that they have been forgotten to time and as many faces and aspects. She lives in the waters, the forests, the mountains and the seas that make up her great body. We call her the Mother, for she is the Earth and is mother to all, but you might know her as Gaia, Demeter or Ceres. We are thrice blessed here in Britannia, as her spirit is strong and can connect with us in a way that is easier for us mortals to understand. Thus it is that we can bond with the sacred, living wood and bend it to our purpose. But no sacrifice comes without price."

"I know," Maia said.

The Priestess regarded her, steadily. "You might, more than most, but the full cost is paid over time and that is what you must be willing to embrace. This is why all candidates must undergo initiation. If you have the courage and the resolve, you will pass."

"What happens if I fail?"

"Your journey on this plane will be ended."

Maia nodded, feeling the familiar sinking sensation. *Here I go again.* Maybe one day there would come a time when her life wasn't hanging in the balance. She met Ceridwen's gaze evenly, refusing to lower her eyes. If the Priestess was surprised at her composure, she gave no sign, but stood abruptly.

"I'll leave you to settle in." She wasn't unkind, just a bit brusque and Maia decided that she could cope with that. She could be about to send her to her death, after all, so it didn't pay to get too attached.

"There are lamps and extra clothes in the chest. If you need anything else, we can provide it later."

"Thank you."

After the woman had left, Maia poked around the hut. There was a bed, with a decent mattress and sheets and several blankets that didn't look too itchy. The pillow was soft and covered with a slip of finer linen cloth. Draped across these was a gown of creamy linen, with a heavier, unbleached woollen over garment and a woven belt in green and brown.

She opened the small chest and the scent of lavender and fresh herbs billowed up. There were three little lamps and a flask of oil to fill them with, plus some spills that she could use to light them. For the moment, she contented herself with filling them all but only lighting one. She would need the others later, when it got really dark. These Priestesses were very unlike some of the others she had seen, riding around Portus in their fancy carriages, or receiving offerings in the temples. She had the feeling that those women had never had to do without. These women led the simpler life of their ancestors.

After debating for a minute, she decided to keep her own underwear and put the other things on top, fastening the belt. It was a little long for her, so she pulled the cloth up so that it hung over a little. Now she would really look old-fashioned. Part of her felt like the first time she had met Matrona, at the Academy in Portus; she hadn't had a comb to her name then, either.

She added some more wood to the fire, hoping that it wouldn't have completely burnt out by the time she got back and grabbed the lit lamp, leaving the other two within easy reach, before taking a deep breath and pulling back the door curtain to emerge once more into the clearing.

There was nobody about, so she took a few seconds to observe her surroundings. She could smell the smoke from the other huts and, beyond them, the forest stretched in a silent wall. The only feature she could see, now fading into the dusk, was the lone hill standing over them, silent and watchful like a sentinel. Gooseflesh prickled along her arms and she turned away quickly, to make for the larger building and the sound of women's voices.

This was the part she truly hated, having to walk into a room full of strangers who were expecting her. To Hades with it! She told herself firmly to get a grip and entered, ducking slightly under the low lintel.

About a dozen women and several small children were clustered around a central hearth. One of them was breastfeeding a baby and Maia could just see the downy head poking out of the sling that cradled the infant. There were no men.

One child jumped to her feet and headed in Maia's direction, calling out to the others.

"She's here!" the girl said. Maia felt herself the subject of scrutiny for a second, before the girl took her hand and pulled her towards the fire.

"Hello! My name's Rhiannon. I live here with my mother, Arianrhod. What's your name?"

"Let her sit down before you bombard her with more questions, Rhiannon," Arianrhod said, smiling at Maia. "Forgive my daughter, she tends to get carried away."

"That's all right," Maia replied. "I'm Maia."

Rhiannon was a gangly girl of about eight, with brown plaited hair and a gap-toothed smile. She opened her mouth, as if to ask another question, then closed it at a glance from her mother.

"You can make yourself useful and get our guest something to eat."

Ceridwen was seated at the far side of the fire, holding a wooden bowl in her lap. A pot of stew simmered near the flames. Rhiannon skipped over and carefully ladled the thick broth into a bowl. A wooden spoon and a hunk of bread completed the preparations and Maia accepted them with thanks. The food smelt good and she was hungry. She found an empty space on the nearest bench and began to eat, keeping one eye on the company.

Rhiannon seemed to be the oldest child there, as the others were only toddlers. Two had fallen asleep on sheepskins spread on the floor and the other two seemed about to follow them, eyes blinking as they fought to stay awake. The stew was rich and thick, with some meat that she couldn't identify, but was probably a bird of some sort. She dipped the bread into the juices, mopping up the bowl before finishing with a sigh of contentment.

"Modren is our cook," Ceridwen said and a stout, blonde woman waved a hand.

"It's very good," Maia said.

Modren dipped her head in acknowledgement, a pleased smile on her lips.

"Would you like some more?"

"No, I'm fine, thanks."

She was wondering what they did in the long dark evenings, when Rhiannon took her bowl and, together with a girl who had to be about Maia's age, wearing a similar pale robe, began to clear away the meal.

"Can I help?" Maia asked.

"Tomorrow," Modren answered. "We all take turns. For tonight, just sit and rest."

One woman brought out some finger weaving, whilst two others began to wind wool into balls. Other talked quietly among themselves, or stared into the fire. Maia could see looms further back in the shadows that would be used in the daytime.

"What happened to your face?"

Rhiannon had sidled up to her.

"I was burned," Maia said. The girl sucked her lip as she thought.

"Did it hurt?"

"Yes. A lot, but it's better now."

"Good. I saw the other ones."

"The other ones?"

"Yes, the other ladies going to be Ships. I liked Briseis. Do you know her?"

Maia smiled, cheered by the mention of her friend. "She's my best friend. She's called the *Patience* now."

"I like that name."

"Perhaps you'll find some one day," her mother said, laughing. The other women joined in.

"I'm sure I shall," Rhiannon said, lifting her chin. "It might be useful."

Maia suppressed a giggle. "It can be," she agreed.

"It's just that I hate waiting for things. I won't be here much longer," she added, quietly, fixing Maia with her big brown eyes as if imparting a great secret.

"Where will you go?"

"I'll probably train to be a Priestess, like Mam."

She glanced at Maia, suddenly shy. "What's it like, being on a Ship?"

"Different. You move about a lot. You might get seasick."

Rhiannon pulled a face. "That doesn't sound good. Did you get seasick?"

"No, I'm lucky," Maia smiled. Rhiannon pulled up her legs and clasped her knees, rocking slightly on the bench.

"It might be all right. I've got to wait for my Potentia to come out, so they know what to do with me. That's if I have some, of course."

"Rhiannon, time for bed," Arianrhod told her daughter. She moved the baby to her shoulder and began to rub its back.

"That's my brother, Mabon. He burps a lot," Rhiannon said.

"Where's your father?" Maia asked. Rhiannon shrugged.

"I don't know. I'm a child of the Goddess. So are the others." She didn't seem bothered. "Have you got a father?"

"I did, but he died."

"Rhiannon! I'm not telling you again."

The little girl gave an exaggerated sigh and rolled her eyes. "I'm not even tired!" Nonetheless, she scrambled off the bench. "I'll see you in the morning."

"Goodnight."

She followed her mother out of the hall. Ceridwen looked across at Maia.

"We bear children for the Goddess, to try and preserve the lines of Potentia, but it's getting harder to find suitable men."

"It's getting difficult to find potential Ships too," Maia said. "There aren't any other candidates at the moment."

Ceridwen nodded, gravely. "Yes. We were lucky to have two others come through lately."

Maia found that she was stifling a yawn. The day had passed very quickly, somehow.

"I think it's nearly your bed time too," the Priestess said, suddenly reminding her of Matrona. Maia thought she detected a resemblance under the tattoos, but couldn't be sure in the firelight. Perhaps her mind was playing tricks on her.

Outside, the wind was rising, but inside was cosy enough and Maia could feel her head start to loll as sleep threatened to overtake her. It must be later than she'd thought, or simply because she'd had a busy day but she could hardly keep her eyes open. Maybe time moved differently here?

The singing brought her back to wakefulness, a low chant that rose and fell in measured cadences. She tried to make out the words and, indeed, some seemed familiar, but different too.

Something about a tree in the forest? The chorus was a simple one and she found herself joining in the refrain, the meaning becoming clearer as she sang.

Rain and sunlight, Tree and leaf,
Sky above and earth beneath.

Later, Maia lay under the warm blankets in the hut, the only sounds the crackle of the fire and the rushing wind outside in the dark.

*

"It is not generally a good thing to be noticed by the Gods."

The Prime Mage's nasal voice cut through the low murmurs that echoed around the Council Chamber of the Londinium Collegium, causing the other occupants to fall silent. Raven sat unmoving, his hands resting on the cool marble surface of the great circular table at the centre of the room. He could feel the late winter sunlight on his skin as it slanted through the clerestory windows and hear the tiny sounds of the other Mages as they shifted in their seats, rustling the papers set before them. He briefly considered using his sightsense, then decided not to waste energy as he knew what he would see, though he did feel a little saddened that he would not be able to appreciate the chamber's tapestries in most of their glory.

"But His Majesty has spoken, so we must decide," Bullfinch continued. He sounded like he'd bitten into a lemon, probably because it was Raven's protégée who'd been accepted. There were whispers already that Maia was no ordinary candidate, though thankfully no specifics had been mentioned. The fact that a Council had been convened to discuss the matter was enough to raise eyebrows.

"Now the question must be, whom shall we provisionally appoint as her Mage?"

Bullfinch was a capable leader, adept at politics and full of the sort of Potentia guaranteed to impress people of authority and lead to fruitful connections, but that didn't mean that Raven could stand the man. Too much time polishing his fancy chair with his backside and not enough dealing with the real world. By now his nostrils would be flaring wide enough to house a large family and he didn't need to see them to know. He always reminded Raven of a fussy old dame forever waiting for the worst to happen; peevish when it didn't arrive and jubilant when it did. Still, he reflected, someone had to attend all those committee meetings and he was just glad that it wasn't him.

A sense of mischief made him decide to throw not only the cat among the pigeons, but strap a couple of explosive grenadoes round its neck for good measure.

"I offer myself for the position," he said calmly.

There were quite a few murmurs of surprise and Raven could almost hear the creaking of vertebrae as heads swivelled in his direction. His opposition to many of Bullfinch's initiatives was well known and the Prime Mage had of late taken every opportunity to have sly digs at his former mentor. Besides which, despite his great age and long service, Raven had absolutely no intention of retiring to a quiet corner. This was surely a solution to the fact that his current assignment at the palace was almost ended and Bullfinch would want him out of the way. Where better than fulfilling his obligations on active service far out at sea?

"You, Raven? Surely not!"

"The hardships of life at sea would be too much –"

"Your advanced years –"

The confused babble left Raven unmoved. He cut it off short, raising a hand to forestall any further objections.

"I am not yet in my dotage, gentlemen, despite my many, many years of service. Who is better qualified to tend to a young, untried Ship than one who is already conversant with her history and nature? She knows and trusts me."

There was a great deal of muttering. Raven engaged his sightsense at last, outlines springing into focus like a reverse charcoal drawing, with details but no colour. That, alas, was beyond him. The five other Council members were looking to their leader, who was sitting in an attitude of thought, fingers steepled before him. Raven noted that he'd been right about the nostrils.

"An interesting proposition."

The Prime Mage was clearly weighing the advantages. Raven could almost see the little cogwheels whirling and meshing in his brain. Would he agree, or would he leave himself open to a scenario where the ancient Mage would continue to be a thorn in his flesh? Bullfinch was astute enough to know that Raven still held a lot of influence and respect both at court and in the Senate House. The Master Mage waited for the result, idly thinking that his answer should emerge from Bullfinch's mouth on a strip of paper like one of the new calculating machines.

"I am persuaded by your reasoning," the Prime Mage finally acknowledged, with a calculated show of reluctance. "Very well, I recommend this appointment to the Council. Unless there are any other suggestions?"

The Prime Mage's tone of voice made it abundantly clear that he would rather there weren't. Negative mutterings and the shaking of heads answered him.

"Good. That's sorted then. I shall communicate our decision to the Admiralty."

'*Our decision*'. Raven snorted inwardly. One more reason to heartily dislike the man. Bullfinch's gaze raked the table.

"If you think it best, Prime Mage. I'm sure that we all support your wise judgement," a small, balding man offered unctuously.

"Thank you, Lapwing," Bullfinch said, clearly satisfied that the matter had been resolved. "I think that concludes our business for today."

He rose and the others followed suit, bowing politely. Lapwing hurried to his side as the Prime Mage swept out, trailing authority and importance.

Kite and Yellowhammer, more of Bullfinch's cronies, bowed to Raven then followed Bullfinch, but Chough and Dunnock sidled over to the Master Mage.

"Can you believe Lapwing? What a lickspittle!" Chough growled in disgust, his black eyes narrowed. "We'll have to find a way to cut him down to size. So, preparing for sea-trials then, Raven?"

"I think it best," Raven answered, jerking his head in the direction of the departed Bullfinch. "I'm tired of sniping from the shadows."

"He'll be glad to see the back of you," Dunnock agreed.

"I'm hoping for a far-off posting myself. I wouldn't have taken this seat if I hadn't had my arm twisted by the moderates."

"Someone needs to keep an eye on him," Raven warned. "His role is to guide, not dictate policy."

"Nobody's told him that. I still think he was constructed in Vulcan's workshop, not born to mortal woman," Chough said.

They shared wry smiles.

"Someone has to chair all those meetings," Dunnock said.

Raven harrumphed.

"I'd like to see him facing down a kraken."

"He'd drown it in paperwork," Chough grinned. "So, a potential new Ship! What's she like?"

Raven smiled. "Determined and tough. I'm quite looking forward to serving aboard her. I've a feeling that it'll be interesting."

"I'll say!" Dunnock agreed. "Do you know more than they're saying about her? There are rumours -"

"Which are totally unfounded," Raven said flatly. There was a short silence as the other men exchanged glances.

"Yes, right. Of course," Dunnock said quickly, before suddenly adding "Oh blast it! I'm supposed to be meeting Sparrow for lunch and he'll be waiting. Want to come?"

Both Raven and Chough accepted the offer.

"Certainly. Then it's off to the palace for me," Raven said.

"Still tutoring the Princess? Surely they've come a marriage settlement by now?"

"It's dragging on," Raven admitted. "Old Parisius should be grateful that he's even being considered."

"Yes, it doesn't look very hopeful that he'll get an heir," Dunnock agreed. "Still, it seems you've planned ahead. Bullfinch just couldn't resist the temptation, could he?"

Raven grinned. "I was counting on it."

The Master Mage was glad that he still had friends on the Council, even though his vacated seat would doubtless be filled by another of Bullfinch's toadies. All in all he was glad to be out of it.

As to whether he would be successful or not, that would be up to Maia.

VIII

Despite his expectations, Milo's stay in the capital had dragged on through into Februarius; not that he was complaining. A warm room in town was infinitely preferable to being parcelled off to scour the bleak countryside, plus it gave him time to catch up on his network of contacts and informants. He continued reporting in to his superiors at regular intervals, but so far it seemed that everyone had hunkered down for the winter. It had been a cold, wet and miserable season.

The damp was pervasive and Milo wished for a few crisp days, or even some snow, though the aftermath of that would be just as bad. Still, if it had snowed, people would doubtless be complaining about that instead. It was a standing joke in the Empire that Britons were obsessed with the weather.

He was crossing the Forum at dusk when his speechstone activated, its warmth flaring against his upper arm.

<Blue here,> he Sent.

The central operator's voice came over the link.

<Agent Blue. Unauthorised teleport activity has been detected in a block near Hadrian and Vallum, co-ordinates 86 by 41. Investigate and report back immediately.>

<Acknowledged.>

He signed off, changing direction and quickening his pace. Those co-ordinates were too near the palace for comfort and nobody should be portalling in or out of the city without official sanction. As he went, he contacted Caniculus.

<Blue to Green.>

The reply was immediate.

<Green here. What's up?>

Milo explained.

<I'm heading for the co-ordinates now. Have you heard anything?>

<Not much. I'm still at the palace. It's probably a glitch in the system again.>

<Again?>

He could sense his fellow Agent's amusement.

<Apparently. Hart was sent to check the same thing out last week, but didn't find anything. It must be your turn to draw the short straw. Charge 'em extra for wasting your time.>

Milo snorted. <If only. I'd better check it out.>

He ended the Sending and slowed, ears and eyes alert for anything out of the ordinary. It wasn't unknown for there to be false alarms, but it paid to be cautious. Or rather, he was paid to be cautious.

There was still a large number of hooded figures about, most of them hurrying to get home before the heavens opened up again. Milo crossed at the intersection of the two streets, using the stepping stones to keep his boots out of the mess of dung, rubbish and dirty rainwater. It was quieter here, near where the old Londinium wall and ditch had been before it was filled in and built over; badly in some places. He wouldn't like to be living in one of these properties that had been hastily raised on weak foundations.

The old sections of wall had largely been incorporated into new buildings, but traces of the ancient stonework remained in patches here and there. He leaned casually against one piece and scanned the rows of shops, most of which had living quarters above. Unless they expected him to knock on every door, what else was he supposed to do? Even then, any guilty parties would hardly admit to breaking the law.

He'd hang around for a while longer, then report back.

The rain was starting in earnest now and he was just debating whether to head for the nearest shelter, when his eye was caught by a flash of intense light from a nearby grating.

What on earth?

He sidled over and crouched down at the base of the wall, trying to peer through the metal bars into the cellar. The sign above proclaimed it to be the premises of a well-known Naval outfitters.

Fortunately, Milo had more resources than the average Agent. He summoned his Potentia, feeling it whisper across his skin like a static charge and muttered a word.

Before him, the wall faded into a latticework of hollow bricks, giving him a view into the room below. The scene wasn't totally clear, but he could make out stacks of boxes around the sides, leaving the centre of the floor clear for the circle that almost filled it. The lines of Potentia were dimming as it powered down, having completed its work and Milo cursed silently. Five minutes earlier and he'd have caught them when it was charging. Still, half a loaf was better than no bread and his intuition told him that the space was still occupied.

He concentrated his sight and vision, focusing on any sounds and movements, before coming to the conclusion that there was only one person. Milo doubted that the suspect would leave by the front; it was far more probable that he would try to slip out the back, which wouldn't be well-lit.

A whispered word broke the spell and he moved quickly down the narrow side passage that led to the rear of the building, praying that he'd be in time to intercept whoever it was.

As he'd hoped, there was a set of double gates in the wall of the back alley for loading and unloading. He slid into the deepest shadow he could find and waited.

It wasn't long before quick, light footsteps echoed through the yard, heading in his direction. Milo's hand slid to the cosh he kept in one of his capacious pockets. Sure enough, one of the gates began to open with only the tiniest groan of metal and a slim, hooded shape squeezed through.

He darted forward and struck the figure, hard. It staggered, one hand flailing to keep upright but the man didn't go down. Instead, an eerie green light burst from his fingertips, aiming straight for Milo. He barely managed to throw himself to one side in time, hitting the ground with a thump.

The stones at his feet bubbled and fizzed, melting almost instantly into a puddle of stinking green slime.

Milo rolled, trying not to breathe in any of the acrid fumes and threw up a shielding spell, the purple glow lighting the figure's retreating back. Cursing, Milo leapt up and followed, careful to keep the spell at the forefront of his mind.

Whatever magic this man was using hadn't been taught at the Collegium.

The figure ran like a startled hare, weaving through the maze of back alleys and piles of rubbish waiting to be carted away. A light rain had begun to fall, concealing the sharp edges of the blackened brick walls in a soft mist that aided his quarry.

Milo threw out a hand and called up a sun orb that zipped ahead, bathing the area with warm, yellow light. He squinted through the murk, orienting on his target, before spitting out a word. White fire burst into life, streaking away like a miniature comet. A second later, it slammed into a protective shield of the same strange Potentia and exploded in an eruption of sparks. Milo could just make out the man, standing beyond it, arms raised. An eerie chant floated through the air towards him, not in the familiar Latin, or even Britannic, but an older, harsher language that made the hair rise on the back of his head and set his nerves jangling. He threw up his own shield once more, waiting for the counter-attack and hoped that his defence would be strong enough.

Instead, the space between them ripped open, like a ragged tear in the weave of reality and *something* emerged.

Milo backed away hastily, struggling to process what he was seeing. This was no ordinary summoning. There was no containing circle, no protective artefacts; one second he was facing a man - the next he was staring at a horror from his worst nightmare.

The thing stepped delicately through the rent, its long, curved claws clicking on the cobblestones. It appeared to be made out of the bones of several creatures, bound together by Potentia and all glowing with the same sickly hue as the alien magic. There were too many joints, Milo thought, unable to tear his eyes away from the grinning skull that bore no relation to anything remotely human. It looked like a cross between a giant wolf and a bear, as if its creator had wanted to combine the worst of both. Pale embers glowed in its empty sockets as it swung its head to orient on him and jaws gaped open to display teeth like scythe blades.

Fading footsteps told him that the suspect had scarpered, leaving him to face the thing alone.

His brain raced frantically through his options. Running would be useless; this creation was built for speed. Its teeth and claws would make short work of him before he could take half-a-dozen steps. He would have to act before the creature got its bearings. It seemed a little confused by its abrupt entrance into the alley, as if it had been dragged from some place far removed from the normal world.

That gave him an idea. He drew his pistol, aimed it at the skull and fired, praying that the metal would be enough to disrupt the magical energy.

The report boomed through the alley and he heard the crack as it smashed into the bone. The creature backed off, shaking its head as if in pain and Milo didn't waste the chance.

He ran to the nearest wall and leapt, grabbing for the top and hauling himself over, thankful that it wasn't studded with glass shards, or something equally lethal. Behind him, the creature's light dimmed momentarily, before flaring to life once more. Milo caught a glimpse of it starting after him as he dropped to the yard on the other side and made for the next wall. Perhaps it couldn't climb.

A loud clattering and scraping soon disabused him of that idea, as the thing's skull appeared over the top of the wall, its claws gouging out huge chunks of brickwork that fell to clatter in the alley. Someone would have great trouble explaining that in the morning.

"*Merda!*"

He scrambled up another wall, and found himself looking down into an enclosed yard – a perfect killing ground for his pursuer. It would be a death trap. Milo swore again and hurled another fire spell. It barely slowed the thing down, but gave him another couple of seconds to think. He had to dispel the magic somehow. He forced himself to concentrate, only too aware of the eager scrabbling as the thing closed the gap between them.

There was a way. One chance for him to survive this and Milo knew what he had to do. He sent a frantic prayer up to Mercury and headed in the only direction open to him. As he'd thought, the narrowness of the wall tops hindered the creature; its long frame was more suited to a chase on open ground than negotiating the crumbling, uneven brickwork. Now all Milo had to do was stay upright and keep his balance. With any luck, the thing would lose its footing and shatter on the stones below.

His breath heaved in his lungs and he could feel his heart pounding as he came to the edge of the wall. It was a full ten feet from the ground. He could take the risk and jump, but a broken ankle would mean certain death.

Milo glanced over his shoulder. The creature was trotting after him like a favourite hound, its skeletal tail wagging happily as if aware of his predicament. It wasn't taking any chances either, counting on him to either fall or weaken enough for it to finish him off. The steady clicking was relentless and Milo doubted that it would tire. A creature such as this, powered by magic, wouldn't stop until it had completed its task or the light of the rising sun broke the spell. It was just his luck that dawn was still many hours away. It had all night to catch him and rip him to bloody shreds.

Milo swore again and dropped, hanging from the wall for a second before letting go and rolling. He fired off another spell, blasting the bricks to shards and dislodging the creature. A rattle of bones told him that it had landed hard on the other side but he didn't presume that it would be stopped for long. These things had a way of reconstituting and now there wasn't much of an obstacle left between them. He staggered to his feet, feeling a twinge of pain shoot up his leg. He hadn't escaped unscathed after all, but a twisted ankle was the least of his worries. A clacking noise told him that the creature was clambering up the pile of rubble and there was no way he could beat it on the flat.

Ten yards to go.

He shot across the last bit of ground and launched himself into space, feeling the sharp tug as claws ripped into the back of his coat. Then the filthy, freezing water of the Thamesis closed over his head.

Milo surfaced, flailing, eyes screwed shut and thankful that he hadn't swallowed any of the noxious muck. Beside him, a strange jumble of assorted bones sank gently to the bottom of the river, the magic that had animated them dispelled by the running water.

It took Milo all his remaining strength to drag himself onto the foreshore, every muscle aching with cold and exhaustion. He allowed himself the luxury of a minute to lie there and gasp like a landed fish, before staggering upright and taking stock. He'd lost his pistol, sucked down to lie in the depths of the dark water, but his speechstone was still intact. Everything had happened so fast that he hadn't had time to call anything in. He thanked the Gods that he'd been near the river.

<Blue to Control.>

<Control. Go ahead, Blue.>

<Portal activity confirmed, but suspect escaped.>

<Understood.> Control didn't sound too pleased. <Status?>

Milo resisted the urge to laugh hysterically.

<The suspect's using Fae magic. All Agents must proceed with extreme caution.>

He felt the annoyance turn to consternation.

<Are you sure?>

<Of course I'm bloody well sure!> he snapped. <He summoned a thing made of bones through an unwarded portal and it damn near ripped my head off! I had to go swimming in the Thamesis to get rid of it!>

There was a brief silence and Milo felt the stab of fear that the controller couldn't hide.

<Er, understood, Blue. Report in as soon as possible.>

<Yeah,> he Sent, adding a mental growl. <Blue out.>

The controller was right to be afraid. Milo grimaced and tried to stop his teeth from chattering. It would be a long walk home. There was no way that any self-respecting carriage driver would take his fare, even if he could find one at this time of night. Plus, he would definitely need another coat. He tipped the water out of his boots and shrugged out of the sodden garment. Three long slashes ran right down the back of it, collar to hem.

"Better my coat than my back," he muttered, wringing the water out, then draped the clammy fabric over his shoulders. It was time to get into the warmth before the cold did the creature's job for it.

He sighed and squelched off into the darkness.

*

"Good morning, Maia. Did you sleep well?"

Ceridwen was seated in the great house eating breakfast, when Maia came in and helped herself to food.

"Yes, thank you."

Over on the other side of the fire, she could see Rhiannon waving. Maia waved back, thinking that she would join her, but the Priestess called her over.

"We must talk. No, not here," she explained, as Maia looked for somewhere to sit. "After you've eaten. Come to my house. It's the one with the oak branch above the doorway."

Maia nodded, wondering what the woman wanted. Probably more Mystery stuff she decided, to prepare her for whatever came next. She was already resigned to days of ritual and purification.

"I'm learning to weave!" Rhiannon announced, as soon as Maia sat next to her.

"You'll need patience for that."

The girl grinned.

"I know. I can already spin."

She produced a drop spindle and some fleece, unwinding a little thread to show off her prowess.

"It's very fine."

Rhiannon beamed.

"Can you spin?"

Maia shook her head, her mouth full of porridge.

"What are you good at?"

She swallowed. "Cleaning mostly, as well as laundry, ironing and mending. I like embroidering too, though I don't get much chance to do that."

Rhiannon pulled a face. "I hate laundry, but I'll have to learn how to do it properly. Still, you won't have to do any of that when you're a Ship, will you?"

"I suppose not."

Rhiannon bit into a huge slice of bread and butter and chewed thoughtfully.

"I might like to be a Ship."

Maia glanced at her. "I think you'd be better off being a Priestess."

The girl pulled a face. "It would mean I'd never go anywhere. It must be exciting, travelling to different places."

"It's hardly seeing the sights," Maia pointed out. "It's not as if you can go off inland."

The girl looked disappointed.

"That's too bad. I'd like to see all the different plants and animals. Like elephants. Have you ever seen one?"

"Once," Maia told her, "in a parade. A man was riding on it."

Rhiannon's eyes opened wide.

"And was it as big as they say?"

Maia had been about six, but she remembered the great, grey beast plodding patiently down the street.

"It was enormous."

Rhiannon nodded, satisfied.

"And monkeys. I'd like a monkey, but Mam says it's too cold for them here." she scowled. "She won't even let me have a dog. It's not fair!"

Maia made sympathetic noises, watching out of the corner of her eye as Ceridwen rose and made her way outside. As much as she'd have liked to stay and chat, she thought she'd better hurry.

Rhiannon's full mouth stopped the questions for the moment and gave Maia time to finish her porridge.

"I'd better go and see what Ceridwen wants," she said, scraping the last spoonful out of the bowl. The youngster nodded.

"All right. See you later!"

Maia smiled at her beaming face and wondered whether Rhiannon had Potentia. If she did, it wouldn't be too long before it manifested and she would be marked, as Briseis and Tullia had been marked from childhood. She probably wouldn't have any choice as to her future, either. Maia added her bowl to the pile and went outside.

Ceridwen's house was set slightly apart from the others, though it was the same size. Maia approached it with trepidation, eyeing the branch and wondering if it was one of the ones that talked. As she got nearer, she saw that it hadn't been sawn off, but must have fallen or been shed as the end was ragged and splintered.

She knocked, expecting to be summoned within, but instead the door opened and the Priestess came out.

"I thought we could go for a walk, instead of sitting in a smoky hut," she said. "Will you be warm enough, or do you need to fetch a cloak?"

"I'll be fine," Maia replied. The day was quite mild considering it was still Februarius, though she knew it could turn cold again at any time.

They walked in silence for a time, until they came to the edge of the clearing. Before them, the trees stretched upwards, their skeletal trunks and branches forming a barrier, but Ceridwen walked on. They strolled along a small path that led into the forest.

"You don't seem totally committed to life as a Ship," the Priestess said abruptly.

Maia took a deep breath.

"It isn't that. It's just…well…I wasn't given much choice."

Ceridwen gazed ahead, into the depths of the silent woodland.

"Maybe you should consider an alternative path."

Maia was surprised. She'd assumed that there wasn't one.

"I don't think I can."

"I could petition on your behalf."

Somehow, Maia didn't think that the King of the Gods would be in a mood to listen.

"I don't think that would work."

"Really? The Mother can be merciful."

"It isn't the Mother I'm worried about."

She didn't know how much she could say.

"A God sent you here," the Priestess said, an edge to her voice. "I have been warned of interference. Which one?"

Fear stabbed into Maia like a blade.

"I can't say."

"Powerful?"

"Very. No one more so," she added, daringly.

Ceridwen turned to her, searching her face.

"You are under a Doom. I felt it when you arrived and there have been other portents. So, you feel that you have no choice?"

"I can do this, or be killed."

For a second, anger bloomed on the Priestess' features, before fading. Maia knew that it wasn't directed at her.

"Then you must go on. But I warn you, you can have no doubts. Sometimes, the fear of death is sufficient to allow one to push through, but something tells me that you've already passed that test."

A memory of burning heat and icy water made Maia shudder.

"At least I know what awaits me if I pass," she said, remembering the new vessel. So what if it was so big that she wouldn't know what to do with it? She'd learn in time.

"Yes. That's why they show you the vessel, to focus your will and stiffen your resolve."

There it was again, Maia thought, that almost familiarity.

"You remind me of someone," she said, hesitantly and Ceridwen laughed.

"Yes. I am related to Helena Quintilla. We are both Priestesses, but she went out into the world, while I elected to stay. She has told me of you, but I wanted to judge you for myself."

The resemblance was plain, once she looked for it. The same nose and chin, though Ceridwen's hair wasn't curly and her eyes were rounder. The blue lines of her tattoos shadowed her face, breaking up the outline.

"Does Matrona have tattoos, too?"

Ceridwen smiled. "Yes, but not where you can see them."

"Is she your sister?"

"No. She's my, let me see now. Great great granddaughter. Yes, that's it."

Maia felt her jaw drop in amazement. She would have sworn that the Priestess was only about fifty, if that.

"The Mother grants us long life, so we may serve her and bear many children."

"How many children have you had?"

"Nine, all dead now save the last, though their descendants live on. I am done with childbearing now." Her eyes were briefly distant, remembering the babies that were lost to her. "I must admit that it was hard to let my youngest go, but he has his own destiny to fulfil."

Maia felt chastened. She had been so busy bewailing her own fate that she hadn't stopped to consider that others were in a similar situation. How many people's lives were shaped by forces beyond their control?

"I don't want to let everybody down," she admitted.

"Never mind that," the Priestess said. "You must do what is best for you."

Maia shrugged. "Then it's in my best interests to become a Ship, isn't it? I suppose I could always retire after a few years."

Ceridwen frowned. "Do you know how many Ships have retired successfully in the whole history of the Navy?"

Maia searched her memory. Had Master Sulianus mentioned it? She came up blank and shook her head.

"One. And that was after four hundred years and an awful lot of persuasion. There was another, but she went back – couldn't cope with being flesh again. And, at the rate the Navy is expanding, it's very unlikely that they'll let anyone else go without a very good reason."

"Can't the Ships just refuse to follow orders?"

A bleak look crossed the older woman's face. "It's counted as mutiny and not only for the Ship. The Navy will hang her entire crew if she refuses to comply."

Maia felt sick. The thought that a Ship would be forced to watch as her men were executed in front of her would be too much to bear.

"Do they have no recourse at all?"

Ceridwen gestured helplessly.

"If they become truly unhappy, they can choose to return to the Mother in death and thus the Navy loses them anyway. There is only so much that mortal mind can stand. They remain women after all, even if the centuries take their toll. It's hard to remain unchanged, while those around you come and go, year after year."

"*Blossom* didn't mention this," she said lamely.

"She wouldn't. Firstly, she has her instructions and she's *very* good at her job. Secondly, Ships don't like to talk about it. They're a closed group in many ways, mostly because only a Ship can truly understand what another is going through. The Navy has so-called 'experts', but they're all men." She sniffed in contempt. "As if they could know anything!"

"Were you a Ship?"

"No, but I am linked to them, through the power of the Mother. I am, if you like, a go-between. It's another reason for my longevity, but even we Priestesses don't live as long as most Ships."

"Do you tell all the candidates this?" Maia asked.

Ceridwen gave a wry smile.

"Actually, no. I just think that you deserve more of the truth. I believe that you can handle it."

Maia sighed. "Why doesn't it get easier?"

"If I knew that, I'd tell you. Life is a road we all travel, whether our way is strewn with petals, or jagged thorns."

The winding path led them through the thick trunks to another glade. Early flowers were just peeping through the damp, leaf-strewn ground, splashes of pale yellow and white against the earth tones.

"See?" Ceridwen said, smiling down at them. "Soon, it will be spring and the Maiden will be returning to us once more."

Maia could only hope that she would live to see it.

"When will I be entering initiation?"

"In a few days. There are ceremonies, though probably not as many as you expect."

Maia nodded. She still felt uneasy among the trees, as if she were being watched by unseen eyes.

Ceridwen spoke suddenly.

"Fear is not the only enemy."

Maia's hair stood on end and a chill ran over her skin. It wasn't quite the Priestess' voice.

"What do you mean?"

"I'm sorry?"

Ceridwen seemed genuinely surprised, then her eyes widened.

"Did I speak?"

"Yes."

Maia swallowed. Her throat was dry and her heart was pounding.

"It wasn't me. Whatever was said was a message from the Mother. No," she said quickly, forestalling Maia's explanation, "don't tell me what she said. It was for your ears alone."

"I didn't understand it."

"You may, later. That's how these things work."

A riddle. Of course it was. That was how the Gods spoke and it was only afterwards that anyone understood what they meant. Why should the Mother be any different? It wasn't helpful at all.

They walked back to the huts in silence.

*

It was early morning and the sun was just appearing over the horizon to shine its pallid light on the city. The Government Offices were already swarming with clerks and Agents as Milo arrived to make his report. He was shown through without delay. The first question was the one he'd been expecting.

"So, it was Fae energy?"

Milo shifted in his seat. It had taken him a long time to get warm after his soaking and he feared that he was about to come down with a cold. He could only pray that he hadn't picked up anything else from the foetid brew that was the Thamesis these days. Even the River God had retired upstream, abandoning that stretch long ago.

His questioner fixed him with a piercing glance from pale blue eyes. Favonius was the Chief Agent and spymaster, answering directly to the Senate. He would be reporting everything, probably as it was happening. His square face and blunt features hid a razor-sharp mind and an excellent grasp of the political situation. Fae activity in the heart of Londin meant nothing but trouble for the realm and he wasn't one to underestimate the danger.

"I taught him well." Raven's dry voice interjected, as he entered the room. "Agent Milo's description was definitive. Nothing else uses that particular Potentia signature. Also, the thing he described was one of their constructs. They excel at moulding flesh, blood and, in this case, bone."

The old man took a seat and fixed his sightless eyes on the senior Agent.

Favonius pressed his lips together.

"Thank you for arriving so promptly, Master Mage. You can understand why I'm loath to admit it. It all happened barely two blocks from the palace!"

Raven raised an eyebrow.

"The Major Fae have been gone so long that it's difficult to contemplate their return, if that is in fact what's happening here."

"They're moving something and I doubt it's Naval uniforms," Favonius said. "In the meantime, the location's the only lead we have. Milo, I'm tasking you with making enquiries. You're the one best suited to this, but you'll have back up standing by, if you need it. We can't afford to let the suspect slip through our fingers again."

"I understand."

And it would be his head on the block if he failed. This was beyond top secret. Should anything happen to him, such as capture, he could expect no support. Plausible deniability was the name of the game here.

"I'll assist you in whatever capacity I can," the Master Mage told him.

Milo felt a spurt of gratitude that the old man still fought his corner, even after he'd been kicked out of the Collegium, though he'd remained tight-lipped about the reason why. Milo had been no worse and a good sight better than many of his peers, but he'd been the one to fail. The School for Agents had welcomed him with open arms, but that still didn't ease the pain of what might have been. He doubted that Mages spent so much time freezing cold or running for their lives; that was when he wasn't almost dying of boredom waiting for persons of interest to make their move. Still, he could have ended up on the streets as just one more friendless lad with a singular lack of prospects.

He left Favonius' office with relief, following the frail figure down the corridor to the small office that the Mage used while he was in the capital and wished to avoid the Collegium.

"Shut the door after you and pour us a drink, won't you?"

Raven sank into his cracked leather chair, while Milo busied himself, pouring them both a generous measure of *aqua vita*.

"This should help keep the cold out," Raven observed. "Have you managed to warm up yet?"

"I spent several hours at the baths," Milo admitted," plus I had an Adept check me over. That water was disgusting."

"Hmm. They need to get on with that new sewer project, before we all die of the stink," Raven agreed. "The river deities are slow to act but they won't be silent for much longer."

"I thought they'd decamped."

"For now, but their absence lessens the protections built into the city. Another reason why enemies can crawl in undetected. Believe me, I don't want us to go back to horseshoes over the door and a knife in every cradle."

Milo remembered that these were ancient remedies against the Fae, now looked on as superstition. At this rate, it looked like they'd be making a comeback in the cities as well as the rural areas.

"Perhaps they were just smuggling goods?"

The Master Mage snorted. "What would the Fae want with things made by mortals? They have their own Artificers and you know that anything made of iron hurts them. It's been our only defence down the ages."

"True. But if it was spies…"

"Well, that's up to you to discover, isn't it? I can help you there. Go to the cupboard in the corner and bring out the carved oak box with leather hinges."

Milo put down his glass and did as directed. The box was long and rectangular with a domed lid, about half as long as his forearm.

"Put it on the table and open it."

Inside, nestled in a lining of dark blue velvet, was a row of three stone discs about half the size of his palm and intricately carved in twisted knot patterns. A feeling of great age emanated from them, as if they weren't of modern manufacture but worked long ago.

"Gifts from the Gods."

"Sorry?" Milo jerked his gaze away from the intertwining shapes.

"Singing stones. They were created many centuries ago, probably even before Artor and Merlin dealt with the last Great Fae Incursion. I've had them in my possession for a while now, hoping they'd never be needed again."

"What are they for?"

Even as he spoke, Milo sensed the answer.

"They detect the proximity of Fae magic. Time was that every great Britannic family had at least one of these, to act as an early warning and to root out those that had fallen under spells. They averted much harm, but there aren't many left these days." He sighed. "People have forgotten."

Milo picked one up, admiring the designs. It felt cold under his fingers, the stone rubbed smooth by much handling.

"Well, eight hundred years is a long time. These will come in useful."

"They will indeed, starting right now. I'm relieved to see that you haven't been contaminated."

Milo shot him a look.

"Did you think I was?"

"Possibly. You could have been glamoured or replaced. The Fae are masters of disguise and infiltration."

"And if I had?"

"It would have burst into a chorus of 'Hail, O glorious Britannia!'"

"What?"

The ancient Mage's face slowly cracked into a smile. Milo rolled his eyes in exasperation.

"Forgive me," the old man chuckled. "No, nothing so melodic, but it will emit a high tone that only the holder can hear. Take it. If you get close to anyone who has been exposed, it will sound off."

Milo slipped the disc into an inner pocket.

"I've a feeling that these will shortly be in high demand." He frowned. "I'll need other weapons too. I don't want to be caught out again. I lost my pistol in the river, but the ball barely slowed it down."

"Lead?"

"Yes."

"Won't work. You need iron."

Milo sighed. "They don't make iron pistol shot. It's not dense enough and it wrecks the barrel."

He thought for a moment.

"I could get a sling and have a go with those ball bearings they use in the new engines."

Raven shook his head.

"You'd need time and distance to use one of those. The same with iron-weighted bolas, though they might come in handy. If push comes to shove, I'd carry a heavy nail, or a horseshoe. Knuckledusters are useful too, plus any knives or swords you have handy."

Milo nodded slowly.

"I think I'll buy a set of throwing knives. A sword's a bit obvious, unless you're a king. I hear that Artorius wears Excalibur at every opportunity."

Raven grunted.

"He does. Nothing like a nice, shiny, magical sword to give a young man a sense of his own self-worth. Under present circumstances, perhaps it's just as well it's there to provide protection, as long as it doesn't go missing. It can't do any good stuck in the Royal Treasury."

"Plus, he'll be surrounded by his Knights, even if the post is mainly ceremonial these days," Milo pointed out.

"That too," the Master Mage admitted.

The King wouldn't be chased by murderous Fae constructs into a stinking river, Milo thought ruefully. It was all right for some. Young Artorius probably didn't even know how to really use the ancient weapon.

"I must admit, I don't envy you," Raven said. "Where are you going to start?"

"With a visit to Magonius'. If the owner's involved, I should pick something up there. It could even be an employee using the premises after hours, so I'll check out the workshops round the back. I might get lucky."

Or then again, the perpetrator might have already abandoned the place.

"Yes, there should be some traces of the energy left. Well, all that remains is for me to wish you good hunting."

"Thank you."

"I'll be on hand, should you need me."

"I just hope that there are no more nasty surprises."

Raven raised an eyebrow.

"Has anyone mentioned that you're probably in the wrong job?"

Milo was tempted to make a rude gesture, but the old man was laughing again.

"Yeah. Find me a better one, will you? Something that involves lounging about on silk cushions all day, while beautiful women feed me grapes."

"I'll see what I can do."

"Or, failing that, one that keeps regular hours."

"You'd get bored."

"Hmm. No chance of that at the moment. Maybe I am in the right job after all."

As he clasped the stick-thin fingers in a gesture of parting, he reflected that boredom was the least of his worries.

IX

Maia spent a great deal of time over the next few days trying to work out what the Mother had been trying to tell her, without success. She was happy to join in doing the chores of the community, falling back into the familiar rhythm of her old life. It was a relief to do domestic tasks rather than poring over lists and instructions and it certainly gave her hands something to do, even if they weren't as deft as before. Occasionally, she could even forget her coming ordeal for whole minutes at a time, before the reality of her situation reared its head like a grinning spectre. She decided to resign herself to her fate, whatever that might be. Nobody could say that she hadn't tried to escape it.

Ceridwen didn't speak to her so frankly again, for which she was grateful, but the waiting was starting to get on her nerves. This was life or death to her and here she was, busy washing pots and helping with the cooking.

The other women were kind enough but there was always an invisible barrier between them. They knew she would be leaving them soon enough and that would be that. She doubted that she would ever see any of them again, though perhaps she would share some sort of link with Ceridwen? The woman had called herself a go-between. It was easier to imagine herself already installed in her new vessel, exchanging gossip with *Blossom, Patience* and the other Ships, whilst speculating about her new Captain. She already missed the open sea. Nor had there been any sign of her sister. Pearl had told her that she wasn't allowed to interfere.

She was helping to hang wet clothes inside the hut put aside for that purpose, when she heard Ceridwen calling her outside.

The Priestess was looking thoughtful as Maia approached her.

"Thank you for helping out," the older woman said.

"It's not a problem. I'd rather keep busy," Maia replied. "It's what I was always used to, well, until these past few years, that is."

"Of course. You came from humble beginnings."

"I know how much work goes into running households," Maia replied, evenly.

Ceridwen's mouth twitched.

"Unlike some, you mean."

They shared a look. Somehow, it wasn't likely that Tullia would have pitched in, especially after her brief experience of being forced to do menial work.

Maia waited for the Priestess to continue.

"As you will shortly begin the Trials of Initiation, I thought that you might like some time to yourself."

Maia frowned. "What would I do?"

Ceridwen spread her hands.

"Whatever you want. If there's a particular food you'd like, it can be provided. Maybe you'd like to rest, pray or walk in the forest. Ships are never alone, so this may be your last opportunity."

A trickle of apprehension ran down Maia's back. This was too much like the condemned prisoner's last meal. She glanced over her shoulder to where the other women were working, before coming to her decision.

"I think I'll go for a walk. I haven't really ever had the opportunity to explore the woods. I'm just afraid that I might get lost. I'm more used to cities."

The Priestess smiled, her face lighting up.

"Have no fear of that! You're under the Mother's protection. Moving through her lands is a form of prayer in itself and I think it will do you good. There are several paths and they will open to you as you need them."

"What lives in the forest?" Maia asked, curiously. "Do I have to worry about wolves and boars and such?"

Ceridwen was clearly trying not to laugh. "There speaks a true city girl. No, you need have no fear in this vicinity. There are some wild places where such creatures are protected but, as you have learned to your cost, there are few creatures as dangerous as humans."

Truth indeed. The look of homicidal rage on her former mistress' face still occasionally haunted her sleep. Even a wolf wouldn't have been that vicious. Maia hoped that whatever remained of Marcia Blandina was locked in the deepest pit of Tartarus.

Something must have shown in her face.

"I'm sorry. I didn't mean to re-open old wounds," Ceridwen said, hastily.

Maia shrugged.

"It happened. It's over now. I'll just take whatever food's on offer and go for a stroll. I like looking at the trees and the flowers."

When she entered the kitchen hut, Modren was there, already packing a basket. She decided that the Priestesses must have some way to communicate amongst themselves.

"Here you are, Maia. There's fresh bread, butter and cheese and a couple of apples, as well as a little treat."

The brown-haired woman had wrapped the items into little cloth packages, tucking them neatly into a willow basket. She went to a shelf and selected a thick glass bottle, sealed with a wooden stopper.

"You'll need something to drink, too. I made some mead last week – don't worry! It isn't the strong stuff."

Maia thought that she'd need a pack mule at this rate, but didn't object. It meant that she could stay out longer and who knew what she could find, out in the woods? She doubted that there was really a means of escape, but some part of her couldn't help but wish for it. She thanked Modren, who bustled off to stir her pots. The rich, savoury smell of the roasted meat promised a good meal later. Maia picked up her basket and set off, popping into her hut on the way to grab a thick blanket to sit on.

Rhiannon was nowhere to be seen, for which she was grateful. She didn't fancy being bombarded with more questions and chatter at the moment. Ceridwen had been right; she would benefit from some time alone. Now, which way to go?

The forest stretched before her, in all directions. She set her face to what she decided was the west and marched off.

The path wound lazily around the trees and she followed the meandering trail. Rays of early spring sunlight lanced through the branches, promising life and warmth to come and she realised that it must be the month of Martius already. The world was still turning, even though she felt like she'd been removed from it.

A sudden thought caused her to reach out to Raven, but she couldn't get through.

So, it was true. She was in a place apart and there would be no communication but what was permitted by the Mother. She snorted to herself. Just when she could have done with a friendly word or two. She hadn't realised how much she'd come to rely on the blind old Mage until he wasn't there. Maia hoped she'd see him again.

The path led past a small clearing surrounded by slim birch trees and full of birdsong. Small winged shapes flitted from twig to twig in sudden blurs of movement. Maia decided that she'd walked far enough and her arm was beginning to ache from carrying the basket. It was time to lighten her load and it had been a few hours since breakfast. Hadn't Modren mentioned a treat?

She spread the blanket out and flopped down, gratefully, before investigating each parcel. The smell of new-baked bread made her mouth water and she used her little eating knife to cut thick slices off the round loaf and slather them with rich, yellow butter and crumbly cheese.

The light mead fizzed pleasantly on her tongue, a perfect accompaniment and she alternated a bite of her bread with pieces of the wrinkled apples, preserved from last year's harvest. The honey cake was a welcome surprise. She hadn't been able to hide her sweet tooth and she savoured every mouthful, all the more delicious because it might be one of the last meals she ever ate. It was a sobering thought.

Replete at last, she lay back, wrapping the blanket around her legs to preserve the warmth and stared upwards to where the branches met the sky. A few little clouds scudded past, overlaid by the silhouettes of birds. They'd be busy getting ready to find a mate and nest. A robin's song burst from a bush, to be challenged by a rival nearby and she thought of her friend and wondered what he was doing. Probably working on yet another of his strange contraptions.

It was calm as she lay under the trees and Maia realised that this was probably the furthest she'd ever been from another human in the whole of her life. When she was a child she'd lived in the Foundling Home, crammed in with all the others in a dormitory, and when she'd been sent out to service she'd shared her room with another girl. At Blandina's, she'd had a cubby hole in the kitchen. It had been warmer there, even if she'd had to put up with the cook's snoring.

Poor Chloe. Maia hoped that she had a better place now, where she wasn't chained to the stove. She'd never had the chance to find out how they all fared. Surely they'd rebuilt The Anchor by now, as well. Maybe, if she actually got to be a Ship, she would be in a position to help them all? It was yet another incentive to get through her initiation.

She was just beginning to drift off, despite the freshness of the air, when a small rustling noise alerted her to the fact that she wasn't by herself after all.

For a few seconds she felt resentment that she couldn't be left alone, even here, then she decided it must be an animal attracted by the scraps she'd saved for later.

Maia carefully cracked one eye open. A little bundle of wind-blown leaves was rolling over the ground towards her. When it came to a halt, she could see that inside was a little brown figure, about a span high and shaped roughly like a human. Its clothes were made of leaves, bits of bark and twigs and feathers were knotted in its wispy hair. Two black beady eyes, like a mouse's, were fixed on the cloth wrapped food.

Maia hardly dared breathe. She'd heard tales of Minor Fae, small sprites of the earth, different to their more powerful and scarier brethren but with their own brand of power, though she'd never known anyone who'd actually seen one. She remained still, trying to keep her breathing even, but the tiny sprite paused, its pointed nose twitching.

Maia opened both eyes, but didn't move. The black eyes locked on hers.

"Are you hungry?" she whispered. "It's all right. Go ahead."

She didn't know if the creature understood her until it made a dart for a piece of cheese, grabbing it in twig-like fingers. A morsel of bread followed it, both stuffed quickly into its leaf clothing. When she didn't object, the sprite grew more ambitious. The apple was a sizeable weight, but it managed to hoist it up onto one shoulder, like a miniature Atlas.

Maia pressed her lips together to stifle a laugh. This little creature, male or female, she couldn't tell, was determined to make the most of this opportunity. It must make a change from living off acorns and roots, or whatever sprites ate.

The final prize, the largest piece of honey cake it could manage, went partly into its mouth, almost obscuring its entire face, then, with a muffled chirrup that she interpreted as a message of thanks, it gathered up its leaf ball and whirled away into the undergrowth.

Maia finally burst out laughing. It was good to meet another opportunist out here, but where there were Fae, there lay the unknown.

She dismissed any thought of trying to find her way out of this strange place. Despite Ceridwen's assurances, she had the feeling that it would be a very bad idea indeed.

*

Londin was its usual noisy crowded and smelly self. Milo rode through the streets, weaving through the carts, carriages and the odd steam wagon clattering ponderously along. Ahead of him was the sign of The Cunning Fox, one of the few places in this area where he knew he could leave his horse with the assurance of getting it back on his return. He trotted into the stable yard, dismounted and allowed his horse to be led away, hooves clopping on the cobbles.

"Will you be wanting a room, sir?" one of the lads asked him.

"No, thank you. I have lodgings already. Just keep my horse in readiness. I'm not sure how long I'll be." He handed over a few coins, then set off purposefully towards his goal.

Anyone seeing him would notice a lean Naval officer, his coat buttoned up against the chilly spring weather and on his way to order or collect some item of apparel from the foremost outfitters in the City. Milo had a number of disguises he used as appropriate and, for this mission, he'd decided to be an officer in need of a hat.

Hidden about his person were various devices that would sniff out inimical magic and those connected to it. There was no guarantee that the outfitters would turn up anything, but it was the logical place to start.

The busy road bore little resemblance to its deserted, night-time face. The large shop window was made of clear glass panes, through which he could see some tastefully arranged coats and jackets. Advertising wasn't necessary, as everyone who worked for the Navy and could afford the prices, bought their apparel from Magonius of Londinium and had done for the last two hundred and fifty years. An officer could get everything he needed right here, down to embroidered underwear should he so desire and, though there were cheaper places, none was as prestigious.

Just the place for an up-and-coming Ship's Lieutenant to purchase a smart and impressive hat. He mounted the short flight of steps and entered.

His arrival was announced by the silvery tinkling of a bell, which in turn produced a short, portly man, who appeared from the depths of the shop as if by magic.

"How may I be of assistance, Lieutenant?" he asked, smiling politely. Milo fixed him with a patronising eye, as befitted his supposed rank and listened for any alert from his plethora of invisible charms.

"I require a new hat," he announced, gazing about him in a casual manner.

"Of course, sir. We have a wide selection that can be customised to your requirements. I take it that you are looking for a bicorn? They're the latest fashion."

Milo's devices remained silent. He would keep up the charade for a while, but he was ready to pull out his authorisation to gain access to the parts of the business that customers didn't normally see.

"So I hear. I've a friend who's just purchased one and I'd like something similar."

The salesman thought for a moment. "Would that have been one of our new styles, with a black silk cockade and matching silk lining? They're much in demand at present."

"That's right. He's very pleased with it and, as I'm due a promotion…" he let the words trail off and the man nodded understandingly.

"Indeed sir. Our hats are very striking and of the highest quality."

"Are they made here?" he asked casually.

"Oh no sir. We outsource them from very reputable suppliers. They use only the finest beaver from the New Continent."

Milo looked impressed. "And the silk trimmings?"

"Yes, we do finish the hats here, sir. You can have whichever colour you want, though currently black is the most fashionable."

"Will it take long?" he asked.

"Well, sir, there is a waiting list, but we can hurry it through for a small consideration. Say…a week?"

Milo pretended to consider it. "And the cost?"

The man named a sum that was half a common working man's yearly salary. Milo hid his horror and nodded as if unsurprised. "Very reasonable. I am persuaded, though alas, I haven't the time to be fitted at present. I shall return when it's more convenient."

The salesman's face never moved. He was very good at his job and, after all, today's Lieutenant could be tomorrow's Admiral. Milo really was impressed this time.

"We await your convenience, sir. In the meantime is there anything else you require?"

"Not at the moment, thank you," he said, with as much dignity as he could muster. He wouldn't be the first young officer whose aspirations outstripped his pocket. The man bowed and saw him out with as much care as if he'd purchased the whole shop. That was what he called great service.

Now, to proceed to his next course of action. A nearby alley provided some shelter as he quickly stripped off and turned his coat inside out, losing his previous identity with ease. His old hat converted similarly into a floppier, wide brimmed version and that, together with a change of stance and a different gait, changed him into an ordinary workman who had never been anywhere near the Naval Academy. He folded down his boots and dragged them through some nearby mud, giving them a good covering to complete the illusion, before making his way around to the back of the elegant frontages. This was where the real work happened.

A pile of old wooden boxes had been stacked at one of the back gates. He snatched one up, bending his shoulders under the fake load and made his way round to the rear entrance of the premises. A cart was being unloaded, the horses waiting patiently as men stripped it of its contents and it was easy to slip in amongst them and continue to the brick-built workshops. The first one was a tailor's, with rows of men cutting and sewing cloth, each in their own section, followed by a smaller place where pinch-faced women sat squinting over embroidery, needles moving continuously in and out of the fine fabric. He waited for the stone to sound an alert, but there was nothing.

"Oi! What yer got?" a voice bellowed.

He turned, to find a slight young man in a leather apron accosting him.

"Stuff fer 'ats," he grunted in return.

"Up there."

The man pointed further up the yard and Milo scuttled off in the new direction. He found the right workshop and was simultaneously alerted by a sudden, high tone in his left ear.

He peered through the window. There were all kinds of hats stacked on shelves, waiting for the final touches before being sent out to their new owners. All were military styles and some were very elaborate, trimmed with swan feathers and jewelled medallions. He had the feeling that those were for the fashionable set, rather than the men who wore them in force ten gales at sea. The rich ladies of the court liked to follow the mannish style, as preferred by the Princess Julia and clearly hats were one of the must-have items of the season. Magonius would be making a fortune, though he doubted that the men and women labouring in the workshops would see any real benefit other than having a steady income if they were free. They were probably paid by the piece, so they would work all hours, taking as little time off as possible and in constant fear of failing vision or accidents. It was more likely that they were enslaved or indentured, then they wouldn't have to be paid at all.

Such was the way of the world in the great and glorious Roman Empire.

Milo pushed open the door, noting that there was only one exit and he was standing in it. The workers barely registered his presence, continuing with their work, until one man gestured to the corner.

"Just stack it there."

He put the box down carefully and straightened up. There were about twenty people – trade was brisk and there was plenty of work for skilled finishers. Some were busy arranging the elaborate pleated cockades, whilst others were stitching in the silk linings. He moved over to the latter, as if to admire their work, when the tone abruptly rose in volume, becoming a sustained, high-pitched note of alarm.

The woman at the bench was scrawny and careworn, thin brown hair escaping in rat tails from a knitted woollen cap. He couldn't see a slave chain, but she had all the marks of an indentured servant. She glanced up as he approached, but Milo moved quickly. He slapped a set of iron cuffs on to her bony wrists before she had time to squawk, whilst with the other hand he pulled out his badge of authority.

"Nobody move!" he commanded. "By order of the Crown!"

The man nearest the door shot to his feet, only to find his way blocked by three burly officers. Milo had back up and his speechstone was linked to another that the Inspector of the City Polis had in his pocket. The said Inspector was even now ordering his Sergeant to round up the workers. Startled and terrified, they filed out meekly but not so the captured woman. She screamed and began to flail at him, desperate to escape, until a well-placed blow to her cheek knocked her to the floor. He dragged her back up, handing her over to two waiting polismen who gripped her firmly by the arms.

"Hold her still," he ordered. Who knew what she still had on her? He pulled a facetted crystal from his pocket and ran it over her clothes, watching for any change in colour as she slumped, semi-conscious, between them. As it touched the clothes at her waist, it flared a vivid green and he knew that he had found his proof.

A hidden pocket held a small silk pouch. Milo pulled on a pair of gloves before extracting its contents; several carved sticks and an oddly-shaped stone that he suspected was a portal activator.

The woman raised her head and stared at him defiantly. A thin trickle of blood ran from her cheek where he'd hit her.

"What are these?" he demanded.

Her grimy face twisted into a sneer. "May the dark Gods eat your soul!"

"I think we've heard enough," the Inspector said over his shoulder. "Take her away."

Milo watched as the woman was dragged outside past the other workers, who were lined up against the opposite wall.

"I'd better check them too," he said. A few minutes later, he'd drawn a blank. It looked like none of these people had been involved, and, judging by their expressions, they were all bewildered by the sudden turn of events.

Raised voices at the end of the yard nearest to the shop made everyone look around. It was the salesman, striding briskly through the crowd of workers and ignoring the polismen's attempts to hold him back.

"These are my premises and my workers! I demand to know what's happening here!"

So, he'd been served by the current Magonius himself. Milo faded unobtrusively back into the crowd, as he didn't want his cover blown.

"One of your workers has been arrested for opening an illegal portal on your premises," the inspector said firmly.

Magonius stopped, his bluster abruptly derailed.

"An illegal portal? What on earth?" He looked round at his cowed workers. "I don't understand!"

"I am Inspector Cyndrigus of the City Polis. Your workshop is linked to an attempt to sabotage national security. My men are going to take you and your workers in for questioning. Anything you say will be taken down and may be used as evidence against you. Do you understand?"

All colour had left Magonius' face now. He swallowed and nodded before regaining some composure.

"Naturally my staff and I will assist in any way possible, Inspector," he said, clearly shocked. Milo didn't think he was bluffing.

"Your co-operation has been noted, sir," Cyndrigus told him before signalling to his men to lead everyone to where the black painted Polis wagons stood. Others took the names of the workers who had stopped their activities and come outside to see what all the fuss was about. There would be no more fancy hats finished today.

Milo slipped away into the crowd, pleased with the result. Not all jobs were this simple, though he had the feeling that this was only a tiny thread pulled from one big piece of cloth. The rest of the material wouldn't be so easy to unravel and who knew where the clue would lead?

This sort of magic spoke of subtle and twisted minds who would stop at nothing to undermine the rule of law.

*

They came for her before first light, moving through the silent clearing like ghosts in the mist.

At first, Maia was disorientated as she was pulled from a deep sleep, then the walls of the hut sprang into focus and she found herself squinting against the light of torches.

She obeyed the summons, throwing on a cloak and slipping her feet into her shoes, then followed the silent women into the forest. Two cloaked figures glided in front and she felt the other two take up position behind her.

In case I run away.

The thought was a tempting one, but where would she go? The danger wasn't from these women; it was in their interest to see her safely through initiation, just as it had been in the Navy's interest to train her. Ceridwen's remarks about the Navy had taken her aback, but she had soon come to realise that they were true, even though *Blossom* and Captain Plinius' care for her had been real enough. Good heavens – the man had wanted to adopt her! Still, they were bound to others, just as she was bound by the will of Jupiter. Now, she would have to answer to the Mother as well. Yet another God to add to her tally.

As they walked through the darkness, she wished that she could speak to her sister Pearl one more time. She wondered if Aura was present, though the stillness of the air spoke of that Goddess' absence.

She suppressed a shiver and concentrated on the way ahead. It seemed well-trodden, without stones or too many tree roots to trip over for which she was thankful, but the chill was unwelcome after her warm bed and the thought of what might await made her feel vaguely nauseous. They walked for several minutes, heading deeper into the forest, past the gnarled trunks of mighty trees that were definitely getting larger as they went. Between them, she glimpsed the lighter bark of graceful birches, striped in silver and black, though the ancient oaks predominated.

Maia was beginning to think that they would never stop, when they emerged into a clearing. Tall stones marked the end of the path and a couple of huts crouched to one side, almost hidden by the surrounding branches. In the centre of the clearing stood an altar, a simple stone that thrust up through the earth like the curved back of a half-hidden creature, caught mid-leap. She couldn't see it clearly enough to make out if there was anything carved into it. Maia couldn't imagine anything more different from the painted marble and incense-filled temples she was used to. There was little here that was fabricated. The flickering torchlight made the women's faces appear forbidding and remote and she could see that they were marked with the same designs that swirled across Ceridwen's features.

She allowed herself to be led to a hut where she was bathed and given yet another robe to wear, this time in the same earth colours as the Priestesses. She gathered it with a woven belt made of leather and wool. Next, she was given a bowl of something warm to drink; a thin, creamy porridge, flavoured with some herb she couldn't identify, which filled her empty stomach. Then, the chanting began. Maia tuned out most of it, as it wasn't in any language she knew, though some of the words seemed vaguely familiar and she thought that it must be an ancient form of Britannic. She was led around the clearing several times, just as the sky began to lighten and the first chorus of birdsong greeted the dawn.

Eventually, Maia was taken before the altar. Colour was beginning to return to the world with the rising of the sun, bringing into focus the old stains on the stone's surface. This was a place of blood offerings.

"It is time for the sacrifice."

Ceridwen's voice made her start. Maia looked around to see which animal would be brought forth for slaughter, garlanded and prepared, but there was nothing.

She looked at the older woman, bewildered.

"You are the sacrifice." Ceridwen told her. "Your flesh, blood and bone will be offered to the Mother."

She gestured and two women stepped out of the line and braided leaves into her hair while Maia stood, too frightened to move or speak, as if caught in a spell.

Their fingers were cold against her skin as they marked her forehead and cheeks with a red pigment, ochre, to symbolise that she belonged to the Mother.

"The offering is sanctified!" the Priestess declared. "Great Mother, we call upon you to bless us, your children that we may share in your bounty and beneficence. Take this woman unto yourself, O Mother of All, so that she may enter the Mystery that is the living wood. Guide her steps and fill her heart with courage."

Maia watched her with frightened eyes, waiting for the knife across her throat and the warm spurt of blood. Would she even feel it? She had seen enough animals go to their deaths. Surely the authorities didn't permit human sacrifice? She forced her knees to lock, keeping herself upright with all the willpower she could muster.

Ceridwen drew a knife from her robes. The blade was stone, not metal, chipped to a fine edge.

"Give me your hand."

Maia held out her left hand. The Priestess took it, turned it palm uppermost and, in one swift movement, drew the knife across.

Maia stared as the cut began to well with blood, followed swiftly by the pain. It was all she could do not to shout out at the suddenness of it. Ceridwen took her hand and held it over the altar stone. A thin trickle of red brightened the ancient mark, adding to the countless layers on the surface and doubtless splashing over Tullia's and Briseis', as well as every other woman who had come this way over the centuries. In times to come, hers would be covered too, forming the indelible stain that marked the bond between mortal and Divine.

As quickly as it was done, it was finished. A woman bound her wound with herbs and a soft cloth.

"The Mother accepts your sacrifice. Now, you must find your way to her. Come."

Once again Maia found herself the centre of the procession, but this time other women joined them. She recognised Modren and Arianrhod amongst them, all accompanying her to wherever the final stages would take place.

They returned to the main clearing and Maia cast a longing look at her little house, to no avail. The chanting women passed between the buildings and began to climb the upward slope beyond, towards the hilltop and the mysterious copse that stood stark in the morning light.

The path wound in a spiral, ascending by a few feet each time until Maia could see above the treetops to the unbroken forest beyond. There were no signs of farms, towns or villages and she wondered just where in the country she was. It was a long gentle climb and she was glad of the food she'd been given. She could smell smoke and the scent of crushed grass beneath the feet of the women and, just as the sun began to warm her face, they reached the top.

If anything, the trees here were even older than the ones below. Most of them looked half-dead, their twisted branches ending in bleached shards and hoary trunks pocked with holes and fissures. Some younger ones were growing just out of reach, as if fearing to approach their elders too closely and content to wait their turn to be ancients. The weight of aeons hung heavy on their branches.

"Maia, your way lies through the oak," Ceridwen said, pointing to the biggest sentinel. A huge void gaped where the heart of the tree had rotted over the years, forming a cave-like hollow, dark and secretive.

"Yes," Maia whispered.

This was where the ordeal began.

"There are three trials. When one is finished, another door will open. Keep going. Whatever you see or hear, or *feel*,"

Ceridwen emphasised, her eyes deadly serious. "*Keep going. Do you understand?*"

Maia's mouth was dry. The dull resignation she'd been locked in for weeks fell away and she realised that she did want to live after all. She wanted to see her friends again and share in their adventures. She wanted warmth and company, even if, at the end of whatever awaited her, she would no longer be fully human.

She wanted to be free of the Doom she was under and to Hades with the Gods and their cruel judgements.

"I understand."

"Then go and be reborn. May the Goddess guide your steps."

It was hard to move, as if her muscles didn't want to follow her commands.

Pull yourself together! Maia told herself firmly. She forced herself to remember the smell of her new vessel. Her enormous, beautiful, state-of-the-art new vessel, waiting for her in the dockyard. It would be hers, as long as she could keep her nerve. What had she got to be afraid of, anyway? Some old women and a hole in a tree? How hard could it be?

She lifted her chin and fixed Ceridwen with a defiant stare.

"I'm ready."

The Priestess smiled and Maia nodded back. She squared her shoulders, marching forwards over the beaten earth and entered into the darkness.

Her vision was instantly flooded with the green-tinted hue of sun through leaves. A heady, verdant scent filled her nostrils, mixed with the rich dampness of earth after rain. All of a sudden, she knew that she was *elsewhere,* in another time and space. She'd crossed through a portal, one so subtle and powerful that she hadn't even felt it.

After all, the Gods played by different rules.

Ahead of her, outlined in the eerie half-light, stood a familiar door. It was so incongruous in this place that all she could do was stare at it for what seemed like an age. The last time she'd seen it was when she'd left to come to Londin for her final training aboard the *Blossom.*

Maia Gemma Abella Valeria took a deep breath and pushed open the door of the Portus Academy.

X

The cell was small and windowless.

Dank flagstones sloped slightly towards the centre, where a rusty iron grille was set into the stones; all the easier to swill away blood and other waste from countless interrogations. The imprint of untold hours of questioning had somehow left their mark in the thick air, seeping oppressively into the atmosphere to weigh heavy on all those who entered.

Milo resisted the constant urge to clear his throat. He stood in a corner, careful not to let his new coat brush against the walls and watching silently as the harsh light crawled over the body tied to a chair. It picked out a shabby, worn undershift and lined skin, sallow from the lack of fresh air and decent food. Her dark, greasy hair fell unchecked, veiling her bowed head in a tangled curtain that obscured her face. Across from him, Favonius gazed on the dismal scene dispassionately.

"It will go easier with you if you tell us everything that you know now."

Crispus, the Royal Interrogator, spoke softly and, not for the first time, Milo wished the woman was a slave to be compelled into speech instead of an indentured servant who would have to be persuaded. The law was clear on that point and breaking it, even in such a worthy cause, would backfire spectacularly if word got out. Magic was forbidden, but physical torture was another matter.

"What's your name?"

The woman raised her head, glaring at her captor with dark, hate-filled eyes.

"Morgan," she said, calmly.

It was a common enough name in certain parts, but it set alarm bells ringing in Milo's head. Morgan was a form of Morrigan, the powerful Goddess of War, revered both in Britannia and across the sea in Hibernia. She was rumoured to be especially courted by Separatist organisations. The revelation, true or not, wasn't lost on the other men in the room either.

"So, Morgan," the Interrogator continued. "Do you know who I am?"

The woman said nothing, nor did she show any further emotion other than a faint contemptuous curl to her lip. The bruises on her face stood out as darker patches against her pale skin.

"No? Well, my name is Crispus and I work for the King."

He sounded like a friendly neighbour passing the time of day or a local Priest asking after the welfare of his followers; not a man who specialised in winkling out secrets from unwilling mouths. He looked like a Priest too, in his dark brown robes and neatly shorn hair. If Milo hadn't witnessed his work with his own eyes, he wouldn't have believed what this man was capable of. It looked like Morgan, if that was her real name, was about to find out. Milo's role was to watch for any signs of magic. He wasn't Raven's favoured Agent for nothing and he stood ready with certain devices should the suspect have any nasty surprises.

Morgan slowly and deliberately spat on the floor.

"Now why would you do that?" Crispus asked her, feigning shock. "Don't we all love our Sovereign Lord?"

"The first Artor betrayed us all," she said clearly, using the old name. "He should have driven the foreign scum back into the sea. Instead, he abandoned his people and wasted his power rescuing a decadent and corrupt Empire. He should have joined with Alaric and the rest to pick Roma's bones!"

"If Artorius Magnus hadn't saved the Empire, we would have been overrun in our turn," Crispus told her reasonably, like a schoolmaster correcting an errant pupil. "The reforming of the legions has protected us for hundreds of years."

"Enslaved us, more like!" she growled, her eyes flashing in the harsh light, her hatred and anger showing at last. "The Old Gods would have given us the strength to deal with any invaders!"

"As they did when the Romans came?" Crispus asked her mildly. "Advanced technology and a will to win often trumps divine intervention, you know that. Besides which, the old Romans had plenty of allies here that welcomed them."

"Traitors!" she shrieked suddenly, the light of fanaticism blazing forth. "As you are traitors to the tribes of Albion!"

Crispus regarded her steadily. There was no further doubt as to her guilt or motivation. Now all that remained was to extract as much information from her as possible.

"Who, or what, were you transporting?" he asked.

Morgan only smiled.

"You won't get anything further from me. Do what you will, you'll learn nothing. I'm immune to pain."

This was so easily tested that Milo had no doubt at all that she was telling the truth. He moved over to Crispus and whispered in his ear.

"Check for tattoos."

The interrogator nodded and pulled the woman's shift away from her neck. Milo craned his neck and saw the strange swirls of blue that covered her back, snaking round to cover her breasts and belly. His heart sank. She must have prepared for this assignment over many months, if not years, to cover herself like this. Nothing they could threaten her with would bother her in the slightest. Bribes and promises wouldn't persuade her either.

He exchanged a glance with Crispus. Their time could be better spent elsewhere.

"Well, it seems you've thought of everything," Crispus said. "Good day to you."

He walked out, leaving her to glare after him with a look of triumph on her face. Milo and Favonius followed him up to more comfortable surroundings to plan their next move.

"That's Druid work," Milo said, as he accepted a glass of wine, "and no ordinary Druid either. She must have been across the sea."

"Maybe, but we can't prove it," Crispus said sourly. He seemed resigned to the fact that he wouldn't get anywhere with torture and, judging from the tattoos, magic wouldn't work on her either. Someone had planned this very carefully.

"Did you find anything else?" Favonius asked.

"No. Apparently, she kept to herself and has only been there a few months."

"Jupiter blast her! I'll place a ringer," Crispus decided. "A few days in the dark and she might spill her guts to a sympathetic ear, especially if she thinks there's a chance of rescue or escape."

Favonius grimaced. "Unfortunately that takes time we haven't got and we can't afford to wait to find out what she knows. A trial is out of the question." He rubbed his chin thoughtfully, falling silent, his pale eyes unfocused as he listened to instructions none of the others could hear. After a short time he nodded, as if agreeing with the unheard speaker.

"Do what you can, as quickly as you can," he told the Interrogator.

"Maybe something in her food?"

Favonius shot him a look.

"Would you eat anything given to you here?"

"She'll die quickly then," Milo pointed out.

Crispus shrugged. "We can force feed her if necessary, but I've a better idea. She might not feel pain, but she can watch as I slowly remove her extremities, piece by piece."

He beamed at them both, his good humour restored.

Favonius frowned. "I don't care what you do to her. Drug her, chop her to pieces, whatever. Just get something out of her."

Crispus nodded, his smile growing wider.

As Milo left the Justicia offices, frustration gnawed at him like a persistent rat. Without information their hands were tied. He'd have to follow the only lead they had; Morgan's tattoos. They were somewhere to start and might provide some answers. The look on Favonius' face had given him the distinct feeling that failure to come up with anything concrete wasn't an option.

He had to discover just who, or what, had been travelling through those portals.

*

The Portus Academy looked just as she'd left it.

Maia looked around in bewilderment, expecting Matrona and Branwen to come and greet her, but the place was silent and empty. For a moment, she was tempted to call to them and announce her arrival, but surely if they were expecting her, they'd have been here already?

A niggling voice in her head insisted that the so-called 'trials' were just a sham, something to test candidates' resolve and not really anything of substance at all. Maybe she'd been smuggled back to Portus to wait until she could be installed, with nobody the wiser?

What was she supposed to do?

She walked down the corridors and entered the main hall. Yes, it was all just as she had left it; the black and white tiled floor and the ten statues, each depicting a Royal Ship. She remembered how afraid of them she'd been at first when she knew she'd been sent to the Academy under false pretences, a candidate with no Potentia. She'd hated to walk between the stony faces, scuttling through with her shoulders hunched and her eyes averted.

Perhaps Matrona was in her office? She started to move, hoping against hope that this was all quite normal and her sudden reappearance would be explained away over chai and cake.

Slight movement in her peripheral vision brought her to a sudden halt. The statue of the *Augusta* was looking directly at her.

One by one, the other statues followed suit, their heads swivelling in smooth motions to pin her with fixed stares. Maia's heart leapt in her breast, as, simultaneously, ten arms raised in gestures of forbidding. She could see that they were stone no longer, but living wood, real Ships not just images.

The *Augusta* spoke first.

"Intruder!"

"Unworthy!" That was the *Diadem,* the first Ship she'd ever seen. The wooden face was set in lines of disdain.

"How dare you presume to think that you could ever be one of us?"

That was the *Victoria,* her feathered wings flexing. Maia could feel the draught they were causing and took a step back in horror.

"It's not too late for you, child." The *Imperatrix* sounded almost sympathetic. "Leave now, before you embarrass yourself any further. Nobody expects you to succeed, anyway, so it's best for all concerned if you abandon your attempt now."

The other Ships nodded in agreement.

"She speaks the truth," the *Augusta* said.

"B-but Jupiter said I have enough Potentia," Maia stammered.

All ten Ships burst into mocking laughter.

"You? A kitchen maid?"

"Poor deluded little skivvy!"

"As if you could ever be like us! You haven't even finished your training!"

The *Justicia* leaned forward, her scales swinging from her hand. "You don't have a chance. *Blossom* told me that personally. You don't have what it takes and Captain Plinius agrees. He feels sorry for you."

Maia gulped, searching each carved face for any sign of support.

"Off you go," the *Diadem* said firmly, "and we'll say no more about it."

Maia glanced over her shoulder towards the main doors. They were open, showing the view of the harbour beyond. It would be so easy to run out and away into Portus. The kind ferryman would give her a ride. She could make her way back to The Anchor and pick up her old life. It would be a relief to be free of all the pressure.

"That's right," the *Diadem* encouraged. "You'll be free."

A warning note sounded in Maia's fuddled brain. She forced her thoughts to stop racing round like a terrified mouse. How had the Ship known what she was thinking?

She pinched herself, hard enough to cause a bruise. The scene before her didn't waver; it all still felt real, but, then again, it always did in a dream, didn't it?

This was her nightmare, dredged up from her subconscious. She remembered feeling this way. Insignificant. Pitiful. Unworthy. The statues had never been Ships. These were her own fears made manifest.

"You're not real," she stated. "You can't stop me. Whatever I was before, I'm not that frightened little girl anymore."

She glared at each one, daring them to contradict her and, slowly, the Ships' features relaxed, as if they were machines that had been set in motion but were now winding down. Their gazes lifted and they became immobile stone once more; just inanimate statues set on plinths, to remind everyone of the might of the Britannic Royal Navy.

Maia took a deep breath. This had been the first trial. Whether by some strange magic she was really in Portus, or locked into a fantasy, she didn't know and it didn't matter.

Ceridwen's words returned to her. "*Keep going.*"

The space before her abruptly shimmered and another door appeared. It was quite ordinary looking, such as could be found in a well-to-do house, with painted wooden panels and a brass handle. She'd seen many just like it over the years.

Maia touched the handle and it swung open.

*

The woman was dead. Milo regarded the flaccid corpse dispassionately as it lay on the stone slab, part covered by a coarse sheet.

"Cause of death?"

Crispus shrugged. "Unclear. If you want my opinion, she willed herself to die as quickly as possible. We got no further information from her, though I took a few fingers and toes for the look of the thing."

Milo kept his revulsion to himself. Morgan wouldn't have felt anything and must have known that she wouldn't get out alive. This level of fanaticism was disturbing and he had the feeling that she wasn't the only hostile agent in the city, though just how many of her kind walked the streets of Londin was as yet unknown. It could be two, or two thousand.

"The Mages have drawn a blank on tracing her movements," he said. "It appears that she was protected by something powerful that they can't penetrate. We're presuming, from what she said, that she was linked to the Separatists, but how Fae magic has come to be involved, we don't know. They could be stirring up trouble out of sheer malice."

He met Crispus' eye and the older man scowled.

"I'd better clear more cells. She won't be the last. Oh and see if you can't get your Collegium friends to find a way to break those tattoos, or we won't get anything out of the next one either."

Milo grunted.

"I'll do my best. At least the damned things are visible, though I've a suspicion that they go deep. You'd better order a post-mortem and make sure that you get a specialist Mage in to perform it."

He'd heard that sometimes protections could be placed internally, magically etched into bone and organs. The procedure was said to be agonising and potentially life-threatening.

"Right. Good advice," Crispus said, once more sounding like someone's kindly uncle and not the most cold-blooded servant the State had at its disposal.

Milo nodded and left with the only clue he had been able to obtain; a partial copy of the tattoos taken from the body. It was time to find out more, even if he had to return to face someone he'd hoped never to have to meet again. Bitterness threatened to overwhelm him but he seized the emotion, locking it back in the depths where it belonged.

He had no choice but to tear open old wounds, even if he felt sick at the thought.

Duty always came first, whatever the cost.

*

A loud rattling and the smell of cooking jerked Maia from sleep.

She yawned, stretching stiff limbs and trying to remember her dream. She hadn't been here, that was for certain.

The sight of her left arm and hand gave her pause. Maia stared at it, disconcerted. The smooth skin seemed odd somehow, as if she'd been expecting to see something else.

"Come on, sleepyhead. There's lots to do today. You can admire yourself later!"

Maia blinked and rubbed her eyes. Chloe was standing by the stove, her chain clinking as she arranged the pans over the fire. It had been this that had woken her up.

"What time is it?" she asked the slave.

"Time you were moving. The mistress is hosting a party tonight and you know what'll happen if we're not ready."

Maia repressed a shudder.

"I was dreaming," she said, screwing up her face in concentration as she tried to remember. "I was…going to be a Ship. A big Ship."

Chloe's bark of laughter brought her up short.

"That's a new one! A Ship? I'd rather be on one, sailing far away from here. As if! Now stir yourself! There are floors to scrub and windows to clean, not to mention all the dirty pots. We've got a few hours before *she* wakes up, so you'd better work quickly."

Maia dragged herself from the thin mattress and went to splash her face at the pump outside in the yard. She couldn't say why everything felt so wrong today. It was a day like any other, apart from the fact that Marcia Blandina was hosting a lot of very important people this evening. She'd talked of nothing else for weeks, according to Flora.

A few mouthfuls of bread and cheese served as breakfast and, while she ate, she found herself hoping that the guests wouldn't be particularly hungry. It might be a good opportunity to steal some food when the plates were cleared; if the other, more senior servants didn't get to it first.

"Oh, hello Maia."

It was Xander, passing through the yard, on his way to the market.

"Hello Xander. Busy already?"

He pulled a face.

"It's going to be one of those days, I can feel it already. It'll take all of us to pull this one off." He grimaced. "I'm to help Chloe with the cooking and pick up some ready-made stuff."

Maia sighed.

"I was just thinking about all the food."

Xander grinned. "I'll try to save you some."

She smiled back at him, then began to fill buckets with water. It was time to scrub the floors and woe betide her if she missed even the tiniest bit.

She was on her hands and knees, halfway through cleaning the entrance hall, when she became aware that she was under scrutiny. She peered surreptitiously through her hair, to see the bulky figure of the Cyclops leaning casually against the main doorjamb. He was grinning, his lone eye watching her every move. Maia tried not to show her fear, concentrating on scrubbing at the patterned mosaic instead, even when she sensed him heading in her direction.

A pair of boots appeared right in front of her, forcing her to stop. She kept her eyes lowered.

One boot lifted and prodded her in the side.

She scooted backwards as quickly as she could, glancing upwards. The Cyclops stood there, his arms folded over his bulging belly. A vague sense of something wrong, out of place, called to her, vanishing again before she could grab hold of it. Something about…the arena? Why was she thinking of the arena?

"Come 'ere, girlie," he said, his voice hoarse. "Give us a kiss. Don't be shy!"

The Cyclops bent down to grab her, but she evaded his clutching hand, staring up at him in fright. His grin vanished, replaced by an ugly scowl.

"Yer don't know what's good for yer, do yer?"

He kicked the bucket, spreading a huge puddle of dirty water across the floor.

"Oh dear! What a shame. Looks like yer'll have to start all over again!"

Maia felt like screaming. She was in so much trouble.

"What's this?"

The shrill voice cut through the Cyclops' laughter.

Marcia Blandina was standing at the entrance to her morning room, her eyes flashing with rage.

"She's making a mess of her work, mistress," the slave said.

Blandina's face lit up with insane glee.

"So she is. Bring her!"

An image flashed through Maia's mind. Blandina, lying in a pool of her own blood, her head caved in.

She shook her head to dispel the image, but it remained, somehow superimposed over the scene before her, just as strong hands hauled her roughly to her feet and dragged her into the other room.

"Hold her still."

The Cyclops gripped the back of her neck, forcing her to bend over a couch, as Blandina opened a cupboard and removed a whip made from thin birch twigs.

"I've not had the chance to teach this one a lesson yet," she announced.

Maia tried to twist out of the Cyclops' grip, bucking and kicking, but he was too strong. Again, the picture in her head rose up, like a cork bobbing on water and this time she seized it.

What was she doing here? They were dead. Both of them, years before.

Even as the realisation hit her, the Cyclops' hold slackened. A smell of charred wood filled her nostrils and orange sparks floated lazily past her. Maia threw her head back and whirled around.

The slave was gone. In his place stood the *Livia,* her blue eyes blazing in triumph, even as her Shipbody burned. Marcia Blandina moved to stand with her, her head now misshapen and bloodied.

The door to the entrance hall was open.

"Run, my baby," the *Livia* said sweetly, as Blandina advanced on Maia, her whip raised high. "You mustn't let her catch you. Run!"

Maia checked. She was right. The way was clear and this time there would be no doorkeeper to stop her making a break for it. She stepped backwards, slowly, towards the door.

Blandina's mad smile widened and Maia knew that she was making the wrong move. She was going backwards. Why shouldn't she go backwards?

"Run!" the *Livia* urged her.

No, this was wrong.

"You're all dead!" Maia screamed.

She picked up the nearest object, a small table and flung it at the pair. It crashed against Blandina, who dropped her whip. Several china ornaments followed, shattering against the walking corpse, while the *Livia* watched, seemingly unconcerned. Blandina raised her hands to protect herself and Maia could clearly see the great gash in her broken skull.

"Get away from me!"

Maia darted forward and snatched the whip, using it to keep the apparitions at arm's length. She half expected to see the *Livia* advance, but she remained still, merely pivoting on the spot to follow Maia's progress as if still anchored to her deck.

Again, the air rippled and another door appeared ahead of her. The wood was painted a bright blue and seemed to glow, as if standing in full sunlight. Seizing her chance, Maia edged towards it, still jabbing the bundle of twigs at her former mistress, who backed away, her power over Maia dissolving into nothing.

Just as she reached the unfamiliar portal, the *Livia*'s features animated, eyes wide and lips parting.

"Remember! Fire and mind! Fire and mind!"

For a second, reality seemed to intrude and Maia met the frantic Ship's eyes. They shone with urgency and horrified awareness, as if finally remembering who she was and what she had done. Maia turned and ran for the exit.

Her shoulder slammed into the door as, behind her, the *Livia*'s Shipbody exploded into a mass of flaming splinters.

Warm sunshine enveloped her as she fell.

*

The shop was in a respectable part of Londin, just out of the centre but not so far that any prospective clients would be put off by the journey. Milo noted that the paint was fresh, the windows were clean and some effort had been made to keep the pavement free of the usual filth.

He paused to read the elaborately painted sign before entering, battling against his sudden reluctance to reopen old wounds; "Coventina's Cavern: Magical Supplies for the Discerning Customer." The display inside was the usual flashy crystal and wire contraptions that were designed to lure in the tourists, together with some impressive looking but largely unnecessary ritual knives and bowls, covered with mystic inscriptions. He knew that the real stuff would be in the back, out of view.

Milo sighed and pushed the door open, ignoring the nagging pain in his gut that had come upon him on waking. He must have eaten a bad oyster, he decided. A hanging bell tinkled prettily and a waft of pleasant incense brushed across his face. Rows of cases containing statuettes, potions and protective amulets stretched to each side of him, while, before him, a long counter filled the width of the shop with shelves behind it.

"I'll be out in just a second!" A woman's cheerful voice came from behind an embroidered curtain to the rear. There was a brief clatter, as of a ladder being moved, then the shop's owner bustled in, a smile already fixed to greet her customer. It vanished as soon as she saw Milo, her expression closing down like a door slammed in his face.

"I need your help, Seren," he said. "It's important and I don't know who else to ask."

Seren just stared at him, her dark eyes hostile and full of contempt.

"Please."

"At least you haven't tried to pretend you're sorry," she said at last, her voice harsh with remembered pain.

"You wouldn't believe me anyway."

She jerked her head.

"True. What do you want? I take it that this is official business."

"Yes."

Seren thought for a moment more, then lifted a section of counter and walked past him to the door. She locked it and put up a "back in five minutes" sign. Her movements were stiff, with none of her usual grace.

"It's not like I have a lot of choice, is it? You've got as long as it says, no more."

He winced inwardly at the anger in her voice, but she owed him and she knew it. If it hadn't been for his favourable report, she would have ended up in the arena with the rest of her seditious little friends. It was too bad that he'd had to fool her into thinking that he cared for her, but it was what his mission had demanded.

He pushed aside the thought that, by the end, he actually had.

"A woman was brought in covered with these," he said.

He offered her the folded papers with the copies of Morgan's tattoos and she took them gingerly, holding them by the edges as if not wanting to contaminate herself by any contact with him. She looked much the same as she had then, he thought, even with her long copper hair tied up instead of falling past her shoulders and her smooth face etched with lines of worry and disappointment. She'd done well for herself to build a business from virtually nothing, though she didn't know who'd really funded her first purchase of stock. He'd been careful to act through an intermediary.

An image of her laughing face, aglow in the light of the Beltane fire, flashed across his memory like a bright spark before fading into the past. She glanced sharply at him, as if sensing his regret, then opened the papers.

All colour drained from her face.

"Goddess protect us!" she said in horror. "Are you sure these are accurate?"

She clearly hoped that he had erred, but he nodded slowly.

"The woman was covered in them beneath her clothes. I know they gave her immunity from pain."

"They would, and more besides."

She gazed at him speculatively, as if looking for something that only she could see, then came to a decision.

"Did you touch her skin?"

"Yes," he admitted. He remembered knocking her to the floor. "I felt for a pulse when I knocked her out and I searched her."

Seren pursed her lips. "Do you feel all right?"

He frowned at her. "What do you mean?"

"I mean," she said slowly, "do you feel ill? These are curses as well, set to target any who would seek to harm her."

Milo's eyes opened wide in alarm, then he bent double as his gut abruptly twisted in an agonising spasm. A moan escaped his lips and he felt himself break out in a cold sweat.

"That answers that," Seren said. "You'd better come with me."

She made no move to assist him, but led the way through to the back of the shop, past boxes and bundles of goods and into her living space. It was as much as he could do to stand upright, both arms folded across his stomach as if to keep his innards from bursting through. It felt as if a ravenous wolf was tearing at him from the inside out. He mumbled a healing charm that he remembered from his days at the Collegium and felt the pain ease a little, but he knew it would be back. This wasn't Magecraft but foul sorcery.

Seren pulled out a wooden stool and he stumbled to it gratefully.

"Pull up your shirt," she ordered, all business, as he slumped on to the hard seat. He complied and she hissed at the sight of red, inflamed marks swirling up his torso, similar to the ones on the paper.

"Cursed contagion?" he asked her, through gritted teeth.

"Yes. It takes a while, but once it starts it's hard to stop. You shouldn't have touched her."

"I didn't know what else she had on her. She was using malicious spells to cause harm."

Another wave of pain gripped him.

Seren raised her eyebrows, unmoved. "Why am I not surprised? There's only one quick cure for this and you're fortunate that I have some here. It's not easily come by and usually fake."

As she spoke she went to a covered table in the middle of the room and flung back the cloth to reveal a strongbox. The key was around her neck and he heard her add a spell of unlocking too before lifting the lid and bringing out a small gold phial.

"This stuff costs a fortune," she continued, pouring wine into a glass and tipping out the contents of the phial into the ruby liquid. "I hope your masters think you're worth the price."

He grabbed the glass and downed it in one. Thank the Gods she had some unicorn horn. Powdered or whole, it was a sure detector and remedy against all poisons, physical or magical, but was usually just rhinoceros or narwhal horn cut with cheap drugs and passed off as the genuine article. He shuddered at the cost of even this small amount.

After a few moments he felt the horn work its magic, replacing the clawing and burning with coolness, as if he had just drunk fresh spring water on a hot summer's day. A sense of peace and well-being flowed through him and he sighed with the intensity of the relief. Seren knew her stuff and the mere fact that she stocked the rare substance showed that her business was doing well.

"It's working then," she said drily. "Where should I send the bill?"

"I'll submit it on your behalf as expenses."

His voice sounded far away to his ears, as he drifted on the aftereffects of the powerful medicine. A dreamy smile crossed his face and he seemed to float for an instant, weightless and carefree. He savoured the feeling; it wasn't one he'd felt for a long, long time. When at last it left him, he was clear headed but saddened. No wonder the very rich took it as a drug to induce euphoria. It had had to work hard in his system or he would have been out of it for several hours; as it stood, he'd only had a brief, tantalising taste of its effects. The ruinous price prevented it from general consumption and there were definitely cheaper ways of freeing the mind.

He came back to earth to find Seren had already written a receipt. He took it without looking at it and tucked it inside his pocket – why spoil the moment?

"I just need you to confirm that this is Fae work," he said.

"I'm sure of it," Seren replied, eyes averted. "She must have come over the sea. Did she give you a name?"

"She claimed to be called Morgan. I doubt it was her real name."

"Who knows?" Seren said. "One thing's for sure, this spell is Fae. They delight in its cruelty and spread it like the plague."

Milo suddenly thought of Crispus and felt his stomach drop. He had to warn him.

"One last thing. Do you know what the Separatists are up to?"

She looked at him with wide eyes, suddenly very afraid.

"There are whispers, but nothing I could link to any attacks. You of all people know that I wouldn't be stupid enough to get involved in any of that. I've a good life now and a profitable business. I'm respected."

He heard the truth in her voice and nodded. Seren was no longer the idealistic, naïve girl who had thought that the old lore held the answers to every problem and that the only way forward was through blood and fire.

Besides which, if he'd thought she had anything to do with this, he'd have killed her himself. Now his priority was to warn others. He stood.

"If you hear anything, let me know."

Seren dropped her eyes and he knew that she was still frightened. He pitied her, knowing that her past dogged her steps and whispered in her ear at night, still seeking to drag her down into the abyss from which she had only just escaped. She had to know that she was still being watched, even after so many years had passed.

Once, she had looked on him with love, but those times were gone. Now she feared him, like so many others once they knew his calling and purpose. There was no way back from that.

"Thank you for your help."

Milo retrieved the papers, unable to meet her eyes and left quickly, feeling her watching him go. He knew only too well the terrible hurt he'd caused her, but was helpless to do anything about it now. He'd done his duty to Empire, King and Country, but that was scant recompense for all they had both lost.

*

He was too late.

The covered corpse of the Chief Inquisitor was taken out past him, followed by three others. He could tell that they hadn't been as lucky as he; their death agonies had been terrible, brought on swiftly by prolonged contact. Crispus had paid a high price for his amusements.

Morgan's death had negated the curse, or it would have taken the City Pathologist as well. Thistle, a tall thin man with a long, hooked nose, was drying his hands as Milo entered, having finished his preliminary examinations. He brought to mind the image of a predatory stork as he stepped carefully around the metal slab. The two men exchanged grim nods.

"A bad business," the Adept said. "Why aren't you dead too?"

"Unicorn horn."

Thistle's eyes widened.

"Jove's beard! Where did you get that?"

"Right time, right place. Any later and I'd have been doomed too."

"Well, aren't you the favoured one?" the Adept said. "It's a pity they had none here. It isn't something we keep in stock, alas, nor will it ever be. Do you know how much that stuff costs?"

Milo did. He wasn't looking forward to submitting the receipt Seren had given him. He'd have to just slip it in with the rest of his expenses and duck for cover. Still, it would take more money and time to replace the victims, especially Crispus, who was noted for his skill and enthusiasm. It wasn't a job that just anyone could do, or would want to.

"It worked. Something to bear in mind next time we come across magic like this."

Thistle merely grunted in reply. They both knew that they had more chance of outstaring the gorgon's head than having a purchase order approved for the valuable substance.

"Well, there are several vacancies here, if you fancy settling down to a steadier post," he said, after a while. The pathologist was noted for his gallows humour.

"No thanks," Milo said. "I just called in on the off chance that somebody else survived. I have to make my report anyway."

Thistle raised his eyebrows.

"Good luck with that. I bet they take the cost of the horn out of your wages."

Milo grinned mirthlessly.

"That's my money gone for the next few years, then."

The Adept snorted.

"At least a century."

Milo left, wondering whether Thistle had had this personality before or after he was named. The way things were looking, it might be up to the Gods to avenge Crispus and the others, as mere mortals were getting nowhere. He had no doubt that their intelligencers were more effective than he could ever be. Or maybe they were simply amused by the whole thing?

Perhaps it was time to get on their good side again and provide another sacrifice, while he still had the funds.

XI

Strong arms caught Maia, leaving her breathless.

"Steady there!" a man laughed. "You nearly knocked me over!"

She pulled away in confusion.

"Gemma? Are you all right?"

She shook her head, instinctively reaching out to push him away.

"Oh no, it's happened again, hasn't it? Here, sit down."

She couldn't see his face at first, just a shape outlined by the sun, as if he were bathed in a radiant halo. It was only when he moved that he came into focus.

Clear blue eyes met her own, above a straight nose and firm jaw. They had been crinkled with merriment, but were now shaded with concern as he guided her to a cushioned bench and wrapped a shawl around her shoulders with deft fingers.

She was in a garden. Before her, geometric flowerbeds and carefully tended hedges stretched away to form an elegant parterre, whilst, in the distance, rolling hills disappeared into the blue haze of the horizon. Her companion bent down to retrieve his hat, placing it back on his dark, wavy hair before sitting down carefully beside her.

"Where am I?" she whispered.

Why was she here, with this handsome young man? He seemed to know her, though he'd called her Gemma, not Maia.

She stared down at herself in bewilderment. Her gown was made of patterned silk, with an embroidered bodice. She'd been expecting something coarser, made of wool, not this fine, expensive fabric. Her gloved hands bunched into it, testing its solidity.

"Come on, we'll get you back to the villa. You need to rest."

She raised her eyes to his face.

"Who are you?"

Pain shot across his features.

"I'm your friend and I'm going to look after you. You've been overdoing it lately and that's why you're not feeling well."

His voice was soothing, but she didn't trust him. She was relieved when he sat back away from her, giving her more space. Maia frowned, trying to orient herself. Her head felt packed full of musty feathers, like a lumpy, worn-out mattress and her memories, usually so clear, refused to line up in their usual orderly fashion.

There was something familiar about him, though.

"I've seen you before," she said, groping to place him.

His face lit up in a broad smile.

"Yes! You know me!"

Some part of her did. It was more his voice than his appearance but, again, the knowledge eluded her. Why couldn't she remember him? Of all the difficulties she'd faced in her life, forgetting had never been one of them.

"Can you remember your name?"

Of course she knew her name.

"I'm Maia Abella," she said, confident in that fact at least.

Emotion shone in his eyes. Was it fear?

"You *were* Maia Abella," he said. "Now you use your real name. Lady Gemma Valeria, of the Family Valerius. You're not that poor little foundling girl anymore."

Gemma Valeria? Yes, she knew that name. It was her name, wasn't it?

"You're getting cold," he said. "It's not very warm, even though it's Junius. I thought the sun would be out today. Can you stand?"

He held out his arm to support her as Maia struggled to her feet. Neat gravel paths bordered the garden, while, behind her, the land rose in more terraces. She couldn't see any buildings at the top, though there was some sort of summer house at the corner of the parterre. It was all lovely and perfectly maintained.

"I think I'm all right," she insisted, just as her legs started to give way.

He caught her effortlessly and, despite her weak protests, swung her up into his arms, cradling her as though she were a babe. She clung to him, trying to keep her wits about her but they, like her thoughts, remained a jumbled mess.

Her rescuer strode along the path, gravel crunching beneath his boots and turned on to a set of wide, stone stairs that ascended through the terraces. The heady scent of roses and lavender drifted in the air as the sun emerged from behind a cloud.

Two men hurried over to them, smart in their livery of green and gold.

"Warn the house. Your mistress is unwell," the man said shortly.

The men exchanged worried looks, before rushing off towards the building that was coming into view. For a moment, she thought it was a temple, before realising that it was a very large house, built in the new classical palace style, complete with portico. More people began to emerge through the huge front doors, one of them an older woman with silver curls peeping from beneath her starched linen cap and her wrinkled face creased with worry.

"Oh, Master Quintilian! How is she?"

"It happened again. She has no memory of who or where she is."

He passed through the doors and entered the building. Maia saw a huge, sweeping staircase, pictures, statues and mosaics, all flashing past and then she was in a smaller room being lowered to a couch. The woman tucked a blanket around her.

"She's freezing and as white as a sheet! I've sent for Adept Poppy."

"Thank you, Efa. I'm sure she'll soon come round, but this was a bad one."

"She was doing so well, too," the woman said sadly. "Still, I suppose it's to be expected with all she's been through. I'd hoped she was improving."

"She was…is," Quintilian said firmly.

His piercing blue eyes fixed on hers and she noticed how thick his eyelashes were.

"Ah! Here's the Adept now."

Quintilian moved aside, to be replaced by an elderly man with a bald head, neatly trimmed beard and dark eyes.

"A little relapse, I see," he murmured. "I'll prescribe a tonic to calm the nerves and help my lady regain her faculties. It's been a while since she's had one of these episodes."

"Yes," Quintilian agreed. "This seems to be a severe one. She didn't know who or where she was. She referred to herself as Maia."

The Adept's face grew thoughtful.

"I see. As I said previously, she has a diagnosis of brain injury. Being starved of oxygen for so long often has these sort of side effects."

"I understand."

He turned his attention to his patient.

"Now Lady Gemma, can you sit up? Excellent! Drink this, that's it. This will make you feel better."

Maia felt too weak to argue. The cool liquid slipped down her throat, the taste of honey masking the underlying bitterness of the herbs. She felt her limbs began to relax immediately. Wherever she was, they knew her and seemed to care, fussing over her like she was a queen.

She blinked, drowsily.

"That's helped," Poppy said. "You'll be feeling better in no time."

She nodded. The light shone on his bald head, brown and glossy and a tiny memory sparked. A large room. People. Danger.

Her eyes opened and she heard herself gasp aloud. Quintilian was by her side immediately.

"She remembers something!"

"Probably a repressed memory. It will pass," the Adept assured him.

Maia tried to hang on to the spark, but it faded and was gone, slipping away like a fish in a stream.

"I can't remember!"

"It will all come back to you," Quintilian said, soothingly. "You're at home, your home and you're safe. That's all you need to know for now."

"I wasn't here. I was…" she trailed off, then flung herself upright. "Blandina!"

"She's dead. She's long dead Gemma, and her crony with her. They were executed in the arena."

Her memories were beginning to come back into some sort of focus.

"She had a whip. And she was…"

Her hands flew to her throat.

"Yes. She was strangling you when the polismen arrived. The slave, Xander, managed to knock out the doorkeeper and run for help. You were nearly dead. Your brain was starved of oxygen and that's why you sometimes forget."

Yes. She could still feel an echo of the pain as the woman tried to squeeze the life from her. So Xander had got help?

"Then you were taken to the Adepts and your true identity was revealed through a test."

That seemed right too.

"Your parents were dead and there were no other relatives, so you were declared the heir to the Valerius fortune. That was almost six years ago now."

His earnest expression held no deceit.

"My father was a Ship's Captain," she insisted.

He stared at her, puzzled.

"No, he was a Senator. He and your mother died in a tragic carriage accident, but your evil aunt substituted a dead child and claimed it was you. She arranged for you to be abandoned. Her crimes were only discovered when she confessed on her death bed. The estate was held in trust by the Crown while we searched for you."

"We?"

"My father and I. He was your father's oldest friend and swore he would find you. That's when we met. He's at court at the moment, attending the King, but he'll come and visit you soon."

So, Blandina had died in the amphitheatre?

"I don't remember any of that. Was I there?"

"Where?"

"Watching Blandina die?"

"Yes. Her crimes were uncovered and the whole city turned out. It was a special event, just for her and that brute that conspired with her. But let us not talk of such unpleasantness."

"It only seems a minute since she was attacking me," Maia said.

Efa shook her head.

"You poor lamb! It's all fine now. Haven't I cared for you these past years as if you were one of my own? I nursed your father from birth and now I have you. Praise the Gods!"

The woman had tears in her eyes and Maia was touched. Again, there was a sense that she knew this woman – or someone very much like her.

"Why don't I arrange some lunch for you both? You can eat it in here. I'll have the fire made up – it's turned a bit chilly."

"Not enough money for the heating, eh Efa?" Quintilian grinned at her with obvious affection. "Always watching the pennies!"

"Oh, you are a one, master!" she replied, in mock reproof. "As if I need to!"

"It's a good idea to keep the lady warm," Poppy said from the other side of the room. "A chill would only make things worse."

"Thank you, Poppy," Quintilian said.

The Adept bowed and left.

"He got here quickly," Maia remarked.

Quintilian gave her a quizzical look.

"He's your private Adept, living here on the estate."

Maia felt her jaw sag. An enormous house, silk dresses, gaggles of servants and a noble title? She bit her lip. Yes. She remembered being in a big house with lots of servants. They must have been hers.

"I don't understand who you are," she told him. "Are you visiting me?"

Quintilian's face went very still and she felt Efa tense.

"I'm the man who loves you," he said quietly.

She looked at him in shock.

"What? You love me?" She laughed briefly. "How could you love me?"

He shrugged. "I married you."

She shot him a look of disbelief.

"Take off your gloves," he told her.

They were the finest kid leather, creamy and supple. Maia stripped them off, revealing pale, tapering fingers unmarked by any blemish and, on the fourth finger of her left hand, a gold ring, which glinted in the light.

"We're married?"

"Yes and we have a son. He's six months old. We called him Lucius, after your father."

He signalled over his shoulder and a young woman stepped forward, carrying a bundle.

"Here he is! Come to your papa, little man!"

Quintilian took the bundle from the woman. His face softened with love as he tenderly cradled the baby.

Maia's head was spinning. So, apparently she had a husband and a child, as well as the rest. Why didn't she remember? Had she given birth in her sleep?

"Go to your mama," Quintilian said. A chubby hand reached from the wrappings and waved. "See? He can't wait."

Shocked, she took the warm, sweet-smelling bundle. The baby gazed up at her as she cuddled him, his blue eyes open and trusting. She felt emotion threaten to overwhelm her and knew, without any doubt, that this was her child.

Tiny fingers closed on hers. Even his fingernails were perfect.

"He has your eyes," she said.

Quintilian laughed. "Do you think so? I think he has your beauty and I can only pray that he's inherited your courage, too. If so, he'll be unstoppable."

Her beauty. Now she knew he was teasing her

"I'm small, thin and ugly," she told him.

He sighed. "Here we go again! You were certainly thin before, but now you're perfect. Decent food and care have seen to that. You were always beautiful, though. Here."

He walked over to the other side of the room and picked up a mirror.

"Look if you don't believe me."

He angled it in front of her.

"See?"

The woman that was staring back looked a little pale, but was otherwise unrecognisable. The sharp angles and long nose were softened and in proportion to the rest of her face. Even her mouth looked fuller, with a gently rounded chin. Her bones had retreated under a layer of clear, smooth skin, without the dullness that had always made her feel grimy. Large eyes, previously a washed-out shade of grey, seemed darker, the colour of storm clouds and her fashionably coiffed hair was piled high and dusted with gold flecks that sparkled as she moved her head. It was no longer thin and mousy, but a rich, chestnut colour.

The high-born lady, wife and mother met her gaze, slowly smiling at her surprise.

"I think I've made my point," Quintilian said airily. "Shall we eat?"

Baby Lucius gurgled in his mother's arms and she bent to kiss his soft cheek. He smelt of powder and milk. The nurse stood by, ready to take him, but she felt oddly reluctant. It seemed a shame that great ladies didn't feed their own children, but she supposed that she was no exception.

She handed him back, feeling the wrench tug painfully at her heart and her eyes followed the woman as she left the room.

"You'll see him again later, my lady. It's time for his nap, anyway," Efa said, consolingly.

The old servant looked very relieved at Maia's reaction to the child and indeed, seeing him had calmed her. So what if all her memories didn't come back at once? They would, given time.

"Does this often happen to me?" she asked.

"Not for many months," he replied. "Poppy thinks that they'll stop eventually, but whatever you're going through, you know I'm here for you."

He looked at her with such love that she felt herself melt. Of course, it had all worked out perfectly.

Why would she ever imagine that it hadn't?

*

Milo had been hoping that it was only Favonius who was waiting to hear his report, but he was out of luck. He was ushered through into his superior's office on arrival, without being made to kick his heels in the antechamber for once. On entering, he was met with the sight of Senator Rufus and Admiral Albanus, both sitting stiffly upright in their chairs as if the mere proximity of the other was supremely distasteful. The Master Mage occupied the space between them like a referee waiting to officiate at a boxing match. Any violence wouldn't be physical, but it could be dangerous, nonetheless.

"Agent. Please take a seat."

Favonius proceeded to glance through some papers. Milo knew that it was all a sham. The man had a mind like the Cretan Labyrinth and more eyes than Argus. He would already have memorised every detail.

Milo bowed politely to the gentlemen, then took the only unoccupied seat in the room, slightly apart and to the right. Favonius was presiding from behind his desk, as usual.

"We are here to discuss your report and, in light of the ramifications, I thought it wiser to involve others of influence."

So, the information had already leaked, however much Favonius might have wanted to keep it confidential for as long as he could. The Senator would be representing the army in his capacity as honorary Legionary Commander, though he'd seen enough service in his younger days and could be called upon again if Britannia found herself at war. He hadn't met Albanus personally but was aware of his high status at court. The gossip said that he was waiting for the Lord High Admiral, the King's uncle, to retire so that he could assume command of the whole Royal Navy. How he must wish for an opportune storm, though it would take a real killer to sink the *Augusta*.

"Agent, please would you give your report in your own words?"

Milo cleared his throat and quickly outlined the events that led to the deaths of the Chief Interrogator and his men. To their credit, none of them interrupted him, though both Rufus and Albanus jotted down notes as he spoke.

When he'd finished, silence hung in the room, before the questioning began. The first one was predictable.

"You've verified that it was Fae magic?" Rufus asked, his voice shattering the quiet.

"I have verified it."

Raven's dry, whispery voice was an odd contrast.

"Also, the tattoos were proof of their involvement, if more proof were needed."

"Ah, right."

The Senator subsided.

"This thing that was conjured," Albanus' precise voice cut in. "How much Potentia might be used to create such a monster?"

He turned to his left, to watch for the Master Mage's reaction.

"For a human? A great deal. For a Fae Lord, not so much. She must have been a skilled practitioner – or there was somebody nearby who was, if she didn't perform the spell herself."

"But the Agent didn't see anybody else?"

"No." Raven confirmed. "In my opinion, she brought it forth herself, expending all her energy in a final burst. That's why she was captured so easily. If she'd had anything left, she could have brought the whole workshop down on everyone's heads while she made her escape."

Albanus nodded.

"She was relying on her tattoos to protect her from coercion," Favonius said. "It's been confirmed that they went deep into her bones."

"A real fanatic, then," Rufus observed. "But what was her objective?"

Milo forced himself not to squirm. This was the tricky point. They still had no idea what had been transported. The woman had done enough to conceal all traces of her spell.

"Currently unknown," Favonius admitted. The words sounded sour in his mouth. "We're working to establish whether the portal was to somewhere linear, or spatial."

Rufus frowned and Favonius hastily clarified.

"Over distance, or through planes. It seems that the thing that chased the Agent was a conjuration, kept for emergencies in some separate holding space between our world and another. Even if it had been created here, it would need to be stored before use, as without constant input it would collapse and be useless."

"Well, the Master Mage and the Collegium will know more about that than I do," Rufus said. "Just point my lads in the direction of the enemy and they'll give 'em a taste of gunfire."

"That might have worked for Echidna," Albanus interposed, smoothly, "but the Fae are quite a different kettle of fish. Isn't that correct, Raven?"

"Alas, I must agree, Admiral. Our guns, in the main, use lead shot, which is largely ineffective."

The Senator harrumphed.

"So it's cold iron that will take them down? We have larger guns that can fire case shot. A few dozen steel balls will put an end to them."

"But not in a crowded area," Albanus said.

"I'm thinking more of a battlefield situation," Rufus said. "Of course, if we meet 'em at sea your cannon should be effective, but we are talking about a land situation here, are we not?"

Milo felt the tension crackling between the two men. A glaring match was due to start any second.

"Gentlemen. Being an island, we may be facing threats both on land and water, which is why the Crown is most grateful for your valuable advice."

Favonius didn't have to raise his voice, but slowly, two sets of raised hackles stood down.

Milo glanced at the Master Mage who seemed his usual imperturbable self.

"There haven't been any other reports of suspicious activity, which leads me to believe that this is merely the start of something," Raven said. "It's been centuries since we fought the Fae, but they aren't mortal in the sense that we are. They can afford to wait until the situation has changed to their advantage."

"Do you think that the Separatists are using their power?" Rufus asked, a faint frown on his face.

"It's more likely that they're using the Separatist cause to further their own designs," Raven corrected him. "If so, the Separatists are ignorant of the consequences. Fae never see human as equals, merely sport."

"They're not Gods," Albanus objected.

Raven shrugged. "They were worshipped as such, once. Fashions change."

The other four men twitched.

"Your sense of humour will get you into trouble one of these days, old friend," Rufus warned, rolling his eyes heavenwards.

The Master Mage grinned.

"Too late."

Favonius was clearly running out of patience.

"So, gentlemen, you now know as much as we do. I believe that you have your own sources of information and I would urge you to use them in regard to this matter. Maybe it's the start of something, as the Master Mage believes, or it could just be a flash in the pan. Either way, knowledge is power, so the Crown would be grateful for your vigilance. In the meantime, the authorities will have to appoint a new Chief Interrogator. It's most inconvenient."

That's one way of describing it. It's as if he thinks of himself as the government, Milo thought.

Then again, he could be. Everything else was probably window dressing; Senate, King Artorius and all. Favonius was probably working behind the scenes doing most of the jobs himself.

"A bad business," Rufus said. "Have you informed the Imperial Governor?"

"He's aware of the situation and has reported back to the Emperor."

No-one commented, but everyone knew that there would be little help there, unless the Northern Alliance decided to attack. Legendary Fae would be deemed an internal problem for Britannia. There was too much trouble to the north and west to commit troops, even if the threat was more concrete.

Milo resisted the urge to touch the stone disc and run his fingers over the surface for reassurance. He'd tucked it inside a leather pouch around his neck, as things could disappear from pockets far too easily.

"We're on our own then," the Admiral said. "What a surprise. We should withhold tribute; that might make the rest of the Empire sit up and take notice."

"They have troubles of their own," Rufus objected.

"And we've sent aid," Albanus replied, calmly. "It seems that they aren't willing to return the favour."

"Perhaps help will be forthcoming when we have more information," Favonius said. "I would be obliged if you kept me informed of any developments. We've sent watchers to the northlands, just in case and I will instruct Agents to depart for the western coasts immediately."

"The Navy will be standing by," Albanus said.

"As will the legions," Rufus added, not to be outdone. "I would think that the western approaches are the more vulnerable."

Favonius nodded.

"Yes. We suspect that the island of Mona could be their first line of attack, but the coastal border is a long stretch to patrol. Be assured that we will do our utmost, until we have reason to stand down."

"Let's hope that this all comes to nothing," Raven said.

"Quite."

Favonius stood and bowed.

"Thank you for your time, gentlemen."

The Admiral left first. Rufus had a few words with Raven, before following. Probably giving the other man time to leave so he didn't punch him out, Milo decided. Their enmity seemed to be growing worse.

"Milo, if you would stay," Favonius said.

"I'll be off," Raven said. "I have a lot to do."

Favonius looked interested.

"I hear our latest Ship candidate is undergoing her initiation."

"She is," Raven agreed. "All being well, she should soon complete the process and be installed. I need to be on hand when she does so."

He turned clouded eyes to Milo.

"Good luck. I hope you find something useful. Just don't die."

"I'll do my best."

The slight figure gathered up his robes and staff, then exited. Milo could hear the tapping growing fainter down the corridor.

"I have an assignment for you," Favonius said, without preamble.

Here it comes, thought Milo. *Will it be the western mountains or the southern moors?*

He didn't fancy either.

"I'm posting you to Kernow, to keep watch."

Milo kept his face straight, but inside he was cursing. There were decent-sized towns, but it was a long way from Londin. Foxy must have been sent elsewhere.

"You know the place fairly well, which is more than I can say for most of my other Agents. Didn't you work on a fishing vessel for a few months?"

Milo bit back a sarcastic answer. Favonius would know his record backwards.

"Yes, sir."

"Excellent. You should be able to pass as a local, with your talent for blending in."

It wasn't flattery; Milo knew he was one of the best they had, if not the best. He'd mastered the near incomprehensible variant of Britannic they used down there and, if he was currently a little rusty, it would soon come back to him.

"Leave today. Draw what supplies you need from the stores," Favonius told him.

"Understood."

Favonius turned back to his paperwork.

"But no more unicorn horn."

Milo swallowed.

"No, sir."

He'd bought a toadstone instead.

*

The days passed, each more delightful than the last.

Maia, or Gemma, as she now thought of herself, felt stronger than she ever had. Even the weather had improved, turning hot and sunny, so that she could spend time in the summerhouse, playing with Lucius, or hosting chai parties for her many friends.

She hadn't remembered them either, but nobody seemed to mind. They were fond of her and that's what counted.

Her husband was often away, working for the family's interests, but she had enough to occupy her time. She'd been surprised to learn that she was very good at painting and often spent hours sketching views of the estate. In the evenings, she would play cards with her friends, or, if there was enough light, embroider. The work soothed her and calmed her mind, plus there was baby Lucius.

It was bliss.

She truly couldn't want for more.

*

The Admiralty Offices in Londin were packed.

Raven could sense the tension as he walked through the doors and wondered what could be causing it. Purple light flickered in his magical vision as a clerk hurried up to him.

"Greetings, Master Mage. The Lord High Admiral requests that you meet with him, at your earliest convenience."

That explained it. The *Augusta* must be in port and Albanus would be relegated to second-in-command once more. If only the King's uncle would spend more time on land!

"It's convenient right now," he told the man. It was good to know that he was still respected in that quarter.

He followed the clerk to Pendragon's office, a large airy room on an upper floor with a good view of the river.

"Ah, Raven. Good of you to see me so quickly."

Pendragon was standing, gazing out of the window, the spring sun highlighting his profile. He turned to greet the Master Mage, taking his arm in a clasp of friendship.

"Your Highness. I was in the vicinity. It's good to hear your voice."

"Likewise."

The Admiral sighed. Raven sensed that he was tired and concerned about something.

"What brings you to port?"

"Let's have a drink and I'll tell you all about it. In private."

A servant provided them both with wine, before quietly departing. Raven immediately raised the spell that kept them from being overheard. The air around them went flat and a slight echo hung on every word, signifying that it was working.

"My Ship needed resupplying," Pendragon began, once they were both settled. "Plus, I wanted to check out the reports of Fae activity. They worry me."

"Me too," Raven replied, sipping the wine. It was uncommonly good. "There's something coming. I can feel it in my bones."

Pendragon shifted in his seat.

"Damn it to Hades! I was hoping that you would tell me it was nothing of consequence."

"Alas, no. Senator Rufus, Albanus, Favonius and I discussed this only two days ago."

"So I heard. I only arrived this morning. Had a trip to the baths, then came straight here. Londin is alive with gossip. Have you any more information?"

"All available Agents are looking into it," Raven replied.

Pendragon hissed through his teeth.

"Why do I feel that we're on the back foot with this one? And why now? There have been rumblings for the past few hundred years, but nothing of any consequence. Thank the Gods we still have Excalibur. I only hope that my nephew knows what to do with it, other than treat it as a fashion accessory."

Raven waved a hand.

"Perhaps the Fae think we've forgotten them? There's a new, untried King, discontent in the Senate and an Empire barely hanging on by its fingernails. They must think they have a chance to return to their old lands."

"I'm even petitioning the Gods for guidance. They surely don't want to see their worship overthrown."

"If the Empire falls, people will turn to the old ways," Raven said. "The native Gods will gain ascendancy once more and some of them are ambivalent, at best. Linking their worship with other, imported deities has kept them contented and, more importantly, in check. I dread to think what would happen if the ancient ways were to return."

"We'd have a hard time beating off the barbarians, for a start. The treaty with the Alliance would never survive and they're always hungry for more land."

"It would impact on the New Continent, too. We can't abandon our people there."

Pendragon rubbed his hand over his face.

"And we won't. I'm taking the *Augusta* on patrol to the west and reinforcing our line of defence."

"You're not staying here? Some would argue that Albanus has too much influence over the King and we all know he wants your job."

"Oh, I know that. That's why I have several food tasters."

Raven's eyebrows shot up.

"Is it as bad as that?"

"Getting there. I can't prove it, but I know that Albanus has links with some highly dubious organisations. Ever heard of the Heirs of Albion?"

"The ones always banging on about Britannia's ancient past, when everyone ran around covered in woad, bare-arsed naked and waving spears at every opportunity?"

Pendragon chuckled.

"Our ancestors weren't *that* primitive. It's just these extremists. No, I don't think that they're just harmless cranks, but I need proof."

"It's a pity you can't just get rid of Albanus."

"It would de-stabilise the situation further."

Raven grunted.

"In the meantime, I'm here and will do what I can," Pendragon continued. "Any news on the new Ship?"

"Not yet. I'm expecting her to emerge any time now, but the Mother is silent. It seems to be taking longer than usual."

A worm of disquiet writhed briefly in his belly as he spoke.

"They're all different."

"True."

"And we need every one of them. There are new vessels being built as I speak and I'd hate to have them rigged for manual."

"Move some older Ships."

"It's probably the only option, unless we can find more candidates. We're fighting a losing battle against the temples and they have more descendants with Potentia anyway."

"It's a pity we can't use boys."

Pendragon was startled. "We never have before. I assumed it was some requirement of the process? There aren't any female Mages."

Raven cocked his head.

"There used to be. The Romans changed that after the Boudiccan Revolt."

"I never knew that."

"It's not taught in schools."

"Hmm. Worth looking into – the boys aspect, though I don't know how the Navy as a whole would react. Don't be expecting any talented girls to start training as Mages, though, not with the shortage of Ships."

"Bullfinch and his lackeys at the Collegium wouldn't accept them, anyway."

Pendragon's head turned as he glanced out the window, to where his great Flagship was moored. His yearning was almost palpable.

"Your Highness, we need a politician now, just as much as a Lord High Admiral."

Pendragon was silent for a few moments.

"I know and I hate it. It was all so much simpler when Father and Julius were alive. I fear that my nephew is a man of very little sense and my son even less. Even the older Knights can't prevail upon the King to slow down. I put forward a list of potential Captains for the new Ship, you know. His Majesty pretended to look at it, but I believe he's already made up his mind. I expect it will be one of his inner circle."

Raven was shocked.

"Surely not? She's barely finished basic training and will need an experienced commander." He paused.

"I don't suppose that you -"

"Out of the question. I must stay with the *Augusta*. I can't entrust her to anyone else."

Raven raised a questioning eyebrow.

"She's old and she needs me," Pendragon said firmly. "I can't abandon her now."

"Maybe you can talk some sense into His Majesty? Surely Albanus doesn't approve?"

"You can be sure that it'll be one of his protégés who gets the job." Pendragon sounded bitter. "The young fool will probably run her aground or sink her before the year is out."

"I thought you had the final say?"

"She's going to be Royal, so no. It's the King's perquisite. I doubt he'll take my advice, not with that toad whispering in his ear. My only consolation is that you'll be aboard to mitigate the worst of it."

"I'll do my best. All this and Fae as well. It never rains, eh?"

"Rain I can cope with. It's the force ten storms that cause us to wreck."

The Admiral waved at the piles of papers neatly stacked on his desk.

"To tell the truth, I'd prefer a gale than this stuff, but needs must. I swear that the clerks save it up for me on purpose. It's a good job there are some I trust, or I'd have to read them all myself, for fear of signing something I shouldn't."

"How is the Prince?"

"Enjoying himself with his cousin. It's an endless round of feasts and merriment, when they're not hunting. You know that I wanted him to enter the army for real?"

"Not the Navy?"

"I tried that first. He flatly refused and the King backed him up. To tell the truth, I'm not sure he's fit for public office. He's honorary head of this and that, but he doesn't actually do anything except parade around in fancy uniforms. It's a blasted shame that Julia wasn't born male. She's got more brains in her head than either of them, but it's likely that she'll end up married off to old Parisius."

Raven nodded.

"What a waste."

"It's politically expedient."

"Even so."

"It's hard to break tradition. Male Ships? A radical notion."

"I'm full of them," Raven said, drily.

"That's ironic," Pendragon told him.

"Just because I'm ancient doesn't mean I can't embrace the future."

"I always hoped that things would improve," Pendragon said wistfully. "New devices, new lands, the world expanding before our eyes, in all its glory. Now I fear it will all come crashing down, just as it's beginning."

"It will be as the Fates decree," Raven said. "Things go in cycles. Britannia is stronger than ever and I've no doubt that we'll get to the bottom of this incursion. Our best Agents are working on it even now. Artorius will grow up, given time. Trade is flourishing and the Navy is expanding. Plus, I'll be here if you need me."

Pendragon smiled at him.

"You're the one constant in an ever-changing world, my old friend."

"Aren't I just?" the Master Mage replied. "How long are you here for?"

Pendragon thought for a moment.

"I want to be gone in a fortnight. We'll make our way out west, before returning to ferry diplomats down to southern Gaul to discuss the marriage. Parisius prefers the south these days because of the warmth and I don't blame him."

"Enjoy the weather. I hope you're still here for the installation."

"I hope so too. I met the young lady some years back, when she was at the Academy. As I recall, she was covered in paint and glitter. Albanus' daughter was with her."

"The *Regina*?"

"Yes. Her Captain's another of Albanus' acolytes, though I have to admit that Silvius knows his stuff."

Pendragon grimaced.

"I have the feeling that I'm being outmanoeuvred. Soon, there'll be remarks like 'isn't it time you retired, Your Highness?', along with suggestions that I be pensioned off to a villa in the country. Over my dead body!"

His eyes glittered fiercely and Raven was reminded of his warrior forebears. Cei would have made an excellent King, though he would have continually pined for the sea.

"Let me know if I can aid you in any way," he offered.

"Thank you. Keep me informed. I can trust the information you give me, unlike some others."

"I will. Give my fondest regards to the *Augusta* when you next see her."

"See her? I'm still living aboard her. Best berth in Londin!"

Raven nodded, unsurprised. They were a devoted couple, though nobody could be sure for how much longer. He had the feeling that they would carry Pendragon out feet first before he would relinquish his command.

It was time to break the spell and go about his business. The Master Mage had enquiries to make and he didn't dare delay further. His first call would be to Matrona, to see if she knew what was causing the delay. Maia should have been out by now.

He couldn't shake the feeling that something was very wrong.

XII

He was right; Matrona was worried. Raven had known her too long to be fooled by her outward calm and wasted no time in telling her so.

"Helena. There must be something we can do to help!"

She shook her head, her face set.

"It's in the Mother's hands now."

"But you must admit that it's taking too long?"

He could hear the hesitation in her voice.

"Possibly. Everyone is different, as are the demands of the test."

"Oh, come on! You aren't telling me that that empty-headed madam Tullia could pass something that Maia couldn't?"

"The test is different for each candidate," Matrona said, stiffly.

Raven pursed his lips in frustration.

"What does Ceridwen say?"

She sighed. "I haven't asked her. What will be, will be and there's no use making a fuss about it."

"This is not a fuss! It's a legitimate concern and it's better that you deal with me than Pendragon and the Board."

He could feel his anxiety ratcheting up by several notches, not helped by Matrona's evasion.

"And I'll say to them what I'm saying to you. Some candidates are lost. We just have to accept it."

Her voice broke and he could sense that she was trying to hold back tears.

"Did you have any inkling that this might happen?" he demanded, determined to extract every last drop of information, even though he knew that he was being cruel. Helena would be wanting Maia to succeed as much as anyone.

"None. She was bright and determined. Oh, I suspect that being a Ship wouldn't have been her first choice. I know that something happened in Londin and the Gods are involved somehow, but there was no reason to believe she would fail."

Raven mulled this over. As far as he knew, only the five of them, he, Aquila, Vibia, Pendragon and Maia herself knew the details of her Divine heritage and the High Priest and Priestess of Jupiter and Juno respectively wouldn't have let this information slip to anyone.

There had to be a reason.

"Look, I know they have to pass three tests. What determines the criteria?"

"That is a –"

"Mystery, yes, I know. Is it imposed from outside, or drawn forth from within them?"

"I can't tell you. I wish I could, but it's out of my hands."

He knew she was glaring at him, teeth gritted, but it was probable that she was physically unable to speak of it, bound by her oath of obedience.

Raven's brain worked furiously.

"Then I'll have to ask someone who can."

He'd already used Potentia to get to Portus. Now he would use it to get to the heart of the matter.

"Tell Ceridwen I'm on my way. I'll meet her in the usual place."

*

Raven stepped out of the portal and into the deceptive peace of the Great Forest.

Late afternoon sun slanted through bare branches that would soon be clothed with the first growth of the new season and a faint warmth spoke of the promise of summer days to come, but there was still a breath of cold in the glade, as if winter was reluctant to ease its grip.

"Master Mage."

Ceridwen was waiting for him, seated on a fallen trunk, her face half-shadowed by her hood.

"Thank you for agreeing to this meeting," he said, trying to be diplomatic.

"You gave me little choice."

"I need to know what's happening."

He heard her intake of breath.

"The Mother is judging her."

"How? Surely she is worthy?"

He concentrated his sightsense to its full extent. He needed all the advantages it would give him right now.

"It is not for us to say. The Mother spoke to her though me, but I don't know what she said. I admit that I thought it might be harder for her than for those who have had an easier life, but it shouldn't have been a problem. She was strong."

The Master Mage frowned at the past tense.

"So, you believe she's definitely lost to us?"

"It seems that way. I know that she passed the first two tests. The final one must have been too much for her."

"Why?"

Ceridwen shook her head.

"I don't know."

"What are they based on?"

"The scenarios are drawn from their own experiences, hopes and dreams," she said, reluctantly. "If all goes well, the candidates realise that they are dreaming and pass through. I told her to keep going, no matter what."

"She's survived many terrible events in her life," Raven said thoughtfully. "She almost got used to them."

An idea suddenly struck him. If he was right, it would be a cruel irony indeed.

"You said that they are shown their *hopes* and dreams?"

Ceridwen nodded.

"There are many kinds of dreams."

"Indeed."

"Could her strength have been a liability?"

"What do you mean?"

"She has gifts; her wonderful memory, for one. Could it be working against her?"

He sensed her sifting through the possibilities.

"Faultless memory. Yes, that could be a problem. The world thus created would seem more real."

"And one that she might not choose to leave?"

The Priestess nodded.

"It's easier to trap flies with honey than vinegar."

His heart sank. Could it be that she'd created a perfect world for herself? If that was the case, why would she ever want to leave it?"

He came to a decision.

"Thank you for your aid, Lady. I'll take it from here."

The Priestess's head jerked back, like a startled horse.

"You can't interfere!"

Raven raised an eyebrow.

"Really? I'm sure something terrible will happen to me."

"Don't make light of this!" Ceridwen hissed. "There will be a price!"

"There's always a price. I'll pay it."

"Whether you succeed, or not."

"Just so."

"You don't care, do you?" she asked him, curiosity in her voice.

"Not really," he admitted. "It's been years since I did anything really useful."

He heard her sigh.

"You know I can't stop you. If you must, you must, but don't say I didn't warn you. Just don't do it here."

"I wouldn't dream of it."

He'd need to be on home ground to do what he was thinking and he had to act immediately if he was to be in time.

He turned to go, but Ceridwen caught his sleeve.

"Tell me, Raven. How is my son?"

"Serving his country and his people. He's a good man."

"Do you think he'll ever forgive us?"

"I hope so, eventually."

A pang shot through him. The pain in her voice was palpable, even though she'd known that she could never keep the child.

"Watch over him. Please."

"I'll do my best."

As he left, he reflected on the fact that he'd made two women cry in the space of an hour. That had to be some sort of record, even for him.

*

The Master Mage reached his destination just before sunset. Away, to the west, the clouds were tinged with red and gold, parading in a final display as if to defy the fall of night. The shadowed land beneath lay blanketed under a soft cloud of gathering mist.

The hilltop was bare, the grass worn in patches by the tread of many feet over the ages. A ring of stones thrust through the earth like broken teeth, silent and waiting.

This was the place. This was home ground.

He had brought everything he would need in a large cloth bag, which he emptied on to the earth. Twigs to start a fire. A bowl and a knife. An item of clothing. And one more thing, which he handled reverently. This would be the last.

It was time. Here, on the line between the light and the dark, was where he would make his stand.

Raven bent over and removed his boots. If this was to work, nothing could be permitted to come between him and the elements. His robes and undershirt followed, until he stood, naked in the evening light, his withered body exposed to the last rays of the sun.

He was surrounded by air. Earth lay at his feet and beneath that, he could sense the movement of the water, flowing deep underground to emerge in the sacred pool at the base of the hill. All he needed now was fire. He arranged the twigs carefully on the central stone, making sure that they were lodged securely in the shallow central depression and waited.

The sun disappeared.

A gesture, and little flames burst into life, licking at the sticks and giving off curls of blue smoke that rose lazily into the darkening sky. Raven could feel the faint warmth through the thick layers of scarring on his ravaged skin.

Now for the ritual. He had to break through the barriers that surrounded Maia and make contact. If he failed, she would be trapped like a fly suspended in amber inside a world of her own making. He picked up Maia's nightgown and, picturing her clearly in his mind, dropped it onto the fire.

That was for her body.

He Sent out another mental call, as strong as he could, then groped for the necklace she had given him. The little pearls and gems glittered in the firelight; her most prized possession, given in love and cherished in return.

That was for her spirit.

Now to forge the link between them.

He placed the bowl on the stone, took the knife and placed his left hand on the hard surface, before balancing the blade over the topmost joint of his little finger and slamming it down.

Pain shot through his hand, but it wasn't the worst he'd ever had.

He took the flesh and bone, holding his dripping finger over the bowl, then dropped the necklace and finger joint within.

Raven tipped the bloody contents into the fire and hurled his will out into the darkness.

*

"Quin!"

Her husband was home. She flew into his arms, kissing him, despite the fact that this wasn't how noble ladies were supposed to behave. He laughed uproariously, his blue eyes sparkling.

"It's nice to be wanted! Now, let me get my coat off and I'll tell you what I've been up to."

They went through into the parlour.

"How was the court?"

"Boring without you. You must come some time."

"I will," she promised, "when Lucius is old enough to be left. I don't want to expose him to Londin air."

He pulled a face at her.

"Yes, it's getting worse, as is the stink. What would you say if I told you I'd bought one of the new steam carriages? We can go for rides around the estate."

For a brief second, she smelt oily steam and heard excited shouting in the dark, then she shook her head and the image melted away.

"As long as it doesn't cause any damage to the grounds. Those things are heavy."

If he'd noticed her momentary abstraction, he didn't say anything.

"I know how to operate one. I can teach Lucius, when he's ready."

"For heaven's sake," she said in mock reproof. "He isn't even one year old yet!"

"So? It's good to make plans. Maybe he'll have a baby brother or sister to show off to?"

She blushed.

"Who knows?"

"Oh, I nearly forgot. I bought you a present."

She sat upright, eager to see what it was."

"You look like Hector when he smells a biscuit," he remarked.

The wolfhound, sprawled on the rug, raised his head at the sound of his name.

"How very flattering of you, my dear husband! Now you'll have to provide the said biscuit, or our puppy won't be speaking to you."

"You first."

She took the little parcel eagerly. It was tied with a blue silk ribbon and she undid it carefully.

Inside the little velvet box was a string of pearls, alternated with lustrous gems.

She stared at it.

"Don't you like it?" he asked, plaintively.

"I love it," she whispered.

She ran them through her fingers, feeling the smoothness of the pearls. One hand went to her throat.

"My love, why are you crying? What have I done?"

He was distraught. She smiled at him through the tears.

"They're wonderful! They just remind me of…"

A seagull's cry, a city by the sea, a girl with dark, curly hair and kind, patient eyes. She gasped as the images threatened to overwhelm her.

<Maia!>

Who was calling to her? It had to be her husband, but he never called her Maia.

A shadow in the corner of the room grew and flowed into the shape of an ancient man, dressed in Mage's robes. Her eyes widened at the sight of the apparition, as she groped for his name.

<Maia! Wake up! It's not real! Remember!>

Fear is not the only enemy. There'd been an older woman, hair streaked with white, but the words had come from another.

I give you fire and mind! Remember! A blue eye set in a rotted wooden face thrust into her own, as searing flames engulfed her skin.

Pain lanced through her as she stood, watching helplessly as the flesh began to char on her bones, the fat sizzling like an overcooked roast as her body twisted and shrank. She tried to scream a denial, but she was voiceless as the fire tore through her like a savage beast, destroying as it went. The fine clothes turned to black ash, even as her beautiful necklace crumbled into dust that streamed in glittering motes through her fingers.

Everything around her crumpled and tore like sodden paper. The last thing she saw was Quintilian's face before he, too, was sucked away into a black void.

Heat engulfed her and she fell.

*

The fire was out.

Raven stood trembling, tears running down his wrinkled cheeks. In just a few moments, he'd seen through Maia's eyes and knew how she'd been caught. Ceridwen had been right. There would be a price to pay.

For both of them.

*

Maia came to slowly, lying on cold, damp leaves in the dark. Her mind churned and bubbled like a boiling cauldron as she sifted fantasy from reality and found the latter wanting. She was back in the forest and dressed once more in her candidate's robe. A few, faint stars shone through the trees as she stared upwards, barely able to make out the branches against the night sky. Hot tears of shock ran down her cheeks, to soak her ears and neck.

It had all been a dream. A wonderful, impossible dream of love, comfort and happiness such as she'd never known. And now it was gone.

She raised her hands, staring at the puckered scars and the stiffened fingers. There was no more Lady Gemma Valeria, only Maia Abella the Ship-in-training, never to be a wife or a mother, bound to serve and obey on the high seas as the nation demanded.

If she survived this.

The dream was fading already. She clutched at it, trying desperately to hold it close, but it vanished to wisps and faded images that whirled away into the dark.

She shivered and sat up. It was freezing. Maia had no idea how long she'd been lying insensible on the ground, but it was enough to have leached all the heat from her bones. She wished that she had the means to make a fire and warm herself, but she had no hope of that in this place, even if she could find some dry wood.

Get up and move, she told herself. If she stayed like this she probably wouldn't see morning.

Her body ached as she dragged herself to her feet and stood, trying to rub some warmth into her arms and legs whilst she got her bearings.

Trees and more trees, black shadows in the night.

Maia had no clue as to direction, or even what time it was. Had just one night passed, or many? She could remember the other dreams she'd had, with the Ships and being back in Blandina's house. Every part of them had felt real at first, but she'd got through them. Until the last one.

She stifled a sob and began to walk, picking up her feet so they wouldn't be snagged by roots or stones and wiping her face on her sleeve. She'd be damned if she died here. Maybe she could find somewhere to shelter from the cold until sunrise? Anything would do – a hollow tree, a cave, or a thicket? Perhaps she could find a hut, if anyone lived here. She couldn't see any lights through the trees, or any signs of human habitation. It was as still as the grave.

Over to her left, an owl hooted, to be answered by another further off, a mournful sound, but at least a sign that she wasn't completely alone. They would be hunting, calling to each other. Perhaps they were mates.

She sobbed again as Quintilian's face rose before her. He'd been so real and he'd been hers. She'd have been happy to stay with him, free of care, with her little family. It had all been so perfect. Sudden rage filled her as she thought of how she'd been dragged away. So what if it hadn't been real? It had been good enough for her and then Raven had appeared and destroyed everything. Part of her knew that she wasn't being reasonable, but the rest of her didn't care.

A tiny rustling made her prick up her ears, already sensitive to the slightest noise. It sounded like a little animal in the leaf litter; nothing threatening, just a creature moving through the forest. She ignored it at first, but it seemed to keep pace with her, moving as she moved.

"What's there?" she said, her voice harsh.

The rustling stopped and a soft glow began to flicker high up against the trunk of the nearest tree, like an errant candle flame dancing in a draught. As she watched apprehensively, it grew in brightness, illuminating the patch of forest around it. Maia thought she could just make out a minute shape inside it. A tiny face peered back at her and she sensed its curiosity.

Movement at her feet made her jump back, startled. She looked down, to see a familiar figure, dressed in brown leaves. It was like the sprite she'd seen in the wood, the one she'd shared her food with. For all she knew, it was the same one.

"Lost, are you?" it squeaked. It sounded like she imagined a mouse would sound if it had the power of human speech.

"Yes."

It seemed to consider that for a moment, while the other sprite drifted closer to join its fellow, the light changing to a blue radiance that diffused through the whole area.

"Got any more food?"

"No, I'm sorry," she said. So it was the same one.

"It was worth asking. Where're you going?"

"I don't know," Maia admitted. "Are there any other humans around here? Women?"

"Oh. Them."

The tiny creature sniffed.

"You can't go back there. You're here now and it's not there."

"I don't understand."

"You left there and now you're here, where we live. We go there sometimes, but not too often." He smacked his tiny lips. "Good food."

"How do I get back?"

He cocked his head and regarded her thoughtfully.

"There's a gap. We slip through it, but I don't know if you'll fit."

"I can try," she said, hopefully. Part of her wondered if this was another dream. If so, she could wish for a better one.

"I can show you –"

He broke off abruptly. The blue light blinked off.

"What it is?" Maia asked.

"No time! My friend says it's coming! Run!"

The leaf sprite vanished, leaving her alone.

"No, come back!" she called desperately, but they were gone, sucked back into the trees.

She turned on the spot, trying to make out where they went, but the forest was silent. What had he meant? She hugged herself, more afraid than she'd ever been, cursing Raven for pulling her out of the dream and Jupiter for condemning her to go through this. Let the King of Olympus strike her dead – she was past caring.

Maia picked a direction and started walking once more, forcing her frozen feet to keep moving. Gradually, she became aware of an ominous crashing and snapping in the undergrowth to her left, as if something large and bulky was moving to intersect her path. It was getting louder.

A stab of fear shot through her. Maia began to run.

*

The bleeding had stopped almost immediately, not that he had much blood left in him anymore. He was as dried-up as an ancient stick, cracked and brittle with any sap long since vanished over the years. He could have chosen to do away with the pain entirely, but some part of him clung to it out of sheer obstinacy. It was better to feel something than nothing at all. The stump of his finger throbbed inside his sleeve, but it had been worth the price.

Now he was standing in the Londin Forum, watching through his sightsense as the mass of humanity swarmed all around, flowing to either side of him as if he were one of the statues on their plinths. Part of him certainly felt as old and totemic. He sighed. It was ridiculous to stand here all day feeling sorry for himself, but the question was which Goddess should he choose?

Juno was the obvious choice. She'd already shown herself to be favourable towards Maia and had interceded for her with her husband, the normally implacable Jupiter. Perhaps she would help him now?

Or maybe she couldn't be seen to be involved too much?

He ran through the other options. Ceres, the Goddess of the Earth, was another possibility. She was closer to the one that Ceridwen and Matrona worshipped and would surely have more sway. After all, when she was upset or angry, nothing grew, including crops and trees. Then there was Isis, the Mother Goddess of Aegyptus and skilled in magic. Maia had been rescued by an avatar of the crocodile God Sobek and both featured prominently in her grandmother Valerius' tomb. They might listen to his pleas for aid. Then again, she was here, in Britannia, where different powers ruled.

He gripped his staff and offered up a silent prayer to nobody in particular.

"You're in the way, old man."

The flower seller was squatting at the base of the steps leading up to the Basilica, where the Government Offices were housed. She was swathed in a multitude of layers that made her look like a particularly unappetising cloth-wrapped pudding with a head poking out. A battered felt hat, sporting an assortment of motley feathers, was perched on her straggling white curls.

"You'll get run over by one of them new engine things, mark my words!" she cackled. "Squashed flat you'll be, like a sheet in a mangle!"

Raven checked his surroundings. There were indeed a couple of the infernal devices, but they were on the other side of the Forum and posed no immediate danger.

"Is it a warning, madam, or simply a wish?" he riposted.

She grinned at him, her face like an apple left to dry over winter.

"Hah! Saw it happen once, I did. I tell everyone now. They'll crush the life out of anything, so they will, nasty, clanking devices! What're you doing then, Master Mage?"

Raven leaned on his staff.

"I'm just debating which Mother to petition."

The old woman sucked her remaining teeth noisily.

"Hmm. Depends what you're wanting. Me, I reckon you can't go wrong with the Triple Goddess. You've got everything covered then, maid, mother and crone."

"Good advice," he said.

"Of course there's only so much you can do when they fall out amongst themselves," she continued, idly selecting a posy from her basket and offering it to a young man. A coin was exchanged and tucked away in the copious folds of her skirts.

Raven felt a chill crawl up his back.

"And why would they do that, Mother?" he asked her carefully.

"The older ones want one thing, youngest wants another. You know what children are like, don't you? Always think they know everything. Full of bile and spite, she is, because her friend had better things to do than run around after her. Revenge, she calls it. A temper tantrum, that's what it is."

"But people have died."

"Aye."

The old woman looked sad.

"That's what happens when powers are thrown around like coins in the street. They're bound to hit someone."

"Can the Huntress be turned away?"

He felt her eyes boring into him, dark and full of secrets.

"That's not your job, my lad. You've done quite enough, believe me. Others are involved now. Oh, make your sacrifice by all means, but all you can do is pick up the pieces afterwards."

Raven bowed to give her what coin he had in his purse. This close to her he could smell the scent of winter cold, together with the faintest hint of decay, as of life returning to the body of the earth. The feathers on her hat fluttered like a startled bird as she took the money, giving him a posy in return.

"Your offering is accepted."

A harsh cawing made him look upwards. When he turned back, the woman was chatting to a passer-by, her voice light and ordinary.

She wasn't old at all.

He tucked the flowers in his pocket and made his way to the Temple of Juno. It wouldn't hurt to burn a small pinch of incense and, at the moment, he thought in frustration, there wasn't anything else he could do.

*

The bleak moor stretched out before him as far as Milo could see, its edges softened by the curtain of drizzle that was steadily working its way through his outer layers. In summer it might have been a pleasant sight, but now, on a spring day with the daylight fading fast and the cold seeping into his bones, all Milo wanted was to find shelter for the night.

He huddled into his coat collar, quietly cursing the orders that had brought him to this Godsforsaken place in the far south west of the land; ancient Kernow where civilised men preferred not to tread, unless, like him they had business in these parts. They had their own ways down here and only paid lip service to the King in distant Londin, having more in common with their Gallic neighbours across the sea than the eastern tribes. It was a good job that he remembered what passed for Britannic down here, as hardly anyone seemed to speak Latin, or, if they did, they wouldn't admit to it unless they really had to.

He checked his bearings. It was further than he liked to reach a warm hearth and it wasn't fair on his horse either. He'd already driven the gelding harder than was ideal and both of them would be extremely grateful when they got out of this desolate place. Milo knew he was on the right road. He'd left Isca two days before, on the trail of an elusive and illegal arms smuggling gang who were suspected of dealing with the Separatists, or anyone else with the money to pay them. They'd covered their tracks well, but the merchandise had come in by vessel from the west and so he was heading for the mouth of the River Fal by way of the top roads. The more he found out, the more he realised that this was no disorganised bunch of crackpot fanatics, but a well-organised group with some serious financial backing.

Milo dismounted in the lee of a great pile of rocks that gave a little respite from the damp. His horse snorted and shook out its mane, casting a reproachful eye on its rider.

"I know Fido," his master told him. "Life isn't fair, is it?"

A fire was out of the question, but he put a nosebag on Fido and pulled out some bread, meat and cheese for himself. It wouldn't do either of them any good to starve. Man and horse ate whilst the drizzle turned into a heavier rain that would do an even better job of soaking him through. He reckoned that he still had about three hours of daylight left, but after that they would be in trouble if he hadn't found them somewhere to stay. A local had told him of an old, isolated inn where he would be sure of a bed for the night and a hot meal; The Carib Inn – named for the trade with the New Continent. It was surely not too far distant.

He finished the last bite of his roll, wiped his hands on his coat and removed Fido's nosebag. The horse didn't look too happy to be on the move again, but it wasn't as if they had much choice. He patted the wet brown neck.

"Come on, lad. Not far to a warm stable now."

Milo swung himself up in the saddle and they headed off again. The mist was growing thicker now, not a good sign, but the road would be easy enough to follow as long as they were careful. Thank the Gods for Roman engineering.

Behind him, in the deepening gloom, a great hound bayed. It was quickly joined by others, as if a pack were at work. A hunt, at this time of year? Milo glanced around, but could see nothing in the murk. Fido quickened his pace and laid his ears flat. His horse definitely sensed something and he wasn't at all happy about it.

Milo urged him on, hoping that they would meet another traveller, or even the huntsmen themselves, but he was completely alone. The harsh yelping began again, closer now, the sound of excited animals scenting a quarry. Milo's gut sounded a warning. His horse was tired and anyway couldn't outrun dogs. He pounded along the roadway, searching for anything he could use as cover. He needed to get his back up against something to give himself a fighting chance. He had pistols and some of his fire spells, so he could hold the creatures off if he had to, though he didn't give much for Fido's chances.

The gelding was galloping flat out now, his mouth foaming as he fled in panic, but the dogs were getting closer and, from the sound of them, spreading out around him to cut off any escape. He made his decision, chose the piece of ground that looked the softest and launched himself into space.

He hit the verge, a tussock of grass breaking his fall. Fido vanished into the rain, the hoof beats becoming fainter as he galloped for his life. Milo rolled into the ditch, grunting as a hard pistol butt dug into his stomach. That would leave a bruise, but at least he wasn't winded, nothing was broken and he had some cover. He lay full length, heedless of the sodden ground and peered through the coarse vegetation to spy his pursuers. Black shapes streaked across the moor, at least six of them, as big as calves, their effortless lope rapidly closing the distance. Milo squinted through the rain to get a better look and his blood froze in his veins.

They had no heads. Tongues of pale blue flame flickered from their necks, casting an eerie light over the landscape.

Black Dogs. They could be found all over Britannia in one form or another, haunting boundaries and bedevilling travellers late at night. Some were helpful, but they were mostly solitary. He'd never heard of them travelling in packs before, unless they were part of the Wild Hunt, but he couldn't see or hear any horsemen. His pistols would be no use at all. He thought quickly; had they been summoned by an enemy? He could have been betrayed, his mission leaked to unfriendly ears, but in that case why call up these daemons when a musket ball or a knife in the back would have sufficed? It didn't make any sense.

The creatures slackened their pace and advanced, growling in low rumbles that made his hair stand on end. He wondered how they could make noise when they had no heads and dismissed the thought, knowing that he had to concentrate and calm himself. Perhaps he could reason with them? There was no sign of a huntsman, but something had to be controlling them. He drew back his hand to throw a fire spell; something Raven had taught him many years before.

His Potentia and wits were all he had left.

The dogs crept closer, low to the ground, more like big cats than dogs, muscles rippling under rough shaggy coats that dripped with moisture. Their paws were the size of dinner plates and noiseless on the spongy ground. He wondered that they didn't seem inclined to tear him apart immediately and launched a spell which flew through the air with a sharp crack, only to fall sizzling into a brackish puddle. The dog it was aimed at seemed quite unperturbed, continuing to crawl in his direction. He couldn't decide which was worse, the stealthy padding or the fact that it had no head. What was it going to do, without teeth to rend? He came to a decision.

He stood up and glared at them.

"What do you want?" he demanded. "I'm soaked through, exhausted and totally pissed off. If you want a chase, find one elsewhere!"

To his surprise, the dogs hesitated, as if uncertain.

"Well?" he shouted. "Come on, if you think you're tough enough!"

The lead dog promptly stretched, then flopped down on the ground. The others followed suit. Milo stared at them in disbelief before turning his back on them and marching off. If they attacked him, so be it. He just wasn't in the mood and headless daemon dogs weren't the worst thing he'd ever seen. May be one day he'd be chased by something more ordinary.

He intended to make for the road, but found his way blocked by two of the dogs, so he switched direction, heading out across the moor. They moved out of his way whilst keeping pace parallel to his path. Wonderful. They were going to watch as he drowned in a bog or died of exposure. Milo decided to ignore them and pressed on. The damned moor wouldn't last for ever; there had to be paths somewhere and at least the ground was sloping slightly downhill. Sure enough, he found a narrow trail through the heather and trudged along it, the dogs padding along on either side like an infernal escort. Ahead of him he could see a depression in the hills, filled with water. A small pool or tarn, treeless and silent. He marched up to its edge, gazing out at the flat expanse and searching in vain for any signs of life. The hounds paused behind him, flames lowered as if sniffing the ground with non-existent noses. Six tails wagged in unison, happy about something.

If he hadn't been so exhausted, Milo would have laughed. He walked along the banks, sensing the otherworldly nature of the water, as if the veil between worlds was thinner here. The back of his neck prickled – there was an ancient power in this place. He could feel it beneath his feet and hovering within the flat, mirrored surface of the pool. As he walked along the bank, his foot struck something protruding from the peaty mud at the water's edge. It looked like a pitted and blackened stick, long abandoned and forgotten. He grasped it firmly and pulled it forth. It might have some use as a weapon.

It was only when he held it up that he realised that it was the remains of a sword.

The hilt was functional, styled like an old Roman gladius with hints of gold wire still glinting faintly on the hilt, probably from some unfortunate legionary who had come to grief long ago, or cast in as an offering to whatever dwelt here. He checked it over, keeping one eye on his companions. It wasn't broken or damaged, apart from the heavily pitted and blackened blade where the iron had been eaten away. It probably wouldn't be much good in a fight, he thought regretfully, raising his arm to throw it back.

The hounds growled menacingly. He lowered his arm.

"You brought me here for…this?"

The blue flames flickered.

"It's a piece of rusty crap."

The dogs regarded him steadily, their lack of eyes notwithstanding.

He examined it closely. An old sword. Big deal. A thought struck him and he wondered if it held magic. It didn't feel like it had any at all. There were magical swords, gifts of the Gods, but they were either returned, or held under lock and key. Arthur's sword, Excalibur, was held safely in Londin and trotted out for each coronation, or when the King wanted to impress people. This one had the feel of something that had been used; more workmanlike somehow, as if it had been a proper soldier's weapon in its day.

"All right!" he said aloud. "I'll keep it with me. What do you want me to do with it?"

Even as he spoke, the hounds rose and sped away, black outlines that faded into the mist and were gone.

"Oh for the Gods' sake!" Milo shouted after them. He was left alone in the middle of a wasteland, soaked through and charged to carry a useless old relic, with no idea why.

Sometimes he just hated his life.

Just then, the mist began to rise and he thought he could make out a road in the distance. That meant people and wayside inns. He shoved the old sword through his belt, fearing to throw it away in case the dogs came back and trudged off towards civilisation.

Maybe he could strip the gold wire off it and sell it as a curiosity later.

XIII

Her pursuer was gaining on her. Maia could hear branches cracking as it ripped its way through the forest.

She was panting now, breathing harshly through burning lungs as she struggled to suck in enough air to keep her aching muscles going. There was no way she could outrun whatever it was and she was terrified of smashing her head open on a low branch, even though moonlight had begun to filter through the tangle of woodland growth.

Tears of fear and frustration dripped off her chin as she forced herself to stop and take stock. Maybe it would be a good move to climb a tree?

One gnarled old oak had a branch she could reach, so she tucked the skirts of her robe into her belt and jumped as best she could, grabbing on to it then scrabbling with her feet until she managed to haul herself over it and get her knees up. She reached for the next one, scraping her hands on the rough bark.

She'd got three branches up when they appeared.

There seemed to be several creatures. Pairs of dull red eyes came slowly into view, smouldering like banked coals and weaving and bobbing in a strangely sinuous motion. Maia strained her eyes to see them more clearly, then realised that she had to get higher. Heedless of the pain from scratches and scrapes, she climbed upwards, praying that it would be enough.

Beneath her, the things hissed like a tank full of snakes. She risked a quick look below over her shoulder, just as the rising moon illuminated her pursuer.

The monster reared up, balancing itself on a thick, muscular body that ended in a pointed tail. Scaly skin shimmered in the light, gleaming like polished metal wherever it touched, while the rest lay heaped in shadowy coils. It had several heads, sprouting from the body like individual snakes with jaws agape to display deadly fangs.

A hydra. One of Echidna's offspring. The Mother of Monsters was dead, but some of her progeny lived on.

It hissed again and Maia nearly choked on the stink it exuded. Some sort of deadly gas? She pulled the collar of her robe up over her nose and mouth, already feeling faint. She'd never seen one of the creatures, but sometimes small ones were caught and displayed in the arena.

She'd gone as far as she could. The hydra writhed in frustration, striking rapidly over and over as high as it could, which wasn't quite enough to reach her. Thwarted in its desire to tear her to bits, it subsided, hissing softly, its luminous eyes remaining glued to her position. Stalemate. It couldn't get to her and she couldn't escape. Maia supposed that she would need to eat before it did. All it had to do was wait.

Suddenly, warm orange torchlight flooded through the trees and hope rose in Maia's heart. Fire meant mortals. Perhaps it was men who could kill the creature, or the Priestesses, realising that she needed help at last? She squinted against the bright light, trying to make out who was coming.

A slender figure stepped delicately out of the trees, holding the torch above her head. She was clad in a tunic that ended above her knee and was shod in leather boots that moulded to her calves. Two dark shapes padded alongside her like flowing shadows. Maia could just make out the silver bow and the quiver of arrows slung across her back.

Diana bent and stabbed the torch into the ground. The hydra's eight heads whipped around to fix on her, but the Goddess ignored it. She stood, legs apart in an easy stance and shook her head slowly.

"Well, Maia. I have to give you credit for your persistence. I thought you'd be long dead by now."

Her voice was silvery, and edged like the sharpest of blades. Maia glared at her. The Goddess turned her head to regard the hydra.

"I'm so disappointed in you!" she scolded it. "Why didn't you catch her sooner?"

The hydra's heads drooped as it cowered before her, like a hound about to feel its mistress' whip.

"You know what they say. If you want something done properly, you have to do it yourself."

She sighed in mock sympathy. "You don't look very comfortable up there. I think you'd better come down."

Maia swore at her. Cap'n Felix would have been proud.

Diana tilted her head and smiled.

"Now, there's no call for that."

"I think there is."

She really was very beautiful, Maia thought, before remembering Branwen's words. *Handsome is as handsome does.*

In which case, this Goddess should be as ugly as Medusa.

Diana's unnerving expression didn't waver. She reached around to her back and took hold of her bow, testing the string before selecting an arrow from her quiver.

"Then I'll just have to shoot you down."

She nocked the arrow and drew the bow in one smooth movement.

Maia briefly considered her options. She could go down to meet her fate with some semblance of dignity, or she could be dropped like a hunted squirrel. She had no doubt that the Goddess would hit her target.

It took an effort of will to begin the climb down. She had been clinging on so tightly it felt like her fingers had fused to the tree bark and her cramped legs didn't want to move. She had only one strategy left to her now. Maia slid down the rest of the way, landing on the ground with a thump and freed her skirts to fall around her ankles.

The Huntress lowered her bow. This close, Maia could see the unnatural smoothness of her skin and the gleam in her eyes. She didn't have the same overwhelming presence as Jupiter, but Potentia emanated from her in waves. Maia lifted her chin and tried to hide her trembling.

"Does your father know you're here?" she asked.

A tiny frown appeared on Diana's face.

"My father doesn't care what I do to mortals, so long as I obey him."

"How nice for you. At least you got to know your father," Maia replied. If she was defiant enough, perhaps Diana would finish her off quickly. Better that than being torn apart by her deadly pets.

"Your parents disobeyed the law of Olympus. They deserved what they got and so do you."

"I haven't disobeyed any laws!" Maia fired back.

"Your mere existence is unlawful! You should have been destroyed at birth!" Diana spat.

"Yes, we can't have demi-gods running about, upsetting the order of things, can we, child of Leto?" Maia sneered. Her plan seemed to be working.

The Goddess' expression became ugly, revealing her predatory nature.

"Jupiter himself chose my mother. My birth was sanctioned!"

"Well, weren't you and Apollo the lucky ones? Just think – a few hundred years later and both of you would have ended up like me. I wonder how you would have found life in the Home? I can just see you washing clothes and scrubbing floors!"

For a second, Diana looked as though she was about to strike Maia down where she stood. She froze, waiting for the inevitable blow but refusing to give the Goddess a single moment of satisfaction.

Suddenly, the Huntress relaxed.

"Ah! I see what you're doing. Very clever. A quick death, eh? At least you don't want for courage and, technically, you still come under my care as I am the protector of maidens."

She put her bow and arrow away. One of the hounds slunk up to her, resting its head under her hand. Diana caressed its ears and it closed its glowing eyes in pleasure.

"I admire your bravery, especially after all you've been through," she said, her previous rage seemingly put aside. "Because of this, I'm prepared to be merciful, as my father was."

Maia watched her warily. A little voice inside her head was warning her not to trust the Goddess, though, naturally, she wouldn't tell a lie. Just not the whole truth.

"Let me be straight with you," Diana began, in a business-like manner. "We can come to an agreement that benefits both of us. I need to protect my reputation and you don't want to have to spend the rest of your mortal existence as a wooden statue, subject to the whims of men. I know what you dreamed. I can give you that life."

Maia regarded her, stony-faced.

"What do you mean?" she said at last. "Your father gave me a choice; become a Ship or die. I chose to live, so now I must become a Ship. I don't think you can change his ruling."

Diana nodded slowly.

"True. But I can send you back to your dream life. It felt real enough, did it not? I can enhance it and," she added, "I can make you forget that you were ever a Ship-in-training. Just think! You'll be Gemma Valeria again, a noble lady, with a handsome husband and beautiful children. You have one son already. How many more would you like?"

Her words dripped honey.

"I could even make it so that you have Potentia and know how to use it. You could become queen of your own world, for as long as you live."

The Huntress waited, expectantly.

She thinks I'll fall at her feet, weeping with gratitude, Maia thought.

She had no doubts that Diana would do exactly what she promised. It would be her only chance to get it all back and not even realise what she was missing. But for how long? A month? A year? Or just long enough for her to become accustomed to her new life? How much sweeter it would be for Diana to give her everything, then rip it away from her, one piece at a time. She'd be in her own world all right, but one controlled by an angry Goddess with nothing better to do than watch her suffer. It would become another kind of arena, a cage carefully designed for nothing but torture.

"Marcia Blandina," she said.

Diana blinked.

"You must remember her? I think you made sure that I ended up in her house."

Comprehension dawned.

"You mean the murderess?"

"That's right."

Diana shrugged.

"That wasn't me. You can blame the Fates for that one."

As if Diana's enmity wasn't bad enough, now she had come to the attention of the Fates, too. Perhaps she had just been the cause of the woman's downfall. If Pearl hadn't brained her with a statue, who knew how many others would have died? She felt a little better about that.

"Let's see what I *can* blame you for, then," she said. "Item one, you found out about my parents' marriage. Item two, I suspect you made sure that the *Livia* found out – in fact, I think you encouraged her madness. Item three, you made my mother so afraid of your vengeance that she blocked any Potentia I might have developed, leaving me vulnerable and alone. Item four, the *Livia* hunted me down and, lastly, you've turned up in person to finish the job. I think that just about covers it. What I don't understand, is why do you hate my mother so much?"

Diana grew very still and the pale glow that surrounded her shone brighter, so that she looked like a marble statue in the moonlight.

A dog's whine of distress broke the spell.

"That is between Aura and myself."

"I can't remember my mother. I've never spoken with her, or even seen her," Maia said evenly. "I bet you haven't either lately, have you? In fact, I bet she wants nothing to do with you. She must hate you for what you've done. I bet she curses your name every single day."

Diana's throat moved convulsively as she swallowed.

"She left me," the Goddess whispered. "After two thousand years, she left me for…for that *man*! How could she love him? She didn't love *him*. She loved *me*!"

Diana's eyes glittered with tears.

"So now you want to kill her daughter, because you can't kill her. How pathetic! You're worse than Marcia Blandina. You waste your Potentia on petty revenge, when you could be much more. Your life must be so empty, if all you can think of is destroying mine!"

Diana's expression grew stony.

"You know nothing. Last chance. Will you take my offer?"

Maia's lip curled. Powerful Goddess or no, she felt nothing but contempt.

"Not bloody likely!"

Rage flashed in Diana's eyes.

"I'll enjoy watching you die!"

"That's just what Blandina said," Maia retorted. "You're like two peas in a pod!"

Rage overcame her fear. A branch, as thick as her arm, lay on the ground at her feet; she stooped and snatched it up, holding it like a club, the blood pounding in her head and teeth bared in defiance.

Diana regarded her for moment, before stepping backwards. Her attention turned to the hydra.

"Kill her."

The creature's eyes sparked to life and it reared, slithering forwards to strike.

Maia screamed and swung the branch as hard as she could. It connected with the first head, stunning it, but the others writhed around it, aiming for her body. She ducked and whirled, snapping jaws and venom-soaked fangs filling her vision as she waited for the hydra's teeth to sink into her flesh.

The branch burst into flames. The fire grew, burning hotter and hotter, until it became a brand of blazing light. Maia nearly dropped it in shock, feeling the awakened Potentia pouring in a boiling stream down her arms to fuel the makeshift weapon.

The hydra flinched away from the heat and Maia saw her chance.

She grasped the end of the branch with both hands and thrust it into the scaly belly.

The monster's hisses turned to screeches of pain as the fierce light devoured its innards and spread rapidly outwards, consuming its flesh as if it were old parchment. Maia yanked out the branch and swung once more. Four of the heads toppled to the floor, twisting in the heat like lengths of charred ribbon. The rest flailed weakly, their hisses becoming fainter, before the whole mass of it collapsed into a pile of half-cooked meat and bones.

Maia threw back her head and yelled her triumph. All her anger and pain seemed to burst from her in one huge wave, enveloping her body like armour and making her feel invulnerable. The branch vanished into whirling spirals of ash, leaving her hands free. She kicked the hydra's body to one side, hearing the cracking as what was left shattered and splintered under her feet.

Diana's eyes widened as Maia advanced.

"You forgot, Olympian," she heard herself say. "This is a child of the air, descended from the elements themselves."

The words were coming from her mouth, but they seemed to come from elsewhere.

I give you power of the mind. Use it! Avenge my Captain and myself!"

She could see the *Livia* in her head, smiling in triumph and knew that this was the reason that the Revenant had sought her out. Her hatred for the Goddess who had spurred her on to murder had been stronger than death itself and she had called up something greater than either of them to carry out her revenge.

Diana turned to flee, but Maia was faster. She grabbed the Goddess' arm, fingers sinking deep into immortal flesh. The terrified Goddess tried to pull away, but she was held fast.

"Did you think you could escape me, daughter of Zeus?"

Something was inside Maia, something huge, ancient and implacable. She was transformed. Another power ruled here now.

"I am Nemesis!"

Diana screamed, high and shrill like a trapped rabbit and Maia finally understood. She watched with implacable eyes as the Goddess broke free and fled, weeping in pain and fear, the mark of the clutching hand branded into her arm. Her attendants followed her, vanishing as silently as they had arrived, leaving Maia standing over the charred remnants of her attacker.

Nemesis' massive presence lifted, leaving her weak and slightly nauseous.

She stared at her hand. The palm still glowed faintly but the Potentia was fading now, returning to whatever secret place it occupied inside her.

What now? The torch was still burning and she stumbled over to it, glad of its warmth and light. She was under no illusion that she had been the author of her salvation; this had been a long game indeed, a power play of the Gods. She had been merely a piece to be used and moved as each side saw fit, to further their own ends.

Nemesis had been summoned by the *Livia*, but this Goddess' main function was to punish pride. Only one God could arrange for his daughter to be brought to heel in this way. It was subtle, masterful – and deniable. Maia wondered how long he'd had been planning it.

She sank down on to the ground, aching in every bone and feeling empty inside. Everything hurt; her arms and legs were scraped and scratched and her fingers felt like they'd been crushed in a vise. She was hungry, thirsty and wanted nothing more than to get out of this endless forest. What she wouldn't give for honest cobbles beneath her feet and the light from a friendly inn!

She looked around, hoping that a door to somewhere else would magically appear, but all she could see was darkness. There was one thing she could do and that was to get as far away from the hydra's stinking remains as she could. Someone else could collect its teeth if they had a mind – she'd had quite enough of the creature.

Maia pushed herself to her feet, yanked the torch out of the ground and made her way wearily out of the glade. Surely the sun would come up soon.

She walked for what seemed like hours. There seemed to be no break in the forest, though she could have sworn that the sky was slowly becoming lighter. A few sleepy chirps told her that it was almost dawn and her spirits lifted a little at the thought that she could at least start to see where she was going and possibly get some sense of direction.

Rustlings in the bushes made her stop, lifting the almost extinguished torch. A familiar bundle of leaves burst from behind a trunk, resolving into the little sprite. His airy companion peeped out from behind a branch, glowing faintly.

"You're still alive!" he squeaked.
"Yes. Amazing, isn't it?" she answered.
"I thought you were a goner."
"Me too."

He stood on one tiny foot, head tilted, considering her.
"You can't stay here. It's not a place for mortals."
"You were going to show me a way out," she said, remembering. "A gap."

He nodded enthusiastically.

"Yes!" He paused, seeming to confer with his friend. "Come on!"

She followed him as he scampered through the trees, until she spotted a group of large rocks, piled up one upon another, like jackstones spilled from a giant's hand. He pointed.

"It's through there."

Maia looked at the dark entrance, doubtfully. Would she be able to squeeze through the fissure? There was only one way to find out.

"Where does it go to?"

"The women," he stated, nodding. "Them as spelled you. That goes to where they are. Not quite in your world, but not here. It's where you need to be."

She smiled at him.

"Thank you."

"I owe you a debt," he informed her, his black eyes twinkling like tiny pieces of jet. "I always repay my debts, for good or ill."

He smiled, showing sharp little teeth. Maia was glad that she was on his good side. For all his size, she thought that he would be a formidable enemy. She'd heard the stories of what Minor Fae could do when they were angered.

"I count your debt as paid in full," she said solemnly.

The little Fae bowed and she returned it, before walking over and peering into the space between the stones. It wasn't large, but it seemed navigable and at the moment it was the best option she had. The little blue light bobbed over to her, as if encouraging her to enter. Maia turned herself sideways and squeezed into the crack.

It was a tight fit and added to her scrapes, but she managed to wriggle inside, hoping that it widened out ahead. It would be a shame if she ended up stuck in this place, unable to move. She felt her robe catch and tear but she persisted, pulling herself through. She reckoned if she could have remembered her birth, it would probably have been something like this.

After a few minutes of discomfort, she could see daylight ahead and was thankful to see that the passage ended in a larger gap that promised an escape. It wasn't far and she redoubled her efforts, grunting as she edged though bit by bit. Finally, a last push and she was free.

Another blasted forest. Maia could have screamed.

She was sick of trees, trees and more trees. Where were the houses, the people? She looked down at her ruined clothes and filthy limbs. Her stomach rumbled and her mouth was dry. The Gods alone knew how long it was since she'd eaten or drank properly. She certainly felt half-starved and desperately thirsty. Maybe there was a stream nearby? She listened for the sound of running water. She could hear something, for sure. The air felt different here, more natural somehow. Then she became aware of something moving.

For an awful moment Maia thought that Diana had returned and she looked around wildly for another branch. Then, a pair of gnarled hands parted a bush and another figure appeared. It was tall and clothed in bark and leaves, like the little sprite she had met, with twigs and more leaves in its green hair. It emerged slowly from the cover of the forest, as if part of it were coming to life. Maia could see that it was woman-shaped, with human-like eyes that crinkled with warmth as she spoke.

"Greetings, sister. Your journey is almost complete. Welcome to the new day and the rising of the sun!"

Maia could only gape at what she assumed was a dryad, a tree spirit. Hadn't she escaped after all? Was she doomed to wander in these alien Fae lands forever?

"I have called the Priestesses," the dryad continued. "They come."

She regarded the stunned girl with curiosity, before disappearing. Instead, there stood a rowan tree, covered in creamy blossoms. Maia blinked in disbelief. If she'd had the energy, she would have laughed.

*

Voices, women's voices. She was flat on her back, wrapped in something warm and being carried along. Maia opened her eyes. Above her, an upside-down face leaned in, blocking the view of the treetops.

"She's waking up!"

There was a confusion of voices, before a more familiar one cut in.

"We're nearly there, keep going."

Maia turned her head and looked up. Ceridwen was walking beside her. Dark eyes met her own.

"It's all right. You're safe now."

Maia felt like cursing, but lapsed back into darkness instead.

*

She awoke to the smell of food. Hands helped her to sit up and held a bowl of broth to her lips. She drank it down greedily, then leaned back on to propped up pillows. She was in a wooden lean-to shelter, being tended by Modren.

"Hello, Maia," the woman said with a smile. "I'm glad you made it. Ceridwen will be here in a minute."

Maia nodded, not trusting herself to speak. A slow anger was burning within her.

She was sick of being used.

Modren left when the older woman entered. Maia saw immediately that she looked tired and strained, as if she hadn't slept properly for many nights. The Priestess pulled up a little stool and sat, her eyes fixed on Maia's face.

"How are you feeling?"

"Exhausted. Angry. Was it supposed to be like this?"

Ceridwen shook her head.

"No. The Mother is furious. Her ritual has been abused and her sanctuary invaded."

"Diana?"

"The maiden has been dealt with. I am told that you were the instrument of her punishment."

Maia shivered.

"She entered the sacred wood and re-routed the last portal to a place of her choosing, out in the Fae lands. She will be further punished for her temerity."

That was good to know, but it still didn't make things any easier for her.

Maia frowned. "Raven was there. In my dream."

Ceridwen sighed.

"Yes. Interference of another kind. He, too, will pay."

"If it wasn't for him, I'd still be in there."

"Possibly. Your memory worked against you, though you may have seen through it at some point. You passed the other tests, so there's no reason to think you wouldn't have succeeded in this one."

Maia privately wondered if she would have ever managed to get out. She'd been totally convinced, despite the flashbacks. She decided it was better to say nothing. All she could hope for was that it was all over and whatever game the Gods were playing had finally come to its conclusion.

"What happens now?"

Maybe they'd let her go? The faint hope that she might still become Gemma Valeria still lingered, though she would be a poor shadow of the woman in her dream.

"You have passed the trials," Ceridwen said. "Now it's time for your installation."

What had Diana said? She would become a wooden statue, subject to the whims of men. The Goddess was right on both counts, though Ships were much, much more than statues. And she would be more than most Ships.

Anyone who threatened her vessel or her crew would have to kill her first.

Maia stared down at her scarred body. What use was it now? She had another choice – to live as an object of pity among these damned trees, or take to the high seas and be respected, loved and feared.

She'd have guns, too. Lots of guns. And she wouldn't look like *this*. She could appear as anything she wanted. It was time to put her dreams of hearth and home aside forever. Time to make her decision.

*

The clearing was about two hundred feet across, carpeted with soft grass and wildflowers. A sweet smell rose from them which soothed her battered and exhausted senses, but it was the lone tree at its centre which struck her with awe.

A gigantic oak dominated the entire space; its immense trunk dividing upwards into many huge, gnarled branches supporting a canopy of new leaves that fluttered and trembled in the early morning air. Strips of cloth and ribbons hung from the lower branches, tied there as offerings and prayers and so many that some must have been hundreds of years old, their colours still bright and undimmed by time. It towered above the other trees which clustered at the edge of the glade, as though they were keeping a respectful distance from this monarch.

Maia could feel the Potentia thrumming through her feet and her ear tingled where the connecting ring had been. This was the Mother Tree, the one from whom all Ships derived their being and the source of the living wood. She had a sudden joyous flash of recognition, as if sighting a relative's face in a large crowd.

Three figures detached themselves from the shadow of the tree and made their way towards her. Maia allowed herself to be led to the base of the Mother Tree, where she was given a drink of water flavoured with some herbs that she couldn't identify. The liquid was cool and refreshing to her parched throat and she drank whilst resting on a great mossy root. One of the Priestesses sat down beside her.

"You have passed the tests of courage and entered into the heart of the sacred forest," the woman told her softly. "It is now time for you to make the transition to your new life. I ask you again, are you willing to make the sacrifice?"

"I am," she replied, feeling drowsiness wash over her.

The women gathered around Maia as she drifted in and out of consciousness, lifting and carrying her to a place in the clearing not too far from the massive trunk. Gentle hands removed her robes, then lowered her carefully to the ground. As she closed her eyes for the last time, the soil gaped open, roots twisting upwards to cocoon her in a tight embrace, before pulling her down, down into the comforting earth, safe at last.

*

She floated in a dark sea; drifting formless in silence.

Far away, a familiar voice called to her, raised in both entreaty and enticement. It caught and tugged, reeling her in from the lightless depths as if she were a hooked fish at the mercy of a skilled fisherman. It rose in volume, its demand growing more urgent.

"Ship, come forth!"

Raven's voice was a command that could not be denied.

Maia focused on his location, straining to grasp the heart of the living oak that would be her new body. She pushed into it, moulding and sculpting the pliant wood; emerging sense by sense and piece by piece until, finally, she burst out into the light.

Sight returned. Raven was standing before her, arms raised. Faintly glowing channels of Potentia sprang from him, centring him in a purple corona.

He cried out a word. Dazzling light pierced her senses, blinding her. The universe spun in a whirl of kaleidoscope colours before coalescing into solidity, compelling and binding her in its magical weave and settling around her like a heavy cloak. She felt the connection through her whole being, as if all her anchors had dropped at once. Then, it was done.

A new Ship was born.

She was her vessel; its wooden body her body, her muscles rope, her bones great pegged beams, her joints pulleys and rigging blocks. She could sense it all, the weight and substance of it as her awareness exploded outwards.

Cabins, holds, decks and companionways, the wind in the rigging, the furled sails, all were now part of her, just as much as her lost flesh, blood and bone, only tougher, stronger and far more durable.

Goodbye Maia Abella, foundling, victimised servant and abandoned daughter.

Hello, up-to-date, fully armoured Battleship of His Majesty's Royal Britannic Navy.

And the Gods help anyone who tried to use her again.

*

The room was unremarkable, though the two occupants were not.

"The way is blocked," the man said. He sounded nervous, rubbing his fingers together in an unconscious gesture of appeasement.

"Temporarily. I regret Morgan's loss, but she died for a noble cause," his companion replied.

"What now?"

"We proceed with the plan."

The other's voice was liquid and not quite human. The man was used to dealing with him now, though his insides still tried to crawl out through his spine every time he spoke.

"When?"

"You will tell us when the time is right."

A smile like jagged glass flashed from inside the hood.

"I understand," the man said. "The bargain is made."

"And we shall honour it. Make sure that you do, also."

"I will," the man said, petulantly. "Your ancient rights and privileges restored. As long as I get my due."

"Oh, I promise you, you will."

The creature slipped away like a stray moonbeam, leaving the man to dream of all the things that would be his.

Just one life stood between him and everything he'd always wanted. It wouldn't be long now.

And then, not even the Gods could stop him.

Author's Note

Greetings, dear Reader!

I hope you enjoyed Book 2 of Maia's adventures. Check out my website at ***emkkoulla.com*** for more information about the world of the *Ships of Britannia*. If you click on the link on the home page, you'll be sent the link to **a free novella**, *'Son of the Sea'*, a **free short story** featuring the Portus Polis, plus a monthly newsletter. More freebies coming soon!

I would also be very grateful if you could *leave a review*, on Amazon, as this will encourage other people to read my books and keep the Ships sailing. As an independent author, I need all the help I can get!

Comments and feedback are always welcome. You can email me through the contact page on my website, @EKkoulla on Twitter or by visiting the Ships of Britannia Facebook page.

Keep a weather eye open for **THE TRIALS OF NEPTUNE: Ships of Britannia, Book 3**, coming Autumn 2021.

Acknowledgements

I'd like to say a massive thank you to all my friends, who have supported me as I've continued on this journey. This book is dedicated to you.

Natalia Richards, my fellow author, for all her practical help and encouragement. 'The Falcon's Rise' and 'The Falcon's Flight', her novels of Anne Boleyn's early life, are meticulously researched, richly detailed and totally stunning.

Jane Powell, as always, for wanting the next chapters hot off the laptop.

My husband Stephen, for keeping my spirits up.

My fantastic beta readers, Perry, Neil, Sue, Jayne and Kevin, who took the time to read through Prey and point out all the bits that were a) wrong, b) missed out or c) incomprehensible. Any mistakes that remain are entirely my fault.

Andrew Newton, who took my hand drawn map and turned it into something impressive, plus created some great art work to promote the series.

Nick Hodgson, my new amazing proofreader.

Thea, Designer *Extraordinaire*, who takes my vague ideas and turns them into amazing covers. Check out her website at www.ikaruna.eu for more of her fantastic artwork!

And lastly (but not definitely not least), to you, dear Reader, for choosing this book. I am eternally grateful.